BLOODY MOON

A THRILLER SET IN JOHANNESBURG IN 2010

IAN D. CORDINER

Published in Australia by Sid Harta Books & Print Pty Ltd,
ABN: 34632585293
23 Stirling Crescent, Glen Waverley, Victoria 3150 Australia
Telephone: +61 3 9560 9920
E-mail: author@sidharta.com.au

First published in Australia 2022
This edition published 2022

Cover design, typesetting: WorkingType (www.workingtype.com.au)

Cordiner, Ian D.
Bloody Moon
ISBN: 978-1-925707-64-9
pp360

Ian Cordiner graduated as a Civil Engineer at Witwatersrand University in Johannesburg. There was growing political unrest in South Africa and he soon left for the UK to work on major construction projects.

Then, in his thirties, he made a significant career change, joining a leading international business consultancy and migrating to Australia. This move away from engineering was the foundation for decades of business consulting and restructuring advice that led to general management, governance and change management roles in six widely different organisations. He has previously written a memoir, *The Accidental Headhunter*, a thoughtful, yet lighthearted, look at risk and coincidence as they have impacted on his life and those six careers.

With such a diverse portfolio of experience, an approach from Richard King to set up a new headhunting firm (Cordiner King) was risky, but attractive. The firm operated successfully for over 25 years, playing an important part in an affiliation of some fifty international firms. Ian was elected one of that group's ten-member Board.

Ten years ago Ian 'retired' to provide governance advice to a number of corporate and government business enterprises.

DEDICATION

*For all her interest and support in everything I do,
this is for Anne, with my love.*

My sincere gratitude for the insights of a number of people dispersed around the world. My perspectives were enhanced by their sharp observations and support for this project. In particular, some helped me with matters of context, but this is not in any way intended to be a historical work. It could have been set in another country with similar social pressures. I thank them for their help in suggesting many nuances of human interaction.

There are several people to whom I owe much gratitude—

Helen and Tony Fromm, insatiable travellers who took up the initial idea and maintained enthusiasm and encouragement throughout.

Dario Tomat, company director and consultant, with a keen eye for detail and a deep understanding of technical matters on a strategic plane.

Cheryl Burman, author of *Keepers* among other works, living in England, who was an early challenger of the style of this book and suggested helpful changes.

Anthea Serritslev, a South African national with strong political connections.

Dr Mike Richards, author of *The Hanged Man* and other

works, who brought an understanding of high-level political intrigue.

Marinus Endenburg, a civil engineer living in Johannesburg whom I have known for six decades and who has a solid grasp of the background to this novel.

Dr Dan Norton. Company Director and corporate advisor. Chair of several Government Business Enterprises in the utilities sectors.

Dr. Tansy Roberts Rayner, Tasmanian Writers' Centre manuscript assessor, who gave me valuable feedback on an early version.

Kerry Collison of Sidharta Publications, for the encouragement to publish my story.

Marie Pietersz, Editor, for the help and advice provided throughout the process.

Luke Harris, for the professional book cover design and printing.

There are numerous others who have made valuable contributions to the draft and challenged aspects of the story. To all of you, my sincerest thanks.

ONE

Just after seven o'clock in the morning, Richard Curie stepped from the Boeing into an aerobridge tunnel and immediately caught a whiff of the distinctive smell of South Africa. Although it had been well over twenty years since he had lived in the country, there was something so different and compelling about this smell that it drew him right back to his youth. It certainly wasn't putrid or flowery, oily and tropical as in India. Nor was it closed in and dank with the leaves of the English countryside he had just left. There was a dry, dusty quality to the air which one could almost taste. It had been a long, hard, summer in Johannesburg and the impact of the drought permeated his senses. His mouth felt it and the blurred neon lighting of the Customs Hall accentuated it. Even sounds seemed to have lost their edge despite the bustle of the terminal.

This was hardly a time for reflection. He briskly made his way through the official processes of immigration and customs, disconcerted by the presence of so many black officers and how many were women. All those years before the black people, mainly men had the most menial jobs in the airport, working as porters and cleaners. Richard's swift progress to the exit gate was certainly helped by a First- Class ticket and he made a mental note to thank his new client at Green Mines.

Richard had been able to undertake brief research on this company, uncovering some discomforting things about Green Mines and its sole owner, Mr Paesano. The company was not listed on any Stock Exchange, though there was public information available on its mining tenements, joint ventures, and registered exploration licences. It had sought to keep a low profile, but there was plenty of speculation in the financial press questioning several of its deals. And here he was, about to deal with it.

Matters had developed quickly after the initial approach by Green Mines, almost too quickly to suit his conservative, risk-adverse nature. For several years he had been living a tenuous professional life as a geological advisor in his own London-based practice. Recently, he had been doing ground-breaking analytical work on his own account which, while keeping him refreshed and intellectually simulated, didn't seem to have any commercial legs. And, with the global financial crisis still frightening almost every lender in the country two years later, his personal downturn in income had attracted the attention of the disgraced and battling Royal Bank of Scotland. It was threatening closure on his housing mortgage.

He was becoming quite despondent when out of the blue, he received a curt email from Green Mines in Johannesburg, advising him to expect delivery of an important offer he should consider a priority. This was something of a surprise for Richard who had certainly not been chasing business in South Africa, and anyway he had never seen himself as much of a salesman or negotiator. Rather, he had depended on referrals to sustain his business.

After Richard examined this offer for his latest intellectual property and expertise, he knew it would be hard to refuse. His new work was focused on a radically more efficient method of gold extraction from low- quality ore bodies using novel algorithms and models which were complex and data hungry.

Apart from presentations in academic circles and discussions with his technical peers working in two large mining houses, there had been scant response to his research. He was most surprised his methodology, as yet untested and rejected after consideration by major mining companies, didn't seem to have deterred Green Mines from making an extravagant offer.

It certainly wasn't through any 'cold selling' on his part, which he wasn't too good at anyway. It also caused him to wonder why this potential client had opened by making such a generous offer and whether he was being softened up. After the overnight flight where the seating, eating and sleeping in First Class was all he could have expected, he hoped he would be able to keep his nerve during the coming discussions. Recognising his poor negotiating skills, he resolved to stand firm on the draft 'Heads of Agreement'.

While the cabin crew made ready for landing, he reminded himself he was just heading to another job. However, the academic recognition and huge financial reward implied in the document were front of mind and could not have come at a more fortuitous time. His instructions from the company, conveyed in a brief, officious phone call from a Mr Denning, had been clear.

'Dr Curie, arrange your flight with my secretary. On your arrival, there'll be a driver to take you to Green Mines' office.' And that really was all he said.

Jostling uncomfortably through a noisy rabble, Richard was again struck by the number of black people in the welcoming throng. Through the bustle he spotted a line of placard-wielding men and women, and by far the most imposing of them was an immense man, possibly one of the biggest he'd ever seen. Tall, shaven head, sunglasses jammed on top and formally dressed in a dark suit, and on his sign was boldly written 'Dick Curry'.

Richard couldn't help being offended by this show of disrespect for his academic standing. Somewhat rattled, he walked over and introduced himself in a friendly, courteous way, hand extended,

'Good morning. The sign must be for me although my name is actually Dr Richard Curie.'

He immediately regretted this pomposity when the towering man pointedly ignored the proffered hand, gave barely the thin hint of a smile, and curtly replied.

'I'm Shorty.'

After a brief pause, he again ground out 'Shorty' and the trace of the smile disappeared as if he thought Richard might make some frivolous comment.

'I'm here to take you to Mr Paesano, the Boss.'

This driver was plainly no lowly employee and Richard wondered what his role might be. The stiffness of his greeting added to Richard's discomfort.

He tried to control his reactions, looking about him as he followed the titan. In passing, he noticed a ruddy-faced, older man with close-cut hair standing at the end of the driver line-up. The only thing which drew his attention was a ridiculously small placard on which an unreadable name had been crudely scrawled. Richard sensed that he seemed to be taking some interest in them, but the moment passed. Understandably, they would have presented an arresting spectacle.

Ignoring the trolley Richard had commandeered, the giant easily hefted the heavy suitcase. As he did so, Richard noticed his huge hands were shielded by black gloves which looked remarkably soft and out of place. He didn't have time to dwell on this because Shorty led the way at something of a gallop across the car park. He forced his way through and Richard, trailing behind, heard the disdainful mutters of some he thrust aside,

'No sense of respect for others ... Doesn't he know how things have changed? ... Being a bully doesn't give him rights ...'

Shorty just pressed on.

Considering all the other extravagances of this deal to date, Richard expected nothing less than a large Mercedes and there it was, in shining silver. As Shorty loaded the luggage and directed Richard into the back seat, the same ruddy-faced man again came into view, this time climbing into a small black VW some distance away. Richard's latent sense of paranoia surfaced for a moment.

Curiously, Richard thought, he didn't have any passengers in tow, but his attention was diverted by the way Shorty hurled the car towards the exit. It was pulled up in the slow-moving payments queue just as Shorty's mobile phone rang. He was thoroughly peeved by the caller and his responses were gruff and staccato, his anger reflected in the occasional stutter.

'What?... uh ... uh ...Yes! ... Don't you teach me how to ...b-b-bloody drive, Nick ... just you tell the Boss I'm gunna be as quick as possible.'

Looking back to Richard, he growled

'What a dickhead that one. Tells me there's a big smash on the motorway... truck hit a minibus ... bodies everywhere ... I'll have to take a back road.'

Shorty didn't exactly soothe Richard's anxiety as the car picked up speed.

'We're late. Mr Paesano mustn't be kept waiting.'

Crouched over the wheel, he thrust the Mercedes towards a truck and a bicycle on the inside lane of a tighter section of the road and asked Richard in a calmer, more conversational way.

'Do you know how many people are killed on the roads here each year? Not just the blacks, either... it's almost as bad as organised crime ...12,000 road deaths last year and they say about 17,000 murders... oh, and a thousand rapes a week ...'

Richard, an academic who liked statistics, regretted his interruption as soon as the words left his mouth,

'Really? All those victims are as many as the population of a good-sized English town like mine ...'

Shorty grunted ominously,

'Senior police give themselves military ranks. It's not solving anything ... at least a thousand more police face criminal charges this year...'

He snorted and for the first time grinned sourly, briefly looking over his shoulder, 'Including some bloody brigadiers. No one knows what's what, few seem to give a stuff and I'm not one of those few pussies who do.'

At that moment almost to illustrate his point, the Mercedes brushed the cyclist with its wing mirror. Richard glimpsed the agonised face of the rider as it whipped past him. He spun in his seat and looked back to see a tangle of rider and machine skidding off the road shoulder. A car pulled over to help, but Shorty was indifferent.

'Silly idiot … see what I mean?'

He drove on even faster. This lack of interest in the chaos he had caused gave Richard even more reason to worry. He squirmed back in his plush seat. The cool blast of the air-conditioning did nothing to reduce his sweaty concern.

There was much to engage Richard's attention during Shorty's suicidal drive to the city. He tried to relax as he took it all in. Looking out at the passing scene, it was difficult to relate these images to his distant memories. As a teenager, he'd had the protection of a secure home in a quiet, exclusive suburb. Now, there were long stretches of corrugated-iron shanty towns reaching up to the road reserve.

He had attended a country boarding school and had seldom any need to visit the city centre. Who needed it anyway? Now, the frantic traffic and the undisciplined, steely determination of every driver on the back streets to make up for the delay, completely unnerved him. After a while, to break the tension, he tried to make polite conversation and leant forward.

'Shorty, you must be very pleased about South Africa hosting the World Soccer Cup soon?'

His answer was an emphatic put-down.

'Expensive nonsense … billions of Rand … who knows how much is already in private pockets….it'll only increase road traffic. Besides, I am a rugby fan.'

Shorty now focused intently on bullying his way through the crowded, narrower city streets and ignored Richard. Despite his concentration he was also glued to his mobile phone and Richard could tell things weren't on plan for someone.

'It's all taking too long and the Boss is going mad … don't interrupt … well, it isn't my… b-b-bloody fault … you go and fix it up or I'll fix you up, you little rat … no more warnings … you get me?'

Richard noticed how his real anger was reflected in that stutter. An uncomfortable silence followed until the car pulled up in front of a substantial office building in an area which Richard vaguely remembered as the business precinct. For a modern city founded just over a century before, the inner streets were quite narrow and there were few imposing buildings in the CBD compared to any other metropolis he had visited.

This area certainly didn't have any of the élan of the city of London and there weren't men in business suits striding about with that particularly British sense of authority. Rather, there was real sense of nervous energy amongst the jostling crowd heading for work. Unlike its neighbours, the building in front of them had no external signage at all, nor did it have throngs waiting to enter. Shorty waved a hand in the direction of the entry and turned to Richard.

'I'll look after your luggage.'

Richard made a snap decision to keep his laptop, provoking an almost imperceptible narrowing of the eyes and a grunted, 'Okay then …'

Shorty opened the rear door, but it wasn't a deferential act and Richard felt as though he had been released from prison.

Inside the building, he was pleased to see one of the elevators being held open for him. He noted by the lack of access buttons that it was a dedicated service and twenty floors up, he exited into a plain, unadorned foyer with a CCTV camera and three doors facing him, each with key pads and push plates.

After barely a moment, the central door opened to reveal a dapper, fit-looking man, perhaps a little older than himself. For an instant, Richard had a vague feeling that he had met him somewhere long ago, but the memory faded. Again, like Shorty, there was only the merest trace of a cold smile in his greeting, and a thinning of his lips which did not extend to his eyes. He sounded as though he was trying to bring a naturally high-pitched voice down an octave and it became gratingly nasal with every syllable distinct and clipped.

'Hello, we've spoken before. I'm Nick … Nick Denning, Mr Paesano's Executive Officer. Come this way, Dick.'

Hoping he was making a positioning statement, he responded.

'Actually, I'd rather prefer Richard if you don't mind'

This was ignored and Richard's sensitivities were again offended.

It was not a friendly room. Some serious modern art on the walls and a huge fine Persian carpet on the floor left Richard feeling it was in an impersonal cavern easily big enough for a Board Room. However, as Richard was to learn later, Dieter Paesano had no time for formal meetings.

Paesano sat at the far end of this space, behind a large desk subtly placed on a slightly raised platform. He ignored both men for a while before picking up a gold fountain pen and rudely pointing it at each in turn. Without any formal introduction, he said, 'You are late and I have no time, so let's get on with it.'

Richard barely had time to assess the man. There was simply nothing impressive about Paesano: pallid, late fifties, dark hair with some silvery streaks. Richard noted the gold cufflinks, the gold signet ring and the very gold and very expensive watch. His own Rolex Oyster, a graduation present from his parents, was miserly by comparison.

He tugged at his casual reefer jacket, again feeling he had been somehow out-manouvered. The others were dressed as businessmen ready to discuss commercial matters and here he was looking like a field geologist, ready to talk about scientific things. He felt decidedly awkward.

Paesano was forceful and business-like, his near-perfect English not quite masking some Italian undertones. It was neither melodic nor soft; somehow designed to be listened to.

'We won't waste any more time. Just read this final version of the Agreement and, if it covers everything, sign both copies here, here and here, where the tabs are.'

He thrust the papers across his desk and as he did, Richard noticed an ugly, old, lumpy, purple scar running diagonally across the back of his hand. Repulsed, the squeamish Richard hesitated for an instant before reaching out for the documents. Paesano, noting his discomfort, deliberately held on to them in his claw-shaped hand. He released them with a tug and a slight, sadistic smirk and Richard realised he was wearing the scar like a badge of honour, like a duelling scar.

Completely disconcerted, Richard now wondered whether the time had come to negotiate and improve his position a bit, so he cleared his throat and tentatively began to suggest a different arrangement. He stumbled a little as he launched his negotiating pitch.

'There are other companies interested in this … um … intellectual property… err … IP, ready to buy it and hide it away until the gold price changes. I honestly believe it'll be very successful. Perhaps I could share in this success, reduce my fee and take an option, a royalty or a commis …'

Paesano cut him short and his tone, which had been cold, was now quite icy.

' Look, man, I know you are having financial difficulties, but I'm carrying all the risk. I said no negotiation. Take it or get out.'

Richard was startled by the vehemence of this outburst and Paesano's knowledge of his personal affairs. After some hesitation, which was a clear annoyance to Paesano, he retrieved his copy of the draft Agreement from his laptop case to compare changes. Paesano stared hard at him and his silent question simply had to be answered.

'I use this laptop to access my large research database and financial models in Engla…'

Again, Paesano cut him off.

'In which case, you'll be supervised by one of my people. This is highly confidential stuff and I don't want you to communicate with anyone until you are finished … then it will all belong to me … do you understand? As far as I am concerned you can take all the scientific accolades you want, Doctor. They may even help us to sell your ideas … but it will still belong to me. Capito?'

Richard felt he could have been tougher, but the amount of money on offer was considerable and the opportunity to have his research further promoted was a real plus. However, the wind was completely taken out of his sails as Paesano continued.

'I have a very nice, secure place, a house out of town where you'll work in secret over the next week or so. Shorty will take you there right now.'

With that, Shorty appeared through a door which seemed to lead from the general office and Richard was ignored. As was becoming more apparent, the man's role was a great deal more important than simply being a company driver or enforcer. Richard, standing of course, was both examining the Agreement and reflecting on Paesano's abruptness while Shorty mounted the podium and speaking softly, was apparently bringing him up to speed on the 'phone call in the car. While he used the formal 'Mr' in this conversation, he wasn't as deferential as Nick Denning.

While Paesano was distracted, Nick wanted to assert his own self-importance. Before Richard had finished reading the Agreement, Nick moved closer and rather than deepening, his voice rose in pitch as he spoke quietly but clearly.

'I can fill you in on any other detail later at the house, but you must know everything we discuss is confidential. Mr Paesano places a very high value on his privacy ...'

Paesano, overhearing this, ignored Shorty and butted in sharply.

'Si, I also place a very high value on expertise and intellectual property. If you can successfully complete and prove your unusual ideas and then assign this IP to Green Mines, this formal agreement commits me to the $4 million fee for your patent rights as first proposed in the Heads of Agreement.'

He looked directly at Nick.

'If you need tax advice, talk to Nick here. He'll fix you up, but it may mean a couple of trips to Switzerland and you'll be paying him a commission. Cut rate, eh Nick?'

He didn't wait for an answer.

'However, you'll notice you have to negotiate to pay any other scientists' fees from this very generous sum.'

All this fee-sharing arrangement was news to Richard as Paesano continued in the same dispassionate tone.

'I have engaged a first-class research scientist, expert in the field of biological metallurgy. Your close collaboration with Dr Dupain will mean a speedy outcome of this trial.'

Richard had a niggling sense of being diddled by this variation to the draft Agreement, though after all, a major part of this fee pool was still a lot of money. There was another new clause which Nick said was needed to ensure succession rights in the event of one of the parties withdrawing for any reason. It was clear Paesano didn't care about any of this. Everything he said was forceful, in direct contrast to his unexceptional physical presence.

'I repeat. No further negotiation. Once it's all delivered, you'll have nothing more to do with it and, successful or not, you can find your own way back to London. I've already learned elsewhere your work seems well advanced and, realistically, I expect through your collaboration it'll take no more than ten days.'

Richard gasped nervously.

'Really? It will take me a week or so to get on top of the

mineral structures. I haven't examined South African ore bodies since university and ...'

Paesano just cut him off and his eyes narrowed.

'Our researcher has been working on this for a long time and the biological side is well advanced. Initially, the collaborating expert was Professor Claude Guerin, but no longer. Ring any bells?'

Richard had vaguely heard of Guerin but only knew his work had been inconclusive and no one knew his present whereabouts. Paesano was dismissive.

'Useless. Drunkard and a gambler, his input finished long ago and we have our hands around his best research which is being refined by our scientist. I want you to just get on with it. There are bankers and investors breathing down my neck waiting for good news.'

Richard was astonished this was the only reference to the technical aspects of his IP. There were no tight product specifications to be met and trial costs hadn't even been mentioned. Paesano was focused only on timely delivery of the whole intellectual property package which still needed a commercial title. Not a ten- word scientific label. With a touch of vanity, he thought to himself that 'The Curie Process' sounded most acceptable.

Paesano was now finished. He gestured to Nick, flicking his finger to the door and, after looking for another file, resumed reading. During the long walk out of the big office behind Shorty and Nick, Richard had the unpleasant feeling Paesano was somehow sizing him up behind his back. He resisted a sudden impulse to turn around and give a genial wave just to spite the man. He was at least pleased he hadn't thanked him for the First Class trip. How inane would that have sounded? On the other hand, he had managed to endure the whole discussion without once addressing Paesano as 'Mr' or 'Sir'.

He glanced at his watch as they waited for the lift. The whole meeting had taken barely twenty minutes. Intellectually self-confident, he had none-the-less been caught off-guard by a dominating personality. Once again he had to face the fact he'd been a hopeless un-commercial negotiator. So much for standing firm! He could almost kick himself. He had to do better when he negotiated the fee split with the other scientist.

They entered the lift lobby and were joined by a smartly-dressed woman from the main office. Nick instantly engaged her in conversation and it was salacious conversation full of innuendo. The lift stopped on the ground floor and she stepped out while they continued to the basement parking. Nick said, by way of explanation, 'Ros. Works for me in accounts. Thirtyish, top of my age range, but I reckon she's a bit of a goer.'

Richard was disgusted and he could feel Shorty's anger.

'Better be careful about fishing in the company pond. The Boss would be furious if he found out. And if I'm ever asked, I'm gunna tell the truth!'

With that he strode across to the silver Mercedes, ushering Richard into the security of the back seat while Nick slowly settled himself in front.

TWO

The trip from the city to the secure house was a more sedate affair than the hectic ride from the airport had been. Shorty was showing some sign of being more affable, but Nick, with aggravating self-importance, made it clear he had to examine his briefcase full of papers. He ostentatiously transferred an overgrown pistol from an inside suit pocket to the glove box to make himself more comfortable. Shorty gave him a disdainful glance and muttered, 'Fat lot of good it'll do there if we meet trouble.'

Nick just ignored him and Richard gulped slightly at the thought of some unknown danger. He was pretty sure Shorty was similarly armed. They hardly spoke another word to each other and there was a tension between them Richard could nearly touch.

At least the silence gave him time to reflect again on his knowledge of Green Mines and, more specifically, its people. In his gut he was beginning to feel they were unsavoury and even for the potential scientific recognition and significant financial rewards, he doubted he would relish this assignment.

His thoughts turned first to the leader he'd just met, who had been so extravagantly rude to him and with such a domineering grip on his subordinates.

Richard's background research before he left London only produced a murky image of Mr Dieter Paesano, embellished by a few enlightening articles in the business press, courtesy of a determined investigative journalist, Jonathon Franklin. These implied that adverse talk in the finance industry required Paesano to do something pretty quickly in order to reduce investor pressure and avoid foreclosure. Franklin's in-depth article had done Green Mines no good at all.

Paesano couldn't afford more exposure. While he may well be Green Mines' big shot, Franklin suggested the chances were his shady foreign past could come back to haunt him. Creating a tight security screen based on the two tough henchmen now sitting in front of Richard was a smart move.

Hoping to find out more, Richard had tried to call Franklin from England, only to learn he had recently died in a horrific car smash outside Johannesburg, leaving a young family and several open questions at the coroner's inquest. However, there were just so many similar traffic incidents, like the one Richard had recently experienced, that the police did not pursue the Franklin matter with any vigour.

Recalling all this, Richard involuntarily coughed and smothered it as Shorty turned around to stare at him. Richard wished he hadn't as the car veered towards the verge. Shorty pulled it back and Nick bleated.

'Watch the damn road, man.'

Richard, now more on edge, turned his mind again to Franklin's diligent sleuthing. He had actually uncovered quite a lot. Paesano had been born in Argentina in 1951, the only child of a short-lived marriage between an Italian and a German migrant. Apparently his grandparents on both sides had been early supporters of Fascism and were politically attracted to Argentina, seeking better opportunities in the aftermath of the Great Depression. They were all extremely successful and considerable parental indulgence may well have conditioned some of his non-conformist behaviour.

Ready linguistic skill became an important feature of Paesano's international financial dealing. Franklin's article asserted Paesano had arrived in South Africa in his early twenties as a fast-talking conman. The researcher more than hinted at the likelihood his rapid wealth accumulation was related to drugs, mercenary work, and possibly even arms dealing in Central Africa. It seemed Paesano had invested part of his purse to ease his way through many regulatory channels during the demise of the apartheid regime.

In no time at all people were calling him 'Mister Paesano' and he seemed not only to have the ear of several Ministers in the recently elected government, but had also cuddled up to some newly elevated bureaucrats. Any semblance of a formal investigation into his South American and Central African background had been quickly and conveniently snuffed out.

Diversionary driving by Shorty and another robust exchange between the two thugs up front broke into Richard's thinking. His mind now turned again to Franklin's article which had also briefly alluded to both these men.

One had done time for manslaughter after a colourful career in gang warfare: Shorty Mpane was a massive Zulu and absolutely fearless. There were no indulgences in his background. His overbearing and scarcely concealed aggression suggested to Franklin he would do anything for money, power and the approval of the Boss.

Richard noted from the article that Paesano had no qualms about taking him along on his visits to banks, financiers, public servants and regulators, and was prepared to leave him to his own devices in settling most arguments with investors. Franklin had managed to interview some of these investors and smaller mining companies on the promise of confidentiality. They were scared and rightly so because Shorty could never be regarded as a sympathetic listener. Even in such a short time, Richard thought Franklin had drawn a very good pen portrait of Mpane. He felt uncomfortable just looking at the shaven head and thick neck in front of him, blocking most of the view ahead.

The other acolyte was Nick Denning, different entirely. Born Michael O'Brien, he had a protected childhood and well-connected parents. Straight out of a good boarding school, he had served in Angola during his National Service years and made no attempt to deny Franklin's speculation he had killed terrorist prisoners in the Angolan Border Wars. He'd later qualified in law and commerce with commendable results before joining a merchant bank.

Franklin described Nick's financial advice as often too lateral and this had led to 'conflict of interest' problems. There were also unproven suggestions of money laundering and insider trading. The bank making serious money had turned a blind eye to these until Nick had grossly over-reached himself and was eventually shown the door. His parents, the O'Briens, had completely cut him off and they had nothing to say to Franklin except they were pleased about his name change to Denning.

Confidants told Franklin that Nick was at a loose end but certainly not destitute when Paesano came across him in the process of finalising one of his dodgier deals. Although he was advising the counter- party, Nick had been more than happy to play into Paesano's hand for a cut of the action. Paesano added him to his small team and relied on him for all his legal arrangements. These never were very simple, as Richard was coming to realise through his recent personal experience, and again a flash of a distant memory troubled him. He let the thought pass.

So this was the situation in which Richard now found himself. Working in an opulent, secure house with an unknown scientist was an intriguing thought, or at least it should be once he had overcome the troubling fee-sharing negotiations. Despite his growing concerns, there was a very attractive sum at stake and the opportunity to gain scientific acclaim even under Paesano's shadow.

Having met the Boss and not having seen much to commend him, he told himself he must now keep his nose well clear of Green Mines' business and get on with his contract. The sooner he was able to extricate himself from all this, the better.

While Richard had been musing, they'd been travelling for nearly an hour through heavy, undisciplined traffic in a northerly direction. Despite his distractions and the restricted view from the back, he noted how the properties and houses were becoming larger and security precautions more obvious. While he had no idea of where he was being taken, he did pay attention as they passed through two large cloverleaf intersections. He was relieved to at last see a signpost to Kyalami Drive which might help later in his orientation. Shorty steered his way down this smooth, winding, tree-lined road and turned in past a bold notice welcoming visitors to Outlook Rural Estate.

Richard decided to break the silence with a question.

'Why isn't there security at the entrance to this estate? There are so many luxurious houses on such large blocks of land around here.'

Shorty put him down, just pointing to the high, protective walls and massive gates on each.

'We're the same. Gunna take a small bloody army to get in.'

They reached a tight turn on a more secluded stretch of road. Shorty slowed down and gestured at a scarred and blackened tree trunk on the left. The surrounding grass had been burnt, but even in the drought, green shoots were beginning to burst through. A scatter of broken glass glittered at the base of the tree and Shorty turned his head to take a hard look at it.

'That's where that prying fucker, Franklin, died. This journo was snooping around Green Mines and trying to get into our secure house. Bad accident here … driving too fast getting away. Not much left of the car after they put out the fire… or of him either for that matter.'

He gave a brief snort and grinned sourly.

'Only identified him by his teeth … There are others, likely our competitors who won't be so nosey in future!'

The implication wasn't at all subtle and Richard gave an involuntary gulp of revulsion while a chill ran down his spine.

Almost immediately, the car drew up in front of its own pair of imposing, black, steel gates which blocked off any view of the interior. Inward and outward-facing searchlights were closely spaced along the fenceline.

THREE

The gates opened smoothly and quickly to give Richard his first view of the secure house. There were memories of similar places from his youth, but he was in no mood to be nostalgic. He suddenly felt on edge, alone and incredibly tired, and he just wanted to finish his work and get back to London.

The wide, gravel drive followed a gentle curve to a long, large, low-set building. It was brightly white-washed beneath a heavily-thatched roof and there were abundant floor-to-ceiling windows. Richard contrasted this substantial mansion with his own pleasant, Grade ll-listed, small cottage in Kent, burdened as it was with debt.

An extensive lawn, apparently lavishly watered throughout the drought, surrounded the house and stretched right up to the boundary walls. Looking around, Richard could see the mandatory tennis court and a small cabana set away from the house and, with a slight pang, he recalled the lively, year-round tennis parties, so important in his parents' lives. To his left, a branch of the drive led to a set of six matching garages, some other outbuildings which were possibly staff quarters and a dog run confining a couple of large Alsatians.

Richard's overwhelming feeling was this was a place to keep

people in as much as it was to keep others out. Once again, paranoia surfaced for a second and he was troubled, wondering what sort of challenges lay ahead.

The car crunched its way slowly on the gravel up to an impressive front door which had been opened by a young Indian man, dark-haired and quite light-skinned. His welcoming smile was so exaggerated it could have been designed to compensate for the dismal earlier efforts of the others. Shorty. of course, rudely ignored it as he eased his large form out of the car. Two other workers had appeared from the garden and without any greeting at all, Shorty grunted a curt order to the nearest.

'Put Dr Curie's bag in suite C. Oh, and you can let him out of the car now.'

In one way Richard was mollified. At least he wasn't 'Curry' this time, although, on the other hand, he was already beginning to feel like a prisoner. He tried to ignore an aside about child-safety locks which the big man seemed to find amusing.

Nick kept everyone else waiting as he carefully packed up his papers, an act which had Shorty fuming. After his briefcase was in order, he laboriously clambered out of the car and then remembered his pistol. He very deliberately retrieved it from the glove-box, sticking it in his pocket where it made an obvious bulge. Turning to the other groundsman, he loudly ordered him to put the car away, trying to give the impression his was a more important command than Shorty's had been. Pushing in front of Shorty, he led the way into the foyer so officiously Richard easily sensed the other man's ire and the seething animosity between the two.

Inside the expansive foyer, Richard looked around with interest. There were four exits: two doorways and two open archways. Both doors were open and through one Richard could see a sizeable sitting and dining area, and beyond the glimmer of a pool. To his left he saw a large kitchen and pantry with a couple of staff milling about who took absolutely no notice of his arrival.

A bulky reception desk provided a jarring note in the foyer. The Indian was already back sitting at it, presiding over a bank of eight CCTV monitors which covered most of the property, including control over the entry gate. Inside the house, the coverage extended to the passageways and public rooms. Green Mines had gone for the top-of-the-range, and Richard wondered whether other recording devices were concealed around the place.

Nick again exercised his assumed authority and pointed towards the arches and passageways beyond, his sharp voice echoing down the corridors.

'These lead to the east and west wings and each have three accommodation suites. Your suite C is in the east wing and you'll find it's very comfortable indeed. This is five-star stuff. There's also an area where you can take your meals in your room or you can use the main dining room. Oh, and the house staff start promptly at five-thirty in the morning and go home around ten at night.'

Richard thought that some things had never changed over all those years. There were still servants, now called staff, working long hours for low wages and God knows where 'home' was for them, what it was like and how long it took to get there.

Nick detected Richard's look of disapproval and said tersely, 'At least this fucking lot have got a car.'

Shorty had already lost interest in these trivialities and quietly disappeared, so Nick adopted a marginally friendlier attitude and behaved more like an estate agent. Again the high pitch of his voice took away some dignity from his presentation.

'Come look at the view.'

He strode across the living room ahead of Richard and stopped near the wall of glass overlooking a large swimming pool and spa. Beyond was a magnificent outlook to the distant Magaliesberg Mountains. They passed through the imposing doorway onto the verandah and Nick sneeringly pointed out Shorty walking towards the wall.

'See Mpane down there pulling his gun out? That's where he does all his bloody practice. He's in love with his gun, probably because it makes more noise than a Harley Davidson without a muffler. I prefer a silencer myself.'

Franklin's comment's about Nick's National Service experience came back to him and he had an uncomfortable feeling in the pit of his stomach before further talk was drowned out by a thundering volley of six shots. A cloud of plaster dust rose from the brickwork. Shorty strolled over to his target and turned towards them holding up his open hand as he called out in triumph.

'Five out of six, man!'

He swaggered back up to the house and disappeared around the corner towards the garages. Nick sounded frustrated and he had difficulty bringing his voice down, causing Richard to speculate about an inferiority complex.

'What an arrogant bastard. You can tell he hasn't had any military training.'

Richard, his ears still ringing, took in the whole scene before him and wondered how he might describe it to his friends at home. While there were no large trees, the vista was not all lawns as he'd first noticed. Well-tended and sometimes low-hedged garden beds were scattered across the property, and they'd been designed to add interest without shielding the view. The only form of vertical relief in the garden was provided by the tennis court fencing and the lush creeper which enveloped the adjacent cabana.

To Richard's practical mind, the architecture of the house was far more interesting than the grounds. He was impressed by the way the two accommodation wings, each containing three suites, curved around the pool, not unlike the cropped horns of a buffalo, the pool seemingly forming its head and the reception rooms a substantial neck. In front of each suite was a large, shaded deck area which was relatively private and Richard now understood Nick's analogy of a five-star resort.

Morning tea had been ordered and it was some time since his lavish airline breakfast, so Richard was happy enough to leave his suite and join Nick at the table on the central verandah. The two chatted to each other quite amiably for a while seeking common ground before it all became awkward with long silences and Nick fiddling with his phone. Ignoring Richard he ostentatiously began arranging a dinner date. Richard felt mildly disgusted with his oily, superficial charm and wondered who might fall for it. Nick was quick to enlighten him.

'She's a young shag-bag. Pity I'm not allowed to organise a party in this place for you and her pals.'

This change in attitude rocked Richard and as fast as he could, he excused himself to do his unpacking and have a shower. Sensing Richard's distaste, Nick's voice hardened and lifted nasally.

'See you in the sitting room before lunch. Bring a summary of your work as you'll be meeting your collaborator. You'll sort out how you'll work together.'

After a pause, he added with a silly smirk.

'You can also decide how you'll divide up the money.'

Richard reached his suite and the first thing he noticed was his bag unpacked and his belongings neatly put away. Even his shirts and trousers had been ironed. His suspicions were immediately aroused. Was it possible Shorty might have had a hand in this? He didn't have morning tea and he didn't spend much time playing with his gun.

He hurriedly looked through his gear to see if anything was missing. All was well. Nervously, he connected his laptop to the suite's computer/printer set-up and was relieved to confirm the database had not been accessed, but he remained uncomfortable.

Making good use of this break, he quickly printed out the summary IP material Nick had asked for. When he tried to connect his iPhone to pick up messages, all he heard was a faint humming sound. He nearly rang the foyer for a line, but pulled himself up. *Bugger,* he thought. *You've got to calm down and think things through. You're seeing phantoms everywhere.* He set an alarm, stood for a long time under a very hot shower, and laid back on the wide bed. His mind was in turmoil.

First and foremost, Richard was absolutely sure his ideas, untested as they were on a commercial scale, had real value to Paesano. He could easily have learnt through industrial espionage about Richard's professional standing and that he had discussions with a couple of major mining companies. Richard recalled one such meeting with a senior geologist who had been sympathetic.

'There are other people sniffing around this technology at the moment. Please understand while we in Exploration think your ideas have great merit, senior management is only interested in big stuff given the price of gold at present. We haven't got the budget, we can't even take an option and we certainly aren't the people to offer you finance.'

Of course, there was always a possibility a big mining house might buy this IP and mothball it. Richard groaned at the thought. It was his baby and he badly wanted to see it up and proven. It represented years of innovative thinking. The real attraction of Green Mines was a willingness to lay out hard cash, and lots of it, to fund, prove and actually implement his novel ideas. He'd learnt enough through reading Franklin to know Paesano liked to jump the gun and gloried in exploiting the tardiness of his big competitors.

Second, there was the matter of money itself. Hard cash for him! This was a great attraction for Richard because while he had run a successful one-man consulting business on an international basis for some years, his success was measured more by sound reputation than by substantial income. Moreover, a pending divorce settlement to his long-suffering American wife was causing him serious financial problems. All this was topped up by a mortgage which he was finding difficult to repay.

He remembered the comfortable university dalliance during his PhD years at MIT which had drifted into a convenient marriage, celebrated at a vastly expensive society wedding. He now recognised, despite being sexually well experienced, he had been a late developer emotionally. He felt a twinge of remorse for ignoring his mother when she had bluntly warned him a year or so after he married.

'Stop behaving in such an under-graduate way, traipsing all over the world. You have a very nice wife at home and I don't think you'll have her for much longer.'

He knew his decision to undertake an MBA in London was selfish. His wife had flatly refused to join him, even for a year. Not surprisingly, this turned out to be the straw which broke the back of the marriage. The fault lay almost entirely in his camp and the final settlement was ugly. Now, in retrospect, he clenched his fists at the sheer scale of her angry demands. She had chosen outrageous financial revenge despite his generous starting offer. The battle was interminable involving some very expensive lawyers on both sides and his hadn't been as good as hers. *So much for being a nice guy,* he thought, as he considered his present predicament.

Here he was, nearly forty years old, very much on his own and in serious need of financial recovery with an expensively mortgaged house in Kent. While any reasonable proportion of the fee would solve this problem, it was all coming down to valuing the contribution of his fellow scientist. It bothered him he had never heard of another innovator other than Claude

Guerin working in this specific field and Guerin had completely disappeared.

As Richard was lying there wide awake, the penny dropped. He knew he would be hopeless in any fee negotiation. Was this the deliberate introduction of a devious power play which he found distasteful? Was the Dr Dupain who had been mentioned by Paesano possibly associated with Guerin? Questions churned around his mind.

Lacking a fundamental understanding of the geology, statistical analysis, mining or concentrator elements of the process, had Paesano backed by Nick's legalise, cunningly made sure the two scientists had to pool their expertise in a divisive atmosphere of selfishness and jealousy? His mind churned. He was too tired to think straight.

What on earth would it be like working for money-grabbing gangsters who knew little about science and cared for it even less? With growing irritation he read again the seemingly innocuous fee-sharing and succession clauses Nick had subtly inserted into the Agreement. He was on his own now because Paesano didn't have the decency to carve the fee cake for him.

FOUR

The persistent chime of his alarm dragged Richard out of his jet-lagged sleep. He was amazed he had actually been able to drift off under the building tension and he pressed the heels of his palms into his heavy eyes to clear them. He was only properly awake after a long shower and now, dressed in clean clothes, he was ready to meet the mystery scientist.

Almost jauntily he glanced in the mirror, tidied up his tousled hair and polished his rimless glasses. Apart from signs of a slight paunch, he felt he presented quite professionally. And, as people do when they are on their own, he tried a couple of facial expressions in the mirror. He smiled and he scowled and he tried to appear condescending. Then, he gathered up his papers and headed for the foyer where he met the polite Indian and mentioned his poor mobile phone connection. He wasn't completely surprised by the explanation.

'Since that nosy journalist tried to hack into our systems, Mr Paesano is making everyone use the secure house line. We are now having a blanket cut-off zone in place. Just give me your internet address and password and I will be setting up your email. Mr Denning has already been telling me you must only be using the secure data line to communicate to your base in England and I am to be supervising this.'

The prickle of worry which sleep and a shower had eased now returned. Richard was sure he was losing too much control over his own affairs and decided to provide only his business password.

'I understand,' he said, a picture of compliancy. 'Here you are.'

He picked up a stylish pen and wrote '*pg7ddH2*'. To cover his rattled state, he calmly said any messages could wait until after lunch, now certain any message for him would have been read anyway.

He approached the sitting room where he saw Shorty and Nick talking angrily and gesticulating at some-one near the large window. The focus of their annoyance was looking out towards the swimming pool and he wondered what had happened to aggravate them. Was this the scientist? All he could see in the glare was someone above medium height with dark, cropped hair and wearing a long, white, laboratory coat.

Shorty continued his ranting and Richard clearly heard a threat.

'You ... b-b-bloody well won't do it ...'

Again, the angry stutter, but then Shorty spotted him and there was an abrupt silence in the room. The stranger turned around but was still indistinct against the bright backdrop. Richard stepped back in his surprise ... a woman ... in a lab coat ... a co-worker? Nick offered an introduction.

'Dr Richard Curie, your workmate, Dr Margrit Dupain.'

Richard saw the smirking Nick was enjoying a long-planned

gender joke at his expense. The joke wasn't yet over. Before either could respond, he continued with obvious relish at Richard's discomfort.

'Once known as Margrit Paesano. Didn't need the fancy doctor title then; she wasn't important to anybody.'

As Nick knew it would, this extra piece of information completely floored Richard and he could only manage a muted, polite, 'Hello,' which she acknowledged with a cold nod but without shaking his proffered hand. He felt his face reddening and looked away, then looked at her again and not wanting to appear rude, he looked down. Paesano with a daughter? Ex-wife? Guerin?

Richard wondered for a moment whether she had any prior knowledge of Nick's pathetic little trick. After his eyes adjusted to the glare, Richard noticed a lingering look of anger and defiance on the woman's flushed face. An obvious grimace of distaste at Nick's callow comments showed she wasn't a party to his childishness. And, judging by the disdainful look on Shorty's face, neither was he.

On first glance, he was unable to note anything distinctive about this Dupain. Her eyes were hidden behind heavy glasses and her body was shapeless under the white laboratory coat. Tall for a woman and indeed she seemed older than him. Her hands were clenched in anger and she appeared austere and frosty. During a brief moment they openly examined each other and, egotistically, he wondered about her initial impression of him. Could they actually work together?

Richard's catalogue of problems had just grown larger and more complicated: a collaborator who appeared to have had close personal ties to his client in the past. He decided it would be difficult to trust let alone get along easily with her.

Nick, feeling he needed to claw back control of the situation, stepped in to end an embarrassing stand-off with a curt, high-pitched instruction, rudely treating Dupain as an invisible person.

'She'll change out of her ridiculous uniform before she joins us for lunch.'

Without making eye contact or saying anything, she strode angrily off towards the west wing. Glorying in the shock of his announcement, Nick continued.

'I'll fill you in before she gets back'

He moved over to the dining table on the far side of the room and wasn't about to drop his little coup in a hurry.

'Bit of a surprise, eh? Don't worry about her, though. She was his second wife and he gave up marriage after number three, who spent money as if she was on a Crusade. Dieter's like me, man. There's too much other tottie out there.'

Richard smiled to himself at Nick's comments thinking it was Mr Paesano to his face and Dieter when his back was turned. He didn't have any time to mull this over, as Nick expanded on Dupain's background.

'She appears so dull. People say she's completely focused on her research in the biological metallurgy field and has had good training under Claude Guerin.'

Pleasantly surprised by the sudden change of mood, Richard joined in, really needing to know more

'It's a wonder I haven't heard of her. Where's she been working?'

It would tell him where she fitted into the all-important hierarchy of the academic world. Nick opened up.

'She worked with that Professor before spending quite some time at SMGT. You know, that Swiss mob: Suisse Molecular and Genetic Technology. Don't ask me what position she had there. It was something pretty smart to do with gold mining technology. I know bugger-all about that sort of stuff.'

Unstoppable, Nick went on.

'I've heard they've had a shit time of it lately, though. I don't know if you're familiar with this sort of thing where the financial side is modelled like parts of the pharmaceutical industry. You know, the ones which aim to raise funds and debt in speculative money markets rather than do any real work. This is much more in my line than all the mining crap.'

Given Nick's own background he thought it ironic he made his last statement with such a straight face. Richard was surprised by Shorty's deep voice overriding Nick.

'Most of the money these guys make goes off overseas, thanks to friendly bankers. SMGT never produced anything in South Africa except bloody announcements. Smart bastards, eh?'

Unusually for someone normally so reticent he went on and on.

'Announcements about new technical discoveries kinda like yours. Stories about joint ventures with universities, about tests, about changes in bosses and about research which Dupain does ...'

Nick, anxious to lead the discussion, broke in, 'Even things which seem pretty damn detrimental can be pushed as a positive by spin doctors. An IP challenge in the courts can be touted as meaning there's value in a company's research and a tax issue can be portrayed as indicative of actual profits.'

Richard decided to score a subtle point which went down well with Shorty and was initially missed by the wound-up, voluble Nick.

'I guess this happens a lot in your sophisticated business world, eh Nick?'

Having brought the conversation around to his own pet topic, Nick ignored the jibe and was now enjoying himself.

'The SMGT people were even clever enough to appoint a commercial risk manager as a consultant, a retired Colonel called Wilhelm Wolhuter. This is classic stuff: a real teaser which gets every dickhead speculator thinking if they have a Risk Manager they must have something big to risk. Believe it or not, this alone nudged the share price up 3 francs and led to SMGT being able to issue more shares.'

He laughed derogatorily as Shorty took up the theme.

'You know, no one asked what a fucking retired, army intelligence officer brings to SMGT. I'd like to look him over sometime soon. Someone there told me he'd been looking at the old Green Mines' tie-up with SMGT.'

Shorty didn't elaborate and sat down at the dining table pushing the settings aside as he pulled a handful of documents out of his briefcase. His part in the conversation was ended, but Nick was unstoppable in his puffed-up way.

'Lately, SMGT has been running skinny on announcements and now the gold price is firming. The Gold Bug investor interest has shifted back to more direct involvement in mining. Here at Green Mines we've managed to dress things up differently and Dieter has been savvy enough to avoid the stock markets and stick to debt finance and joint ventures. This means, of course, far fewer people need to know what's going on and we all know Dieter doesn't appreciate nosiness, does he?'

There was a hidden warning in this and Richard stiffened. Nick moved closer to the archway leading to the west wing. He clearly thought it was time for Dupain to reappear. There was no sign of her, so he turned back to Richard.

'Didn't you know SMGT was once in partnership with Green Mines?'

Richard, who thought it best not to admit anything about his research, shook his head and Nick continued.

'Well, you think about it, there is a common thread. Both were into exploiting financial markets rather than actually producing the metal. I don't mind admitting I'm part of this; it's not illegal to exploit the greed of others. Dieter knew SMGT was hanging on to some good stuff of Dupain's. He believed it should belong to him. So, hey, hard to imagine, but one thing led to another and he married her.'

Richard blinked at this callous summary. Part of him was beginning to wish he hadn't encouraged Nick to be so expansive, but he needed to hear more and Nick obliged.

'Man, she was well over thirty and I reckon he was just wasting his time. It's not as if she knew the whole picture and this Gen Tec mob promptly fired her anyway because of the conflict of interest. They've been battling me and Green Mines over their so-called rights ever since. The funny thing is this argument has actually pushed up SMGT's share price while our bankers are easing off. It just goes to show everyone's hedging their bets. As soon as he knew he wouldn't benefit from the marriage, Dieter ditched the old bag.'

He paused but wasn't about to stop.

'After SMGT there was no way she could find a job. SMGT doesn't forgive easily and there were no references from the bastards.'

Richard interjected.

'Or from Mr Paesano, I imagine?'

He was rewarded by a wry grin.

'They completely abandoned her project until they saw we had an interest, and then things changed yet again. You gossiping scientists never can keep your damn mouths shut. He heard about your stuff and saw how complementary it is to what she's doing. He put two and two together in a hurry and decided to bring her here. So, I negotiated and set her up.'

Throughout all this, Shorty had been silently engrossed in working his way through a document pile. He occasionally glanced warningly at Nick, annoyed he wasn't getting the message or was choosing to ignore it. Richard was learning more than he should.

'The west wing is her lab, her office, her home. There has been cash in the bank every month and she drinks and eats well. Not a bad life for an ageing foreign bitch who's only dedicated to her work. She doesn't have any close family here and for all I know she probably wishes she was still screwing Dieter. She's certainly not my type; I wouldn't touch her.'

At this, Shorty coughed sharply and looked very hard at Nick who suddenly grasped he'd said far too much. His nasal tones completely dried up for a while and into this silence stepped Margrit Dupain, dressed in casual linen trousers, a loose silk shirt and carrying a manila folder under her arm. Despite Nick's gross account, Richard figured she was about his age. Now he saw her close-up, wearing more flattering, light-framed glasses and without her angry glare, she actually was most attractive. In fact, the person he now saw so belied Nick's descriptions Richard couldn't help but wonder whether the opportunist hadn't, in fact, tried it on and been spurned.

They joined Shorty in the dining room, who without waiting for anyone, immediately began chomping on a bread roll. Nick pulled up his chair and sat down sloppily, but Richard waited until Margrit Dupain was seated. This provoked surprised stares from the other two, put out by his good manners, but she politely thanked him with a slight smile.

FIVE

It was a quiet, dull lunch with only sporadic chit-chat. The food was very good and expertly served. Margrit reminded herself that her ex-husband still appeared to be indifferent to minor cost saving opportunities. In the face of financial disruption on a grand scale, Paesano was still a big picture man.

To her relief, there was not much sign of either minder's usual aggression or one-upmanship during the meal. She knew Nick's and Shorty's phones were unaffected by the Indian's so called 'blanket cut off zone' and from time to time they each got up and went outside to use them. Her own freedom to contact outsiders had been cancelled months before.

She was surprised that Nick was uncharacteristically reticent and only picked at his food while reading a legal document. Shorty's contribution, between bouts of examining text messages on his iPhone and chomping noisily on prodigious mouthfuls, consisted mainly of describing some of the spa's many features.

Although still on edge, given the acrimony earlier that morning, she decided to contribute to the scanty conversation and also draw Richard Curie out a bit. Given the lack of response from the other two, she could see that he was puzzled by her forthrightness. Would he be wondering how she fitted in? She felt it would take time to fully gain his trust and decided the academic world was a place to start.

'My background was in pure science in Geneva, then my Doctoral thesis I undertook at the same University under Professor Claude Guerin. How about you?'

She sensed he knew some of this already and waited for his response.

'Oh, MSc at Imperial College and PhD at MIT …'

Nick who felt out of the limelight broke in.

'All those bloody alphabetical letters. Not as good as a first-class law degree like mine!'

To which Richard added, 'And I also completed an MBA at LBS.'

Margrit was pleased at this subtle show of humour and Shorty, degree-less, also saw the point, spluttering his amusement while Nick reddened in anger. He had nothing further to contribute, so Margrit boldly took the opportunity to broaden Shorty's understanding of academic institutions without putting him down.

"As you would know MIT is Massachusetts Institute of Technology and London has a very good business school."

Shorty just grunted and   after barely half an hour she decided to leave and deliberately excusing herself only to Richard, ignored Shorty and handed Nick her manila file.

'I think this is all you wanted. Now, if you don't mind, I'll return to my work.'

Nick barely looked up and pushed the file towards Richard.

'I can't understand this science stuff at all. I get my kicks out of these commercial papers.'

Richard handed his own file directly to her and politely suggested a meeting.

'Your lab after breakfast tomorrow, Margrit?'

She decided it was a genuinely warm approach and nodded her agreement. But Nick couldn't be seen to lose control and his next command was superfluous.

'You two do that! Dieter wants me to remind you how tight the timeline is. We'll all meet tomorrow afternoon.'

Shorty was now seriously put out and dismissed Nick's presumption of authority, grunting ominously.

'Maybe.'

And the foursome split up. Margrit headed towards the west wing, while Nick and Shorty headed for the foyer with Shorty mumbling over his shoulder.

'I'm off to pick up Dieter now. We're gunna visit some of the mining people and give them a bit of … um … encouragement. We'll tell them we're now finishing things and it's going well.'

He turned and looked hard at Richard, anger rising in his voice.

'It'd … b-b-bloody … b-b-better be. Now get on with it!'

Nick had his own priorities and delivered a lewd closing comment aimed at her.

'You won't see me early tomorrow, Shorty. I expect to get lucky with my little girl tonight.'

How typical of him,' she thought, *and also how revealing of his insecurity,* but her thoughts turned quickly to the elegant, intelligent, but also withdrawn, Dr Curie who was unfailingly polite.

She was glad she had taken the trouble to tidy herself up

after a morning's work in the lab and she was pleased to notice his immediate interest in her. He seemed warm and friendly and a ready conversationalist. She had spent far too much time working or dealing with those two common bullies not to welcome his involvement with relief. How could she gain his trust and share her growing concerns with him?

SIX

Left on his own, Richard remembered the fee split hadn't been discussed, let alone resolved. He was disappointed that he had been unable to get any perspective on Margrit Dupain's personality and this would make fee negotiation a real challenge. So, he thought he should face up to this and strengthen his approach. He mentally designed an agenda for the next day and item number one was the fee split. Then he wandered into the foyer where, in the absence of Nick, the Indian had started loudly and officiously berating a gardener.

Friendly by nature, Richard politely waited for the Indian's showy anger to diminish and for the gardener, looking quite unchastened by the dressing down, to saunter out of the foyer. He asked if there was any mail for him as a way of striking up a conversation, and the Indian was quick to proffer a handshake and introduce himself.

'Dr Curie, I'm Winston Naidoo.'

Richard shook his hand warmly.

'What an unusual first name for an Indian. Are you perhaps Anglo-Indian ...'

He suddenly realised he was being rude, so he hurried on, 'Please call me Richard. None of this doctor stuff for me.'

From the slight shrug of his shoulders and a characteristic sideways shake of his head, it seemed Winston didn't care either way. Richard could see he was relaxing now the thugs had departed and his change of mood was reflected in an easy response.

'Indeed yes, my grandmother was British and came here with my grandfather after the war. They were coming from Madras you know, and this was before apartheid really reared its head in 1948. Our family didn't actually have a bad time of it because we were in that strange political space between black and white.'

Winston was obviously keen to talk and Richard took up the chance to have a more normal conversation in this cloistered place. To widen the discussion, he asked Winston about his training.

'I've been lucky, you know. Because of all the changes under Mandela, I was getting into the University of Natal and I passed the second year of a degree in commerce. I came up to Jo'burg to find work and the first job I found was in security at SMGT.'

He paused, noting Richard's growing interest.

'Mr Paesano saw me there while he was still on friendly terms with that mob and asked if I was wanting a better job. There were some pretty bigoted foreigners at SMGT and I felt this place would indeed be better for me.'

Richard was genuinely interested, but felt Winston wasn't giving him the full story.

'And has it been?' he asked.

Winston screwed up his nose, briefly shook his head and responded almost nervously.

'To be honest, it's a bit of a crappy job although I'm being paid pretty well and I'm having no expenses. Mr Paesano has been promising me a promotion if I do a good job, but I do miss Durban and I haven't been off this place in months. That Mr Mpane is always making things difficult for me and it doesn't help that him and Mr Denning are not getting on so well.'

It was obvious Winston wasn't part of the inner sanctum. In fact, from what Richard had seen, he was just dismissed as an appendage.

'Well, it looks to me like you're doing a good job, Winston.'

Richard nodded towards the bank of monitors and pressed on with compliments, just a little concerned he was sounding ponderous.

'The security setup seems pretty convincing and the whole appearance is great.'

'Thank you very much, sir … I mean, Richard. Indeed, I don't often get told that.'

'Well, I think you should know, Winston, my algorithms are massively data hungry and I do need to access them from time to time.'

As Winston had no idea what an algorithm was, he rather cheekily replied.

'Just remember, Richard, data only and under my supervision.'

Winston seemed happy to shed more light on things although for some reason he dropped his voice a little.

'Do you know Mr Paesano is only renting this place? He is not even owning the mansion in town. The properties belonged to one of Mr Paesano's former business partners who'd caused trouble. The fellow was somehow forced into bankruptcy and then he died. They say suicide but who is knowing …'

His voice tailed off and a shadow crossed his face, but he brightened as he continued.

'Mr Paesano negotiated with the liquidator and arranged to occupy all the properties in exchange for picking up the maintenance charges. A number of foreigners, mainly from South America, are being brought to stay here from time to time, but I am not allowed to talk to them even if I could be speaking Spanish.'

At last Winston had to break off the conversation to answer an incoming call. Open as this janitor had seemed to be, Richard wondered where Winston's loyalties would lie if a real issue arose.

Back in his room, he put Margrit Dupain's folder down near the computer. After the alcohol-free lunch, he felt a real need to relax and poured himself a stiff drink from the bar fridge.

One thing really bugging him was establishing whether Margrit Dupain was a Paesano supporter or a somewhat unwilling resident in the house. Her earlier confrontation in the sitting room certainly suggested the latter. How could he be sure?

Semi-distracted by this, he started to leaf through the documents in her folder. For a start, he noticed how his own contacts and several key issues he had identified were threaded through her papers. Clearly Nick had passed these on to her for inclusion and Green Mines appeared to know a lot more about him than generally available public material. With his reputation for underhand play, Paesano was quite likely to have arranged someone to hack into his client base. Why wouldn't he?

After a while his reading became more thorough and he examined the file with a growing professional interest. The resulting buoyancy of mind had been lacking in his life for a long time. This research was not only elegant, it was also practically focused.

Essentially, Margrit Dupain used her background in biological metallurgy to identify molecules which were cheap to make, and were very efficient in extracting the last vestiges of gold from worn-out, old mines. This was way beyond Richard's initial hopes because her work seemed to cover the whole gamut of issues linking their work.

He thought back to his earlier discussions with international mining companies in London and the way he had been politely put down by their technical staff.

'Richard, the gold price is now at a ten-year low and the ability to drive costs down even in low grade mines could dramatically increase recoverable reserves. Can your IP actually do it? It'll need to be properly tested and we need better proof.'

This would show them, he thought. He now saw the brilliance of Paesano's vision to connect these concepts, linking her work to the algorithms he had developed and going far beyond his own basic processes of analysis towards creating feedback for sophisticated decision making. He rushed through the familiar aspects of her research to concentrate on the most innovative parts.

He was so agitated he had to get up and walk around the room while he considered issues ranging beyond gold extraction from mines and even slimes dams. He was even beginning to envision a positive environmental impact, clearing up mercury and heavy metal residues as well as cyanide and sulphide contamination. All that was missing in her work was the definition of the appropriate ore concentrations to use and he was confident together they could clarify this in the days ahead.

Spurred on by the potential of her research and the progress she had made, Richard had to question his own contribution. After he had abandoned field work and returned to a comfortable office life, an expensive post-graduate degree at the London Business School had helped him to understand many of the financial drivers behind business decisions. He could see how this skill would fit into what he was already beginning to think of as 'The Curie Process'. He naively down-played his arrangement with Green Mines and really ignored her input.

All this raised a stab of real excitement. He knew it would only take a small amount of testing and experimentation to bring their separate ideas together and establish very valuable IP. He again stood up from the desk in his excitement and let his mind roam.

What then? he thought, as his mouth dried. Despite Paesano's propensity to leap in where others feared to tread, Richard knew he was no fool. Paesano would actually apply it in his own rundown mining properties. Now he understood more about Green Mines, he felt fairly confident Paesano would raise more capital and ramp up his own values in partnership with a number of those smaller miners. He was a Gold Bug.

'The Curie Process', after all, would be most valuable to

the independents at the bottom of the food chain, even with a shark at the top. Franklin had learnt how many of these bottom feeders were already being exploited and were growing disenchanted by Paesano's unfulfilled promises. This was the way Green Mines did its deal-making. It wasn't just a mining company by any stretch of anyone's imagination …

He finished his first reading of Margrit Dupain's file and with resumed confidence was feeling more upbeat about the likelihood of a successful outcome.

His mood changed once more. On the downside, what might happen if the process didn't yield an outstanding outcome? Paesano seemed prepared to throw substantial money at the project which was a sure sign he was relying heavily on it. Apart from his own mining interests, he would surely have shown a bit of leg to seduce many small Gold Bug chancers into outlaying funds?

He guessed Paesano would need time to wind down those complex commitments. From what Nick had divulged, these participants appeared to be no cleaner than Green Mines and this added a further twist to a potentially nasty scenario. Paesano could simply not afford to have this deviousness exposed, especially to SMGT or his financiers, and so he'd want to keep his two scientific advisors well out of the way. Were these the reasons behind Richard's attractive fee offer and the secretive way in which he was now being detained?

Richard had been told by Paesano that succeed or fail, he would be heading straight home after the trials. Now having seen first-hand the way things operated at Green Mines, he was not at all sure it was straightforward, whatever the project outcome. And what of Margrit Dupain's prospects? There must be a sizeable risk that together they were both about to discover too much about this unsavoury commercial jungle. He shuddered slightly in his concern,

Aware he was becoming despondent, he turned again to her extraordinarily thorough research and the rest of the afternoon passed quickly.

His concentration was broken again when Winston delivered Richard's pre-ordered light dinner. The conversation between the two was as convivial as it had been in the afternoon and Richard was able to ask him about night-time security arrangements. Winston obliged with some reservation.

'Security is being maintained throughout the night by two guards. They are spending most of their day in the compound over by the garages, which is also where I am sleeping. At night they are on patrol, but the CCTV monitors in the compound are like those in the foyer, so you can rest easy. Indeed everything will be safe and sound, no need even to be locking your door.'

He'd found Winston's last comment ironic as he couldn't see how anyone could get into the property. Playing along, Richard said, 'That's good to hear. Just one thing, though. I'd like to swim sometime each evening and with all this security stuff, will I be able to use the pool at night?'

Winston assured him with a waggle of his head that it would perfectly alright until midnight. Beyond that Richard had to pry the actual arrangements out of him and he replied almost furtively, facing away from the foyer camera.

'The dogs are let loose and I am turning electricity on to the fence. Oh, and I am also switching over to night-vision CCTV.

The mighty Mr Mpane is paranoid and has promised he will kill me if anyone is getting in here. You've already seen him having shooting practice down at the wall. He does it every time he comes out here and he was making a big show of his gun when he chased the journalist off. We all know what eventually happened to him ...'

After such openness, Winston now clammed up.

'I'll send your emails through to you later. Now I'd better be getting back to those screens.'

As Richard waved the Indian off he wondered whether he could be induced to turn a blind eye to the use of an outside line if things became dire. He was certainly very pleasant, but Richard had an uneasy feeling his explanations had been left incomplete. Did he know more about the Franklin matter than he had said? Other than in self-interest, where would Winston's loyalties lie? And if they had both once worked at SMGT, why hadn't he mentioned Margrit Dupain at all? He sat down to his light dinner wondering whether anyone he had met could be trusted. His slight appetite disappeared.

SEVEN

An hour or so later, Richard changed into swimming trunks and made his way through his verandah doors and across to the pool. Even with the garden and pool well lit, the brilliant stars and half-moon dominated the whole sky from one horizon to the other. From the house to the distant mountains stretched a flat plain dotted here and there with distant red lines of fire, marking the progress of autumnal grass burning.

Sometimes there would be a tiny sparkle of orange as a burning tree flared in those lines. However, the winds of the last few days had dropped completely and the fires presented no real threat. The dust had settled and the night sky was now brilliantly clear showing just a few wisps of colour from the fires. Few places he had ever visited could deliver such a spectacle.

Richard had swum a few quite leisurely laps when unexpectedly Margrit Dupain appeared from suite D and walked over to test the water in the spa. Richard gave her a nonchalant wave and studiously ignored her as she switched on the spa pump, took off her white towelling bath robe, and slid with grace into the turbulent water. The noise of the spa was louder than Richard had anticipated and there was no way Winston, if inquisitive, would hear much from them.

For a while, Richard continued his gentle laps of the pool before calling out.

'Very warm in the spa?'

He was just able to catch her reply above the noise as he swam over and stepped into the spa from the pool side. It certainly was agreeably warm as he settled onto the low ledge opposite her.

Through the corner of his eye he caught a quick reflection of light from the corner of the house and he watched as a camera was repositioned. He realised Winston would be watching, and the blue underwater lamps provided plenty of light for his prying. The noise of the spa would frustrate him, though.

His greeting, '*Bon soir*, Margrit,' was his only venture into French. For the first time she really smiled and her friendly response wasn't a correction of his atrocious pronunciation. They began to talk, but found the noise of the spa quite distracting. Richard wondered what Winston's instructions had been, but he quickly turned his full attention to Margrit. Winston, if he were prying, would soon have become bored.

To an outsider they might almost have been a middle-aged, holidaying couple in a fancy resort. There was some tension between them as they sought to find common ground in conversation while the ugly events of the morning rankled. Trust was still needed.

The discussion which followed was all about scientific matters and preparations for the next day. There was nothing in the way of small talk or those things of a more personal nature which Richard wished he had been able to introduce. He really wanted to know more about her life outside the scientific world, but there wasn't an obvious starting point.

He was sure she would have been deprived of meaningful conversation over the past months where her only interactions seemed to have been with the two thugs and hardly with Winston. However, over the next hour their mutual understanding of their project was enhanced. Richard was impressed and certainly wasn't condescending.

'You are right across all of the issues in my work. I wish I'd taken more time on this chemistry side that you have been developing, but I can understand why your research has been kept secret.'

She kept up a barrage of good, tough questions and had a quick grasp of his answers. Time passed quickly, the night grew quite chilly and he noticed the skin on her hands beginning to wrinkle. He swallowed his disappointment when their talk eventually petered out and Margrit got up to leave.

As she wrapped on her white towelling robe, Richard thought she was even more attractive and interesting than she had been at lunch. He wished he'd taken more care of his own shape since becoming so desk, aeroplane and couch bound. He stayed on in the spa a little longer for form's sake, stifling a wicked impulse to wave at any CCTV which may have been used to capture their meeting. It would have made dull viewing for Paesano and his thugs.

When he got back to his room, Richard had a lot to mull over. His main concern revolved around questioning Margrit's potential duplicity and he was suspicious about how her blind allegiance to Paesano might have foundered. It was clear he had tired of her as a woman and her only relevance to him now was the value of her technology. But, had she completely tired of him? Was she a spy in his pay?

At the same time, Richard couldn't help thinking how valuable his own Agreement was to him, and he would not have it jeopardised in any way by Margrit. He rather lazily, and perhaps foolishly, pushed all of this to the back of his mind. Right now, he was keen to focus on the project itself. Picking up her file, he read on for a couple of hours, thinking of her now and then as he made a note about a technical issue.

He had been able to relax a little as he worked through Margrit's file. Around ten o'clock he heard workers depart noisily down the gravel drive, calling out to the guards as they went. Their old car started giving out the characteristic bang and rumble of a very unhealthy exhaust system. The gleam of headlights on the roadside trees plotted its path along the winding lane heading down Kyalami Drive. The gates had closed smoothly after the car left and for a while Richard couldn't help reflecting on Jonathon Franklin and his untimely death not far up the road.

He went back to the file and was still working at midnight. The property lights dimmed and two Alsatian dogs barked their way around the garden. Wide awake, Richard knew he should get some decent sleep before the meeting, but it was some time before he dozed off.

Just as he did, he was jolted back to his senses by the sound of four quick, thudding gunshots away in the distance. He froze as first the lights were turned up, followed by sounds of hurrying footsteps, much whistling for the dogs and, eventually, faint faraway screams of sirens. Everything went quiet again, the outside lights dimmed and Richard was eventually able to fall asleep thinking bucolic England had much to offer.

EIGHT

It was getting light when the workers returned as noisily as they had left and the perimeter lights were switched off. Richard, now wide awake, decided on an early morning swim. He had only managed to cover a few laps, blaming his lack of fitness on Johannesburg's high altitude. His ordered, scientific mind recalled the air was only 94 per cent of its sea level density. No wonder he felt tired after minor exertion.

He was drying himself as Margrit appeared and offered him a perfunctory greeting. She dived into the pool and completed length after length at a steady pace, gliding smoothly through the water. While she was at it, Richard decided to return to his room. Part of him wished he could have watched her athletic performance for a bit longer. It was clear she was not interested in an early morning chat.

It was soon breakfast time. On his way to the dining room, Richard asked Winston about the gunshots in the night.

'Oh, nothing unusual in these parts. No one who is behaving himself would want to be out late at night, as security people tend to shoot first and ask questions later. Did you not hear that police helicopter circling far off?'

Richard hadn't and politely ended the discussion.

After a while, Margrit joined him and, in the absence of Nick and Shorty, the brooding atmosphere of aggression vanished. They concentrated on firming up the science and integrating the technology of their separate components. Moving over to a large coffee table in the sitting room, they worked comfortably together, spreading papers in all directions and focusing on their laptops. Within two hours, a project plan was established and they agreed a ten-day deadline was feasible. Richard played safe by secretly writing in a safety factor which extended the program by two more days. The fee split had not yet been touched upon and he didn't feel inclined to start discussing it yet, given how smoothly they were working together.

After this important plan was completed, Richard wanted to have a look at her laboratory, so they headed off to the west wing. The inspection had barely begun before Nick barged in, saying sarcastically,

'Did you two lovebirds have a good session in the spa last night?'

Neither deigned to reply as he continued.

'I hear you seem to have fallen out over something. Didn't go off together?'

Both were now highly offended and Richard made a mental note to be even more wary of Winston in future. Richard's voice was steely.

'It was not quite what you think. I got a bit of a surprise to see Margrit there and we spoke about the project. We haven't touched on the fee split yet.'

Turning to Margrit he asked, 'I hope this won't poison our ability to work together?'

'We'll see …' she began.

Nick savagely interjected, 'You're dead right about 'we'll see'. You don't have much time!'

Richard thought it would be best to change the subject by handing over their draft project plan.

'Well, we have done a lot of hard work on thi …'

Nick only gave it a cursory glance before commenting angrily on the end date and shaking the paper at them as his voice rose in pitch.

'This won't do at all. Don't either of you understand Dieter's position? He wants action and he wants it quickly. If you don't speed things up, we'll exercise those penalty clauses against you. I didn't design them to be fucking Christmas presents! Now think about the deadline again and get the damn fee sharing arrangement out of the way as well, or one of you will suffer.'

After a few brief words and describing some mythical short cuts, Richard gave Nick the pleasure of slicing two days off the completion date. He knew full well Nick would present this to Paesano as another demonstration of his skill and drive, even though it was plain to both the man barely understood a word of it.

Then, as a further sop to Nick's ego, Margrit astutely suggested he should arbitrate their delayed fee discussion. The sarcasm dripped from him, spoiled a little by his high-pitched voice.

'Okay. That's easy. How will we carve up four million dollars? Ladies first … not you, Curie! What's your position, madam?'

'Fifty/fifty,' was her immediate and provocative answer.

'And you, Curie?' he asked rudely. 'What do you think her effort is worth?'

Richard felt his response was embarrassingly ponderous, but Nick seemed to accept it.

'Well, actually since I own the only registered IP patent, and seeing any settlement comes out of my package, I consider Margrit should get no more than a twenty per cent share. After all, some of her stuff comes directly from SMGT and ...' gesturing around the laboratory, '... she's been well set up and has already been paid by Green Mines. I believe I've been doing all this on my own.'

He conveniently forgot the participation of friendly geologists in the two major mining houses.

To her credit, Margrit came straight back.

'Won't you see reason, Richard? What's the use of finding the most suitable resources in the world if you can't economically beneficiate the concentrates? Clearly I'm the only one who knows how to make it all work if you can deliver the right feed-stock.'

Nick was thoroughly enjoying this as it started to bring out the negotiating lawyer in him. He egged Richard on.

'Can't you see she's making sense, Dicky?'

He added a put down for Margrit.

'On her past form, she'd even sleep with the devil for fifty/fifty. You'll have to do better with your offer, my friend.'

Margrit's angry flush returned and she was only just able to hold back a French expletive. The argument went to and fro for some time until Nick, reaching the end of his notoriously brief attention span, grew bored and angrily pointed out this was all irrelevant to getting a final outcome on time. At this, Margrit appeared to see reason and backed down to accept Richard's final offer of thirty percent.

That the compromise favoured the male seemed to satisfy Nick's chauvinism, even though he saw the whole matter as something of a sham. He knew there was no way Paesano could pay anyone so generously, and there were always the fall-back clauses of his shonky Agreement, or even some other darker solution of Shorty's.

If it wasn't for the chance of something going wrong Richard, who was beginning to enjoy the farce, might have stretched it further. Nick was becoming more of a sulky bully in the process and Margrit was acting peevishly. Still, Nick had another good story to take back to the Boss and managed two more insults as he left them.

'Dicky, you'd better start thinking of this as the 'Curie-Dupain Process' now. It's not all you, you know.'

Richard went red with embarrassment and he couldn't bring himself to look at Margrit, recognising how much he had played down her contribution.

Nick finished rudely, 'Now don't you kids go on fighting while I'm not here to supervise you! Just get on with your damn homework.'

Richard could not let him get away with this and his voice hardened

'That's enough, Nick! I'm now asking you to be polite to Dr Dupain and control your mouth; we aren't your slaves.' The astonished thug turned and walked straight out.

Richard surprised even himself by his reaction to this

altercation and he began to see things differently. However, he was still miffed by the outcome of the fee negotiation.

He disclosed as much to Winston, knowing how quick the relay process would be through Nick and, suitably embellished, on to Paesano. Richard would still show flashes of anger, knowing Nick would find this acceptable and understandable behaviour from a real man.

After a couple of busy days, Richard wanted to patch things up with Margrit. They started to meet at the spa again in the evenings for a short while and, apart from the underlying threat they were facing, these were enjoyable moments under a crisp, clear sky and a growing moon which flooded the lawns with a generous light.

They also spent more time in the lab and Richard gained a real appreciation of Margrit's comprehensive bench work. The final fee settlement wasn't even raised although it still rankled a little with him.

They were able to overcome their concerns about the short timeline by burying themselves in work. They adjusted the project plan, prioritising a number of immediate tasks, while identifying critical blocking points which would need deeper analysis. Richard was from time to time charmingly polite.

'Margrit, now you've mostly completed your research, perhaps you might work up sufficient quantities of biochemical agents for the trial run and I'll nip back and look over some of my older stuff? Then we can finetune things together'

She suggested a more practical approach.

'I'm not quite as far ahead as you think, Richard. While there are things needing my particular attention, we should develop a daily work routine. Perhaps we might work separately, catch up before lunch and work on our own in the afternoons until dinner? We can then work on our own again each night.'

She said that dividing their time like this had a side benefit, providing a comfortable escape from the prying of Nick's direct supervision and Winston's covert surveillance. Richard agreed in the interests of the timetable, although she was pleased to think he may have preferred to work with her.

NINE

Behind his intermittent abrasiveness about the fee split, Margrit sensed this growing personal interest from Richard. Nevertheless, she could also feel he wasn't entirely sure how much to trust her and there were some of his algorithms which remained a mystery to her.

Through not very subtle questioning, he had tried to discover more about her early involvement with Paesano. She didn't want his prying to go too far, so controlled her responses.

'I was particularly vulnerable at the time because my long-term relationship with my professor broke down. Over the years, Claude had grown more distant from me. He had started to gamble in a big way and I was earning very little. He was also taking all the credit for my discoveries. I had to kick him out, and Richard you know how hard it is to get research funding. This work of mine is so absorbing I guess I lost direction and didn't know it. But I needed direction and Claude simply disappeared. I suppose in a way I was financially seduced by Dieter who promised me a lot of support in developing professionally.'

She knew Richard, the scientist, would readily have understood how important this would have been as her research ramped up and told him.

'I really thought Dieter was interested in what I was doing for Green Mines, but he used me and I suppose I also used him. He didn't get all he wanted. Our marriage dissolved; he would have nothing to do with me personally. All communication with Green Mines, and later the offer to continue my work on this project here in secrecy, all came through Nick.'

By the time Richard arrived on the scene, her grasp of the situation had become much clearer and more threatening. She understood it far better than he did. Although he was genuinely sympathetic, she found herself turning to him now as a saviour rather than in admiration of the clever scientist.

Instinctively, she knew he was no forceful character. He was honest and would not be easily bullied and her gut reaction was she was in a much stronger position with him there. He had a sense of humour too and was not above laughing at himself. In banter, she suggested, 'Perhaps this really should be called the 'Dupain Curie Process?''

His quick response came with a chuckle.

'Oh, no! Denning would never approve. I'm the man in this. My name must come first even though he seems to question my manliness.'

She just laughed and repeated with a lift in her voice.

'The Dupain Curie!' And you needn't worry about your manliness.'

She saw how this flirtation obviously startled him but he was becoming more open, sharing things outside his professional life, about his schooling, his failed marriage, his travel lust and his estrangement from his family. This openness about personal matters was unusual in her experience and she found parallels in their lives, in particular their successful academic careers and unsuccessful marital disasters. He seemed to hold high ethical standards and she felt his guarded pomposity when dealing with Nick was only a reaction to the man's scurrilous character.

From time to time, she caught herself looking at him fondly, taking real comfort from their meetings. As each day passed, they came to understand each other better. At one level she sensed his interest, but his reticence still remained.

Finally in the spa on the fifth evening, she was desperate to spill out her deep concerns and try to break through. She saw it came as a real shock to him.

'I am very frightened and you should be too. Why did you get involved with these people?'

His answer, after a startled pause, was to her mind much too glib for their situation.

'It's simple; four million is my total fee for this IP. I need hardly remind you about your thirty per cent of it.'

However, she moved closer towards him and nervously whispered.

'Four million dollars is like a Swiss fairytale. They haven't got four thousand Rand to spare at the moment and even if they had, you won't get a cent. That slick lawyer, Denning, is there to see every agreement ever made gets broken.'

She felt his response was a little too dismissive.

'Well, in itself that isn't life-threatening. Even if they renege on my contract, it shouldn't worry you. Your research is good enough to stand on its own.'

Despite the compliment she wasn't to be stopped. Her voice

was quietly pitched and now desperate in tone. What she said was enough to make Richard's body visibly shiver despite the warmth of the spa.

'Late this afternoon, when they thought I was back in the laboratory with you, I overheard Nick and Shorty. Nick wanted to know what they would do about a couple of scientists no one would really miss.'

She paused and went on falteringly.

'Shorty told him to shut up and to remember Franklin and Guerin hadn't exactly been big problems in the end. He said he'd fix it, perhaps with an explosion in the lab … and I am sure he will. He's truly an evil man and, my God, am I terrified now about what might have happened to Claude Guerin!'

She continued in a more measured, less brittle way.

'When I was married to Dieter, someone we knew in business, but not socially, also just disappeared. I heard rumours Dieter had ordered a killing and Shorty did it. People certainly stopped annoying Green Mines so much for money.'

There was a long pause and she decided to open up further.

'I can't even begin to guess what sort of role he'd had in the South American drug syndicates or with arms dealers. When we were married he used to take telephone calls in the middle of the night and they were full of angry arguments in Spanish, but I heard he is most unwilling to travel there these days. He gets Spanish-speaking people to come here, but I am not allowed to talk to them.

She paused to collect herself and blurted out.

'Really, Richard, I believe he'll do anything and the more money involved, the bigger the risk he'll take. I now think he really was in the arms business and you can be sure he will have hidden some of the money …'

Her voice caught.

'Even in my beautiful Switzerland perhaps.'

Her concerns continued to tumble out.

'He must worry about how much threat I pose. Maybe he fears I may still have links to people in SMGT. They also want this IP.'

Turning away a little, she was now hardly audible as she finished.

'He wants to control all information. It's his power base over people he manipulates. I have come to learn how terrifying he is and yet I was transfixed by this power early on. I am sure he would be surprised by what you have already found out about Green Mines. I think he would discard you too without a second thought.'

She sighed with mental exhaustion and abruptly stood away from the spa. She smiled wanly at him as she left for her room and actually wished Richard, had he been more impulsive, might even have followed her to calm her fears.

TEN

There had been no sign of Paesano after days of very demanding work by the scientists and they were making good progress. Given the importance of the project to him, they were astonished he had vested so much authority in his two minions. At least one would appear unannounced to check on them at random intervals. There was no sign of the philandering Nick at night though. Margrit suggested to Richard a reason for Paesano's seeming lack of involvement in the project.

'Possibly he's on one of those infrequent overseas trips that he hates so much … even those two won't know where. It's amazing he is so strong he can delegate so much to them and his physical presence here is so irrelevant.'

Another day had passed before Nick on one of his rare evening visits quite casually let drop Mr Paesano would be joining them for their morning session.

At precisely 11 o'clock, Richard made his way to the meeting. Winston in the foyer was particularly keyed up, avoiding eye contact and fussing over a minute detail of tidiness in the foyer until Paesano stepped in. He completely ignored Winston's nervous greeting and also brushed past Richard without any acknowledgement. With Shorty trailing behind he headed straight for the dining room. Richard left in his wake, noting in passing that the man was physically out of balance, with a big frame on noticeably short legs. He remembered the podium in Paesano's city office which contributed to this image of vanity and self-awareness.

Maintaining his bluster, Paesano moved straight to the head of the table and was seated before the others had finished entering. To Richard, Paesano sitting actually did appear to be physically taller and certainly more imposing.

The meeting began straight away, if such a process deserved to be called a meeting. There was no pretence of polite talk. As it proceeded, Paesano's complete disdain for formal procedure became evident to Richard. They were there simply to be interrogated and to take instructions, and not to air their views or opinions. True to form, Paesano bullied his way through every matter. Snatching at a copy of the project plan, he began berating Richard in a savage staccato.

'Where are you in this program? I said I wanted action. You can take days off this time frame if you put in more effort. They tell me you're working early and late. I'm not here waiting for some doctoral thesis. I don't want to hear about references or sources or new ideas. All I want is something which works.'

His anger was evident but controlled and Richard noted he scratched absentmindedly at the scar on his hand.

'I'm paying you a lot of money for this IP. Am I making myself clear enough for you, Curie?'

Richard, determined not to be bullied, wordlessly stared straight back at Paesano. There was a brief silence before the acolytes rushed to fill the gap together answering for Richard.

'Yes, Mr Paesano.'

As much as Richard would have liked, he wasn't inclined right then to push his luck by calling him 'Dieter' in front of the fawning thugs. Even so, he knew he had made a statement by saying nothing. If this further aggravated the two henchmen, then so be it.

For the next hour, Paesano went over the whole plan and while he skirted around the scientific aspects, it was clear he understood how each element related to the others. Consequently, Richard was hard-pressed to hold onto safety factors he had built into the timetable.

As the diatribe continued it was clear Nick was also in more than a bit of trouble. Paesano didn't hide the fact he thought his minion, adept and cunning as he was, had lost control of the project through his lazy streak. Then the penny dropped for Paesano. Richard had deceived Nick about the initial two-day saving and the Boss was unremitting, almost vicious, in his annoyance. Nick's ire at having been shown up was palpable and Richard wondered whether he might seek retribution later in some way.

Discussion next moved to the test run of the project and here, in the technical matters at least, Richard was able to regain ground because of the Green Mines' troika's lack of understanding. It came down to practicalities and he had a precise list of requirements.

'... in addition, we'll also need flotation tanks and sample testing gear which I assume would be readily sourced from any one of your Green Mines properties, even if they are derelict. The stuff is almost indestructible ... then here are the specifications for, say, seven tonnes each of five different feed-stocks. They must vary from soft to hard material and of course they must be low grade.'

Richard noticed Paesano's face hardening whenever Margrit chipped in and how he looked away when she set out her requirements.

'I need much bigger containers for all my compounds and now we are upsizing, bigger laboratory scales are wanted, otherwise it'll all take more time.'

The inquisitors were back in familiar and practical territory now. They could see something was happening and Paesano quickly agreed all of this could be easily arranged by Shorty, as could the secondment of half a dozen semi-skilled workers and an experienced foreman.

Dealing with these nuts-and-bolts arrangements seemed to have settled Paesano down. Richard said they would need to visit the site first, and he replied quite calmly for a change.

'I'll leave it in Shorty's hands. It must be done in secret and you can't talk to the people doing the dog work.'

Richard pointed out he and Margrit could hardly avoid giving directions to the workers as they were finetuning the process during testing. Paesano only grunted and looked piercingly at Shorty to confirm his instruction. Through all of this, Paesano deliberately ignored his ex-wife.

She was asked to define her requirements for sample testing and to expand on aspects of the concentration process. Nick, thinking he could sense Paesano's mood, made a wrong call. The sycophant was unable to contain himself and butted in with his grating question.

'What do you need her there for anyway?'

However, Paesano, who still had him in his bad books, snarled back at him.

'What would you know about this, Nick? You stick to the legal stuff.'

Like a kicked dog cowering, he responded.

'Sorry, Mr Paesano.'

This rebuke evidently pleased Shorty and gave him an opening to take centre stage with a complete change of subject. Turning to Margrit without any preamble he asked, 'Do you remember a Colonel Wolhuter when you first worked at SMGT?'

Surprised at being directly included at last, she hesitated before answering. Her face paled for a moment. Richard wondered where the questioning was going and her answer came slowly.

'I believe he was a risk manager or something similar. There were rumours he was there as much to keep an eye on staff as dealing with the external threats from people stealing our work. I didn't personally have any business connection because he would have had no understanding of my project. There wouldn't be any safety issues about my lab work until testing began and yes it could be dangerous. Besides, he was seldom seen about the place. Why are you asking me about him anyway?'

Shorty ignored her question and continued in an even more aggressive, angry manner, 'B-b-been in touch at all since you left?'

Margrit flushed with anger, but retained her natural control as she staunchly denied having anything to do with anyone at SMGT. Richard thought she was good at doing anger, particularly when she turned to Paesano saying, 'You certainly didn't help my standing at all. Why would they talk to me?'

Paesano refused eye contact and merely grunted in reply, scratching again at the scar on his hand. Using this impasse to his advantage, Nick came charging back into the fray, his voice rising.

'We hope not for your sake, because they've named you in their latest claim against Green Mines for stealing their stuff. Their lawyers are trying to find out what you know and we've heard this Wolhuter is also involved in the investigation.'

Paesano clearly agreed and Shorty, of course, was not to be outdone.

'This Wolhuter is gunna need fixing. I can't get a handle on where he hangs out and I dunno what he looks like. He spends a lot of time abroad. So, you tell me if he ever contacts you, Dupain.'

It occurred to Richard if Paesano and his cronies really didn't know much about Wolhuter it was likely they had arrogantly also overlooked Winston Naidoo as a source of information. Richard was not so dismissive. In spite of the obvious risks involved, he suspected the Indian took a keen interest in any intrigue which might have an advantageous outcome for him.

The meeting ended as abruptly as it began. They all stood up and Paesano shrank into his less imposing form. Turning to Shorty, he ordered, 'Nick can drive me. You can tidy things up here with these two. Keep them on their game and let me know as soon as you suspect something funny is going on.'

Then, turning back to Nick, Paesano grinned evilly.

'Two commands for you. First up, ditch the stupid gun and get yourself a smaller one; it won't ruin your suit so much. Secondly, keep your mind out of your trousers and start to concentrate on what really matters around here.'

They walked purposefully into the foyer and Richard was suddenly struck by the thought that for all his overbearing dominance, he had never once heard Paesano swear.

Margrit and Richard had both sensed his escalating impatience and the tension surrounding him. After he left, they looked at one another in silence and, knowing the pressure was mounting, returned to the solitude of their suites to work.

There was a matching tension in the air when late in the afternoon a monstrous flash followed by a frightening thunderclap forced them to abandon their work. It was the onset of a spectacular late summer storm which they watched together in the huge living room. The continuous noise meant conversation was virtually impossible and they drew closer together to talk. The clouds rose to immense heights from a dark base and marched to the horizon. Between rolls of thunder, following each brilliant flash, Margrit captured the moment.

'For me it recalls storms in the Alps, the views there are restricted by the mountains … here it is the towering clouds themselves. You can see higher than any mountain.'

Richard reminded himself that Johannesburg was one of the lightning capitals of the world and he drew her back firmly from the window as another sharp flash struck a tree just beyond the security wall. She seemed to welcome his protection and his arm lingered on her shoulder for a moment.

There was a short burst of heavy hail and the storm was

over within half an hour. The residual smell of damp, burnt air lingered for a while and the sun quickly melted the small, white piles of hail on the deck. The immensity and raw beauty of the storm had brought them closer together; a brief moment of respite from their uncomfortable predicament. Awed by this display of Nature's power, they looked at each other with a new understanding and, without another word, went back to their rooms.

ELEVEN

Richard was by now comfortable dining with Margrit, although their conversation was desultory even in the spa. During one restricted discussion, Richard enquired quietly about Winston. Margrit said she had no solid recollection of him during her time at SMGT and he wasn't surprised because he knew how easily she became oblivious to matters outside her scientific obsession. He envied the way she could forget even her deepest concerns while absorbed in their joint project. Winston would have been crestfallen had he known how thoroughly he was erased from her memory.

Later that night, as Margrit and Richard were heading from the spa to the foyer to place their breakfast orders, they heard a car cruise by. It paused briefly near the gates before moving on and they looked at each other uncertainly. The car made an abrupt U-turn and moved slowly back. Winston was a bit distracted by the staff getting ready to leave for their homes, but he had noticed this manouvere on the night vision CCTV and called across to Richard.

'This is very odd. Come and look at these screens.'

A large car had pulled up behind the staff's old jalopy. Several men got out, one apparently pulling another along. Winston turned on the floodlights at the gate and the camera threw up a white screen as it adjusted to the glare. There was hardly a pause before a volley of shots rang out. Floodlights and camera were smashed. For a couple of minutes nothing happened, then the headlights of the large car lit up the trees beyond the gates. The staff rushed to the kitchen in shock before a wail of fear broke out.

The guards had just started their first patrol and now Winston turned on the brilliant security lights. Both guards started to run towards the gates, pulling out their guns with the dogs barking viciously ahead of them.

To everyone's astonishment, the old car which was parked near the main entrance gate, started with a backfire and rumble. The engine revved to a crescendo and it seemed the car was turning towards the house, generating a halo of light above the gate opening. The car charged the gate. There was a resounding crash and the solid gates remained intact. The car backed away and to the guards' dismay, attacked again with renewed force. This time the left hand leaf of the gate buckled. The jalopy's headlights had been knocked out and the light halo vanished, to be replaced by a reddish glow behind the gates, growing in intensity.

The foyer came alive with frantic activity. Winston shouted an urgent order.

'You two scientists must be locking yourselves in your rooms.'

This was one order which Margrit was all too eager to obey. Richard, showing far more bravado than was his usual nature, lingered long enough to hear Winston make two calls. The first of these was obviously to Shorty.

'Come out here quick, Boss, we're in big trouble!'

There was a very audible response, 'Get the fuck out there and take … b-b-bloody control! I'm on my way.'

Winston seemed to be in no great hurry to join the fray, and Richard listened to his general emergency call before deciding he should get back to watch things unfold from the relative safety of his room. As he began to sidle down the corridor to his suite, he heard Winston quietly make a third call and one phrase caught his attention.

'… you'll indeed be having some real news.'

Richard's curiosity was caught by this remark, but it was soon forgotten as other events began to unfold. In a surreal fashion the situation descended into a confused mess which Richard was only later able to unpick with recollections like random frames in a slide show. He knew he had been truly frightened in the midst of the unfolding chaos and a morbid fascination prevented him from looking away from the horrifying immediacy of the violence.

His abiding first memory was of the thud of a stray bullet hitting the thatched roof above his suite, and while in retrospect this was a minor incident, to him it was symbolic of the horror of the whole experience.

Richard watched as the glow at the gate erupted into flames. In the firelight and garden lighting he could see the guards were now moving forward very cautiously and there were two or possibly three backlit figures at the open entrance. Audible over the growing crackle of the blaze, and even through the double glazing were startling sounds of gunshots fired from a variety of weapons.

One of the dogs suddenly broke off its barking which turned into a gut-wrenching wail and the guards ducked for cover behind the low garden hedging. Richard instinctively crouched lower, aware he too could be a target silhouetted against the corridor lights. He was seriously worried about Margrit before remembering her suite didn't have direct exposure to the gate.

Suddenly he could see a wild eruption of flame and noise as the fire took greater hold. The shoot-out between guards and intruders resumed. He saw distinct muzzle flashes and another stray bullet cracked into the window frame of the neighbouring suite.

A horrifying scream of pain and anguish, cut off ominously by a heavy, muffled shot, was the crescendo of violence. The noise abruptly ceased and the intruders beat a retreat. A few seconds later, car doors slammed and the sound of a powerful vehicle quickly faded into the night. The whole thing had probably only taken minutes and, as it ended, Richard couldn't help thinking if Winston had taken more interest in the passing traffic and less on the spa, it may never even have happened.

A brief and ominous silence followed before sobbing sounded from the kitchen as someone there realised the full extent of the danger they had faced. A general hubbub followed as everyone wanted to have their say about it all at once. As their courage returned, some looked out towards the gate and realised something truly horrible had happened. They could see one guard was stooped over a couple of shapes on the ground and was no longer paying any heed to the departing intruders. As Richard rushed back into the foyer, he heard the guard bellowing.

'My God, Mr Naidoo, this is terrible … come quick!' *Very reluctantly*, Richard thought, Winston left his sanctuary and tentatively approached the gate. By this time, Margrit had reached the foyer and together they watched as Winston took a brief look at the bundles on the ground and rushed back towards the foyer calling out

'Jesus, man! One of the guards has been shot … in the face. I have seen bodies before and I don't think there is any hope for him.'

As Winston went looking for a blanket to cover the body, the scientists still in their swimwear headed towards the carnage. For Margrit, now in control again, this was a characteristic show of compassion, but for Richard it was a barely tolerable act of duty. Margrit quickly realised nothing could be done either for the guard or for the dog lying in the gateway with its companion sadly sniffing at the lifeless body. Squeamish Richard, as much as possible avoiding a close look at either victim, wasn't quite sure which affected him most: the dead man or the dead dog and its distressed mate.

Winston returned again to the foyer and made another call to quickly update Shorty, who was still some distance away, driving with manic disregard for other road users. The big man felt quite out of control in the developing chaos and he screamed at Winston in a fury that he was being less than useless.

Gradually support services began to arrive. A fire truck was the first on the scene, no doubt coming from one of the nearby grass fires. The fire crew didn't have much to do as only the front tyres and upholstery of the old car continued to flare and smoulder. They were decidedly off-hand in dealing with the problem and were far more interested in exploring the rest of the battle scene and especially the bodies inside the gate. While they were preoccupied, an ambulance arrived in a hurry and departed just as quickly when the crew confirmed the human victim was most definitely dead and they had more urgent matters on their agenda.

There was no sign of a police presence and a journalist with a photographer quite deliberately walked straight over to Winston, who seemed to know them well. They wandered in and began to do just as they pleased, interviewing all the staff. Richard and Margrit, fearing the overhanging threat of Paesano's anger, wanted to keep a low profile and avoided the media snoops. Besides which, they felt underdressed in their swimwear and Margrit was beginning to attract attention.

Shorty arrived next and did so in characteristic style. Without pausing to ask after the surviving guard or even casting a glance at the one who had been killed, he flew into a towering rage. He spat vitriol at three neighbours who had been attracted by the excitement and were wandering around, their guns ostentatiously on show. Next he turned on Winston with a mouthful of abuse about his lack of control of the situation.

'You stupid, lowlife, curry-munching Indian. Can't you do anything properly? What the hell am I gunna tell Mr Paesano about all the publicity you've caused? There is no reason for any of these nosy pricks to be on our land.'

He pointed at the two newspaper men.

'Who are these morons with cameras? Get them out of the fucking house!'

Richard, now more appropriately dressed, returned to the scene while Shorty was in full flight. Rather than risk more abuse, he wandered away to see if he could do anything useful. He noticed long grass outside the gates was smouldering and even burning in places. He tried stamping out the flames, while the firemen lolled against their machine waiting for their chief to finish a call.

Eyes smarting in the smoke, Richard made his way along in the shadow of the wall until he caught the unmistakable reek of singed hair over the burning grass. Just as the smell registered, his foot gave way on a large, soft lump, and he looked in horror at a slightly singed, very dead body lying face down.

Everyone's focus was on the bodies inside the gate and this twisted form had not been spotted. Shocked, Richard stood transfixed in the half light of the moon. He tried to control his breathing and suppressing a strong urge to retch, he looked down at the oozing, matted head wound. Regaining some composure, he noted a gun lying on the ground next to the gloved right hand of the corpse and he thought this must be one of the would-be intruders.

He yelled out frantically for Shorty, 'Come here for God's sake, there's another body outside the gate!'

His cry must have been impressive because Shorty stopped abusing the press and lumbered over to the distraught scientist. He glanced at the corpse and grunted to Richard.

'Here's one who didn't get away.'

He was prodding the body roughly with his foot just as the police van arrived and its spotlight threw their grotesque shadows against the wall. He rounded on Richard.

'Shit, man! Get your arse back to your room and don't talk to any of those buggers.'

Any ideas Shorty may have had about concealing this additional problem were dashed by the arrival of the police. The next few hours provided a continuous mayhem of coming and going, of questioning and measuring, and of frequent flashes from cameras wielded by forensic investigators, a rapidly swelling media throng, and inquisitive locals. Shorty had bullied the latter from the property and they were showing a great interest in the aftermath of the gunfight outside the wall with free access to Richard's find.

Shorty was incensed and tried to force the police to move them all along. The Sergeant, as dark as him and as statuesque, seemed unconcerned and officious.

'Cool it, sir. These media people are only doing their job, and anyway we'll need access to as many photos as we can get.'

Clearly the police, despite their growing numbers, had been unable to segregate the authorised from the curious in the swelling mob. They had forfeited any chance to recover unpolluted evidence.

Rather than return to his room as ordered, yet mindful of Paesano's strict instructions about secrecy and Shorty's threat, Richard risked hanging back on the dark fringes of the action where he was now joined by Margrit. Together they listened as Shorty and the Sergeant discussed the case in a stilted, formal way for the benefit of the press. From the way they spoke, Richard sensed this wasn't the first time they had met. It was the longest monologue Richard had yet heard from Shorty and it was calmly delivered.

'Not much work for you here, Sergeant Mgeni. Pretty simple really. You see plenty of these robberies, I guess. The thieves must have heard about the foreign tourists who are guests here and thought it would be easy to skin them out. Must have been a shock to find how tough my guards are and they didn't do their homework very well, did they? This is just an opportunistic robbery which went badly wrong.'

Mgeni nodded his agreement, saying loudly, 'Those robbers would've considered they were geniuses to force their way in using the old car.'

Without yet having collected much evidence at all, let alone any which might suggest an alternative crime scenario, the Sergeant was all too keen to agree with Shorty's proposition.

'You're right, Mr Mpane. It's been a long, tiring day and my boys just want to get off duty. It's obvious to me this was just an opportunistic robbery which went badly wrong. My report to Major Brand, my boss, will just say we must formally identify this body.'

This stilted, manufactured discussion went down well with the media. This didn't completely please Shorty who was used to calling the shots. If previous South African practice had been anything to go by, the matter would have ended there and then.

What is unusual in this case was the rapidity with which the matter gained wide media exposure. Within days and with the body identified, the whole affair took on new dimensions.

TWELVE

Needless to say, no one could find Nick despite Winston's regular calls throughout the night. The message finally got through as he was driving back to his own apartment in the early morning and he diverted his trip. Swaggering in just before 7 o'clock, he demanded a separate debriefing.

'I had to identify myself to the police, dammit, and they wouldn't tell me anything. God-damned cheek I call it.'

Of course, Shorty took real delight in passing this titbit on to Paesano later in the day. First, though, he needed to prepare a report and each employee was given a far more aggressive grilling than the police had used. But they had been too traumatised to notice much and were unable to add anything helpful.

'Why such crude violence?' mused Nick. 'They look like piss-weak amateurs to me.'

They ordered Winston to rerun the CCTV footage and spent some time pondering over the earliest scenes. They could only guess the getaway car was rented and, as such, not likely to provide a lead. However, Shorty wasn't prepared to await the outcome of an inefficient police enquiry and launched his own search amongst car rental companies. He soon found out there was an 'overdue', which had been hired by a Columbian.

All to no avail as the car was found on one of Green Mines' derelict properties completely stripped of anything removable and bare of clues.

Shorty conveyed all this to Paesano and it was received with a grunt which gave nothing away.

'Oh yeah? You two just get back here to Parktown as soon as you figure out what's happened.'

They were quite perplexed by the events and even more concerned about how to manage the repercussions. To get away from prying eyes and ears, especially Winston's, they decided to use an empty suite in the east wing as their incident control room. Their first priority was dealing with the fallout in the morning press and on radio and Shorty felt too much had already been seen.

'How in fuck's name did those two pressmen arrive so soon?'

Nick tried to sound superior.

'C'mon, man. You know they always monitor police communications. They'd have got straight on to Winston's call.'

Shorty was still pensive, but his words were thunderous.

'Something about the slimy little shit I can't put my finger on. Why did he let them in? Anyway, all this crap is in your territory, pretty … b-b-boy. You deserve it after going screwing all night.'

Then another call came through from Paesano. He told Nick yet again.

'Your only job is to shield me from any hint of involvement. I've got a growing press presence outside the office and more here at Parktown and I don't need this publicity. I can keep my head down here and you have to make sure this is off the evening news or at least toned way down.'

In a society with a high tolerance to violence and murder, Paesano hoped this would quickly subside into a one-day wonder. Nick risked a deferential response.

'Yes, Mr Paesano',

He wasn't finished yet.

'For all we know this could be the work of SMGT. Even if they had nothing to do with it, wide press coverage will get them interested in my secure house. The journalists appear to have had open access to the property and I'm told they've even taken shots through the windows of the west wing laboratory. The only good thing is so far there's been nothing said about our two-house guests. Are you listening to me, Nick? Just do something right for once and make sure it stays that way.'

The phone slammed down.

'Yes, Dieter' said Nick, to himself of course.

Unfortunately for Nick, the media was on a roll looking for different angles to this nasty story. There was no doubt Paesano was well skilled in oiling his way through the political, bureaucratic and law enforcement jungles, and he had already been in touch with one high level police contact to convey a veiled threat.

'I think it would be sensible if your people kept out of the limelight down at Kyalami Drive. The police don't need this sort of publicity.'

But it made no difference. The reformist members of the service were keen to show how things were improving and were actively seeking good press.

When the bodies and car were finally moved and the police

had departed, the remaining intrusive, uninvited throng were impolitely ordered to 'Bugger off!' The excitement died away.

With no sympathy from Shorty for the loss of their car, the house staff were told to find their own way home and not be late the next day. He elected to undertake the replacement guard role until the next shift arrived, showing scant sympathy for the shaking man who had to complete his session. To Shorty's annoyance the police now also mounted guard. The media presence had introduced a further dimension to what was becoming a high-profile matter.

Things also began to settle down in the house where sleep had been impossible. Still too hyped up to slot back into normal routine and with no staff on hand, the 'house guests' looked around for breakfast. The large and well organised kitchen was new territory for them and they explored it carefully.

It dawned on Richard that at last they'd found an area which was surveillance-free because no one in the hierarchy would have been interested in what the staff might be saying. Taking advantage of this rare moment of total privacy, they huddled closely together at the island bench to collect themselves. In a sense it was their first moment of physical intimacy but set on a stage of horror. Richard's rattled, unconnected sentences showed how much he had been affected and Margrit let him get it off his chest.

'It was just awful, wasn't it? I don't know whether it had anything to do with us … Why would they involve us in this? Maybe it was your fellow, Wolhuter, whom they've been talking about? I wonder if Winston knows more about him … I'll wait until those animals go off to their meeting in town, then see how much Winston knows … It seems like a lot of trouble for SMGT just to scare us, doesn't it?'

He paused, breathless and his anxiety was obvious.

'Maybe we should just make sure our tests fail and walk away … would they let us go after we've seen all this horror and violence? I sense you've been worried all along and now I can see why … Shorty and Nick don't know the full story either and they look very nervy.'

Richard sympathetically put his hand on Margrit's clenched fist. She moved it slightly towards him and he was startled to realise despite her openness about events in her life, how little he knew of her as a person. Was it she or he who had thrown up this continuing solid barrier in their working relationship?

'Maybe the key is to bring SMGT into this, or have you got something more to hide from me about them? Given the situation we're in now, I simply have to know whether there are any other issues.'

Margrit's face paled and Richard, realising he could have been a touch more gentle, braced himself for her anger. Instead, her response was calm and considered.

'I don't think you've been really open either … we can come back to that. Yes, I do know Will Wolhuter well. I had been hoping to keep open some links with SMGT until Green Mines engaged me full-time. Instead, to my great consternation, I have found myself cut off here. Will is the only one who seems to understand how badly I had been treated by both sides. Believe me, SMGT are not very nice people either. Up to now he has been my only safety factor, although after you arrived, I dared hope you'd be an ally too.'

Margrit continued, her despair obvious.

'Will is no scientist. He won't be up to date on my progress, or the reason for your involvement, or even know who you are. The only SMGT people who have any idea of the importance of my work are the senior managers back in Zurich. From the start they only gave me a little support and left me alone. Long after Dieter succeeded in seducing me away, they realised they may have lost a seriously undervalued asset. They'll be desperate to get their hands on my latest research. It could so easily have been theirs and they would have no knowledge of your work apart from your published papers which are very technical.'

Richard now for his part less tense calmed her with a firm press on her shoulder and took up her hand again. She went on.

'This is where Dieter, who couldn't begin to understand the science, got a grasp of the commercial angle … he is a wicked and creative business genius … and as I have said before, very persuasive. He could immediately see the value of putting our two projects together. Well, soon it'll be clear to SMGT something is happening here. I doubt they'll have known anything substantial about your work … why they would ever have attacked this place is beyond me also. As you know yourself, it's impossible to get any message in or out of here, even if I wanted to, so SMGT would only be guessing how far my work has advanced.'

Abruptly, she changed direction to talk about their thin chance of escape.

'You have no contacts here in South Africa and my only way to get to Will Wolhuter is by phone and we are cut off. I really haven't bothered him up to now and I only have an emergency number which may not be current because he moves around such a lot. I am certain he could find a way to help us because he is so straight. He is such a lovely man.'

Richard felt a surprising twinge of jealousy about this praise as she paused to choose her next words with care.

'We need to know how we stand with each other. As for me hiding things from you, I sense you don't fully trust me and there is a critical element of your analysis which you are hiding from me. Why?'

Richard had no answer and his face reddened as she continued with emphasis.

'We're the only allies we've got and we simply have to be honest. Remember I know him far better than you do. As I have said so often, he is very, very clever. He's also ruthless beyond belief and it won't take him long to see through you and work out you … we … are stalling him. You have no choice but to believe in me as I will in you, once you let me in on every last detail of your work.'

She finished looking directly at him. Richard was now contrite and wished he had opened up first. He had sat through Margrit's monologue feeling very uncomfortable. He should have known she was too clever and too committed to the project not to grasp he was holding back key parts of his IP. He apologised as Margrit listened intently.

'You're right. Up to now my mind has been firmly shut. From all I'd found out about this organisation, I decided early on to trust no one. Lately, I've seen we have too much riding on this project not to fully cooperate. I'm sorry it took a crisis like we've just been through to see things more clearly. We need to start planning a way out of this mess.'

With the air cleared between them, it might have been a good time for planning had not Nick, who had been storming about the house searching for them, suddenly appeared at the kitchen door. Richard gently pulled his hand away from Margrit's and faced Nick without embarrassment and with some annoyance as though he had interrupted an informal debate between them.

Nick was in his most bullying mood. Clearly put out by the trauma of the night, the added furore of his own late arrival at the scene and his impending meeting with Paesano, he was looking for soft targets and his voice almost screamed out.

'Bloody scientists. Doesn't take long for you to lose sight of reality. Why the hell are you two swooning about in here? Do you really think this is a holiday resort and not a crime scene?'

And then, being Nick, 'Don't think you can play nooky on the kitchen table, either.'

While this last remark was directed mainly at Margrit, it was designed to annoy both of them. Richard, though, was learning how to play Nick. Acting out a low-key unfinished argument with Margrit, he turned away from the bully.

'Dammit, Margrit! I've told you a hundred times there's no way those filters could possibly work.'

She was quick to catch on and replied in a bantering tone.

'Don't be so stubborn, they will and you know it, you idiot. After all this is the 'Dupain Curie Process', is it not?'

The ploy worked, and as a non-plussed Nick turned to leave, he venomously called back over his shoulder.

'This isn't the place for scientific debate. You two just get over it, will you? Get on with your work. Just get on with it! There's a deadline waiting, as if you didn't know.'

At this, like a bolt out of the blue, Richard's memory suddenly clicked back to recall the bullying Nick as a high-toned schoolboy tyrant whose voice had never properly broken. He had seen him before: twenty-five years ago Mick O'Brien had made his life a perfect misery. Now here he was as Nick Denning! Funny thing how older boys seldom remember their juniors and the self-focused Nick would never make the connection. Richard certainly had no intention of giving the bully any further advantage, but stored away in his mind this long past episode.

Walking back to his suite, Richard wondered again how he had been sucked into this miasma. Certainly money was a factor and his reward would be considerably diluted by the unexpected contribution he was required to make for Margrit. Still, because they were now in the same boat, her interests had become his and he didn't feel nearly as resentful about that aspect. And there, as magnetic as it ever had been, was the chance to see so many years of research become reality. Who wouldn't find trumping two big mining companies egocentrically satisfying?

A resolution to the ugly side wasn't too clear and every day things were getting worse for the two of them. His mind danced from one scenario to another and he couldn't apply himself to work. He wondered if Margrit felt the same way and decided he would tell her about the impact Nick had on his teenage years.

THIRTEEN

Winston suffered yet another ear-bashing before Shorty and Nick departed in haste for an urgent meeting with Paesano at the Parktown mansion. They decided to share a car into town and Nick tore down the gravel drive. A bit pointless really. He had to pull up abruptly because of the broken gate opening mechanism. The police were unhelpful and this held them up which further increased the tension between the pair.

This would have continued had not a repair team chosen that moment to arrive and set about removing both gate leaves, providing unrestricted views into the property for the sizeable crowd of onlookers. And, there were many curious people because the media had done such a fine job.

Arriving in Parktown, Nick took the car on a long circuit up a narrow back lane to a secluded garage entry, and drove in without arousing any further attention. A tough-looking stranger who had little command of English greeted them. It was obvious he had no idea of their importance and he shook a large pistol in their direction.

'Where you think you go?'

Nick responded making sure the stranger knew he was also armed.

'And who the hell are you to be speaking like that to Mr Paesano's Personal Assistants?'

Shorty, ignoring both, simply pushed past the guard and led the way to Paesano's study where they were greeted impassively.

'I see you've met one of my new guards. I've already hired four of them. They'll do as good a job as your mob, Shorty, don't you think?'

Shorty dropped his head in embarrassment and Paesano pointed a finger at each in turn. Starting with Nick his voice rose.

'I am not interested in your sex life, lover-boy. Where did you happen to be when you were needed during the night? You think it's more important to lavish so much attention on young women than to do your job and answer calls at any time?'

This was almost another statement rather than a question and Nick had no ready answer. It was Shorty's turn for a hammering, but luck was on his side as Paesano's phone jangled on his desk.

'Good morning, Mr Paesano. My name is Major Brand of the Police. Maybe you remember me?'

Paesano did not reply. Instead, he switched over to the speaker phone and placed a finger on his lips.

'Mr Paesano, I thought you'd like to know we have reassessed the incident at your property and have now given it high priority.'

The Major continued.

'As a consequence, I wish to inform you I am now personally in charge of the case and despite the crowds of people who were allowed to mill about the crime scene, we have uncovered additional evidence which is providing valuable leads.'

Brand started his summary in the style of a formal police statement.

'One of the deceased males, whose body was found nine metres from the south side of the gate and outside the property, is an alleged illegal immigrant. Further, the papers which were found on the body indicate the deceased is … was … a citizen of a South American country we are not yet at liberty to disclose. The fact is, Mr Paesano, it's extremely unusual to find so much identifying material on a body, so much that the police are inclined to believe he or someone else wanted his identity to be discovered … unusual in this type of robbery.'

Paesano grimaced and remained silent as Brand expanded.

'This puts a different twist on a case which the Investigating Sergeant first considered to be straightforward banditry with a fatal outcome. We can also tell you the deceased has only been in the country for less than one month, and while investigators have identified him, we are held up until the relevant Consul in Pretoria has contacted next of kin.'

He continued with some pomposity.

'Furthermore, and more importantly, it appears the deceased was shot in the back of the head at close range facing towards the entry gate and this may have been accidental. A weapon lying nearby was a Glock and as you would know …'

He paused deliberately and could feel Paesano's fury.

'… a weapon of choice in the criminal community.'

Paesano was not getting the full story and Brand was trying to extract more from him. There was no response, so Brand continued in the same formal way.

'We haven't worked out which gun killed him, but it was

discharged from close up and behind. I don't believe this was a mutual shoot-out with that deceased guard of yours. Do you have anything which may help us?'

The response from Paesano was stilted.

'No, I am awaiting a report from my people at the scene.'

Brand continued.

'Mr Paesano, we are examining the body of your guard to determine the type of weapons used by the so-called robbers. Witnesses have told us of hearing shots fired from several different guns so this will take time.'

It was all delivered with barely concealed sarcasm. Brand was using his knowledge of Paesano's history when he added grimly, 'Anyway, it was a good head shot in such conditions.'

Brand was really taking great delight in methodically piling layer upon layer of uncertainty onto him, but he didn't respond at all. Brand was quick to fill the ensuing silence.

'My Sergeant Mgeni and your Mr Mpane were on the wrong track with their conclusion about this affray because neither had gone past rudimentary investigation. It was clearly not an attempted robbery as they had so lazily proclaimed. The sergeant has already been made aware of the seriousness and consequences of his mistakes, and I trust you will strongly remind your people they are not detectives and have no business meddling with police affairs.'

Brand wound up the call with evident satisfaction.

'Please be aware the police will continue their investigations into this matter. Also be aware in due course, a full personal statement will be needed from you. Oh, and I nearly forgot, Mr Paesano; surely you will appreciate being informed your deceased guard had a colourful criminal record. I would advise you to be very careful about how you choose your people in future. Good day to you, Sir.'

There now followed a long, uncomfortable silence eventually broken by Paesano and his voice was harsh.

'And when you do choose them, Shorty, make sure they can shoot straight.'

After another long silence in which Paesano again tried to deal with the discomfort of having been so spectacularly wrong-footed by Brand, he swung back into Shorty.

'So, tell me, what exactly did you hope to achieve with the dumb robbery story you and the brainless policeman concocted? Brand seems to be one very clever man who will never let go, and he would have seen straight through you and your rubbish. He'll be even more suspicious of me ... and you. You've left yourself ... and me ... squarely in the sights of that rare thing called an honest cop! I managed to get him stopped before he got too close to the Franklin accident. Who knows if I can do it this time? Never again let yourself get involved personally with the police. After all, you and I both know where it has taken you in the past.'

Shorty looked very contrite during this tirade, while Nick had perked up realising he was no longer the main target of Paesano's wrath. Both were, however, now more confused than ever. They had believed they were across everything in Paesano's world, but much of what Brand had said about a South American was unfathomable. It didn't seem likely they would be enlightened either, as Paesano wouldn't even elaborate on the new Parktown guards. As the pair left the mansion, each was deep in his own thoughts.

Paesano's mind was also deep in turmoil as he began to thread back through his past and present ventures. Who could have a motive for this attack? He knew it wouldn't take long for the police to track down connections to the victim through their sources and Brand would keep him under pressure for as long as he could.

Subconsciously, he scratched at his scarred hand. Now he had to find out more about the dead South American before Brand did.

FOURTEEN

Out at Kyalami on the other side of town, Richard was looking for ways to connect to Margrit's friend, Colonel Will Wolhuter. He went back to the foyer to find the Indian was still in a state of extreme agitation and furious about the racial abuse he had received over an hour before from both Nick and Shorty. The distraught man needed someone to talk to and Richard was ten steps away from the reception desk as Winston began his tirade with shakes of his head emphasising every point.

'That Mpane is a bullying bastard. He may be black, but there is no race would be having him, and he is a disgrace to the Zulu nation. I have never heard him laugh. He seems to be getting real pleasure out of hurting or frightening people.'

He moved on to include his very personal hatred of Denning.

'Those bullies are indeed treating me like an earthworm. They see me as racially inferior because of my parentage. While the Boss doesn't often throw temper tantrums and never swears, he is demanding total loyalty and you would be getting merry hell if you were crossing him. Mpane makes sure some people just never forget and Denning is always telling tales to get people in trouble.'

Winston was still highly strung and looking for solace beyond his anger at the thugs.

'It's not only those scoundrels or what had happened down at the gate. Indeed, I was doing something really foolish last night and I know the Boss will work it out and will be coming down hard on me. No wonder I'm frantic.'

Winston now recognised Richard seemed to be in no mood to be his counsellor and since he had already said too much, he tried to steer the conversation back to his two bullies, but Richard then asked him, 'You've only had two jobs and it seems to me you've had bad bosses in both. Is that right?'

Winston was quick to respond.

'Oh no! It is only the SMGT senior people in Switzerland who are having poor management policy and no connection at all with their people in South Africa. Just like Shorty and Nick here at Green Mines, they were always pushing us about and they were being much stingier about pay. Dr Dupain will be telling you she had bad experiences with SMGT.'

Richard clearly wanted to know more about SMGT and Winston guessed why. Snooping on the CCTV, he had already seen something of Shorty's interest in Wolhuter. Furthermore, his knowledge of the Curie and Dupain fee negotiations and yesterday's round table meeting with Paesano all gave him a broad perspective. He also knew Margrit actually had a solid link to Will and was almost too quick to give Richard more background.

'My direct manager there was very good. It's just that I wasn't seeing much of him. He was often overseas on some security matter or other. If he was in the office he was paying a lot of attention to my professional development. Indeed he was … is … a most considerate person. Name of Will Wolhuter … none of the mister nonsense for him, even though he'd been an Officer in the Defence Force.'

Richard appeared to want even more and probed gently.

'What was this Wolhuter fellow's background? Do you know if he's still in the company?'

Winston had enjoyed a good relationship and again was happy to spell out aspects of the man's past hoping to gain an advantage through Richard's interest.

'Will is being in his fifties and told me he was born into a strictly religious Afrikaner family. His father was a General in the Army and Will himself was in military intelligence, rising to the rank of Colonel. He told me much of this service was in operational areas and talked about the terrible Angolan business where the South African forces were up against those mercenary Cubans and communists on the border.'

Winston paused to look out of the window at the situation at the gate, so Richard pulled the conversation back in the direction he wanted.

'Good heavens, man, you seem to be talking about a saint. Did he tell you anything else about his achievements?'

Winston knew he had Richard hooked.

'You know, for all his brains Will wouldn't be standing out in a crowd. He's average height, sort of stocky, and generally ambles about, but o-my-goodness, can he move fast if he wants to! What is really unusual is he's the least racist person I have ever come across. Not like that monster the Nazi, Terre Blanche who was murdered last week … good riddance. As you know, we Indians are copping it from all directions.'

He delivered this with a penetrating look at Richard, waggling his head again.

'Indeed like all these Afrikaners, he is having a deeply ingrained love for his country, and he used to talk to me about how distressed he was by the level of corruption in politics, bureaucracy and business. I always wish I could be seeing things like him but, from my background my first priority has to be to make a place in life for me.'

Winston was now a lot calmer. He was well prepared when Richard took a careful step onto dangerous ground, sounding a bit stilted.

'I wonder after I finish up here and go back to England, if I might be able to get in touch with this Wolhuter fellow because I know several of my clients would benefit greatly by having access to his expertise and experience. Certainly someone with his credentials would be very valuable. Do you still have his contact details? I assure you I'd be discreet.'

Given this wide interest in Wolhuter, Winston wasn't about to let a possible business opportunity slip past. Through Will, he could become an informant for SMGT as well as a go-between for Richard. If he played his cards carefully he'd be able to name his own price.

So as soon as Richard left for his suite, Winston tried to contact Will Wolhuter. However, he could only leave a fairly cryptic message, introducing a business proposition with a Dr Curie. And, Will was far too busy to take that bait at the moment.

FIFTEEN

Major Brand hadn't been idle after his call to Paesano. While this was now a high profile case, his interest had actually been aroused as soon as he heard 'Kyalami.' Only a few months before there was a tragic accident nearby involving a journalist called Franklin. He had previously been violently assaulted in the same vicinity not many months before his death. A number of things about the fatal accident hadn't added up for Brand and he had decided to conduct his own unofficial research.

Franklin was a devoted family man; a sober, responsible employee regularly in contact with home and office. Yet he had gone completely off the air before his burnt-out car was found on Kyalami Drive. A forensic examiner provided a report to Brand.

The passenger-side door was open before impact. The driver's seat belt wasn't fastened and from what I can tell, somehow the airbags failed to activate. The fire developed more quickly and with greater intensity than in my experience, yet according to your sergeant no fire accelerants other than diesel have been detected.

The forensic surgeon assisting was not prepared to state death had occurred at the time of impact.

However, I am not happy about damage to the skull. It isn't consistent with impact inside the vehicle.

Then a pharmacist turned up who claimed he had filled a prescription for Franklin after his earlier vicious bashing.

It is possible an excess dose of the heavy pain-killing drug I supplied, could have been a contributing factor.

As there was no way the autopsy could have found any traces of that drug in the body, Brand wondered how convenient it was that his sergeant, who had been so ready to close the case, was able to locate that particular pharmacist.

What was irrefutable was the 'accident' had occurred not far from Paesano's country house. Brand was convinced an earlier assault on the journalist was linked to his current investigative research. At the time, it was widely rumoured Franklin's investigation had yet to run its full course and more was set to be revealed.

Brand had covered Paesano in his earlier investigation and encountered a lot of scuttlebutt amongst his colleagues, who warned him, 'You don't mess with that guy.' Out of the blue, his work on the Franklin case was brought to a standstill despite a growing stack of circumstantial evidence. Senior Brigadier Oosthuizen was emphatic.

'All this is taking too long and you have more important cases where the forensic lab is needed. It's a road accident, so close it off now.'

However, there had recently been a remarkable change in attitudes in the police service. Things seemed to have taken an abrupt U-turn following the unexpected retirement of Oosthuizen. Brand was once again given latitude to unravel any tenuous connections around Paesano. Newly promoted Brigadier Mfuleni, who had come to the role having a solid reputation for integrity, told him regretfully that virtually all the files on Green Mines operations and on Franklin's case, seemed mysteriously to have been cleaned out. The new Brigadier was digging into the matter and called him to share his early findings.

'It is likely, Koos, that my predecessor ordered this. He hasn't retired a pauper and he hasn't been arrested like some others in the service. Immigration people are not coughing up any information about Mr Paesano, either. They're saying it is all too long ago. But, I'm sure they're not really trying ... I'd be glad if you could stir the pot for me, Koos.'

The phone rang again a day later. It was Will Wolhuter this time and he had a lot to say.

'Sorry, Koos man, I know it's been a while since I've been in touch. I've been away on a short trip to Europe and you'll be pleased I'm back, because I've got you some leads on the Kyalami Drive matter. You know how I've been working for SMGT on theft of trade secrets? Well, it turns out they're having a big legal barney with Green Mines about intellectual property ownership and it directly concerns that dangerous bastard, Paesano. I think he has a couple of scientists out at Kyalami Drive working on this IP stuff behind the scenes. One has been there for months and I'm now certain it's Dr Margrit Dupain.'

Brand couldn't contain himself and butted in.

'Agh, man, you mean his ex? Didn't she once work for that Swiss mob?'

'She's the one, Koos. I've been trying to get in touch with her but her mobile's blocked.'

Brand tried to interrupt, but Will was on a roll.

'About a week ago, I had a tip-off another scientist was being brought in from England to work with her. I watched the disembarkation, and I reckon this was the guy who was whisked away by a very big, well-dressed fellow.

He barely paused

'Now I'm finding it impossible to get into the place on Kyalami Drive. My contact there, a shifty little janitor, isn't exactly being helpful at the moment and I suspect he's trying to play me off.'

This time, Brand was able to interrupt.

'It's all coming together, man. My slack sergeant hadn't bothered to properly interview the house guests after the shooting; however, he did mention in passing two foreigners whom he dismissed as just irrelevant spectators. He had nosed about the buildings and looked in a few windows and went on to say he thought they were working on some chemistry stuff.'

As he was talking, Brand was growing increasingly convinced his sergeant must have been fingered by someone trying to take the heat off Franklin's assault, the fatal car crash, and now this whole shooting incident. His thoughts turned to Mpane, whom he had previously spoken to on a couple of other matters without satisfaction.

'Hey man, Will, I reckon I know the identity of your big fellow at the airport. Was he black?'

He was indeed and Shorty Mpane was now 'clearly a person of interest' as the police record put it. At this point, Will tried to hose down his friend's enthusiasm because he was exuberantly going off half-cocked and might act too quickly.

'First of all, Koos, I don't think the shooting has got anything to do with the legal fight about the intellectual property. My view of the Swiss is they're too conservative. There certainly are some very tough characters in their international system, but they seem to work under a screen of respectability. They'd know enough about Paesano to want to handle him carefully.'

Brand was now keen to share all he knew, including the identity of the Columbian victim.

'Ja, man, you're right as usual. The IP and the execution are two separate matters, but there is a link in the research of that poor bloody journalist Franklin. It would be good to get all his stuff. I reckon he was digging a long way back into Paesano's past, well before he came to South Africa and became so powerful.'

It was to Margrit's and Richard's peril Brand was inclined now to downplay the IP side. He could not know the truly critical value of their work for Paesano and the risk the two scientists were facing with this absolutely unscrupulous tyrant if things went wrong.

'We lack information here. Brigadier bloody Oosthuizen and Paesano were as thick as thieves and surely salted Franklin's information away somewhere nice and safe or destroyed it. You know, Will, for some reason not everyone trusts us police. This includes Mrs Franklin even though I've provided her and the kids with round-the-clock protection. Do you think you could find a way to approach her?'

Out of respect for his friend, Will agreed to try, but he had other matters on his mind which he considered more important. He felt it was time to tell Brand his role at SMGT was genuine enough, but it was only part-time. It provided good cover for his other consulting work in the Department of Foreign Affairs.

'This is highly confidential, Koos. My focus is on international mercenary activity and ties between gun-running and drug cartels.'

Brand didn't need to know more than this, nor would Will have told him, but he clearly saw where their investigations might overlap.

'This puts new emphasis on my murder investigation, Will. I just wonder if those two boffins have any skin in the game?'

The complex activities out at Kyalami Drive and the reasons behind the collapse of the Green Mines and SMGT joint venture were high on Will's list, and moreover critical in the wider international context. He really needed to focus on the owner of Green Mines and put him under increasing pressure.

SIXTEEN

For his part the owner, Paesano, sitting in Parktown, was in an uncharacteristically agitated state. There were too many unanswered questions. He didn't think the ongoing tension in SMGT over Margrit's work and now the efforts to hide Richard's involvement in the IP project were being handled well enough. The attack on the house troubled him deeply because he felt it showed up abysmal flaws in his self-proclaimed watertight security. Could he trust or depend on anyone?

His gut feeling was SMGT had a role in the shooting affray. Was Wolhuter involved? He knew all too well the free-for-all approach which was adopted by industrial rivals if big money was at stake. He dismissed from his mind those who might work to higher ethical standards than himself.

He called in his henchmen to fire them up.

'Shorty, I want you to go after this Wolhuter phantom, but I don't want you to touch him. Keep your hands to yourself and be subtle for a change. I want to know all you can find out about him and his past and also how I can get at him. Understand?'

Shorty did, anxious to please after his recent stuff-up.

'Right away, Mr Paesano.'

Paesano pursed his lips and added as an afterthought,

'While you're at it, I want you to check out our security people and especially where they've come from in the last year. And, if you think you can be trusted to do three things at once without ruining them all, go straight out to Kyalami Drive and stick the biggest rocket you can find under those scientists. They should soon be ready for the tests so be sure they've got all they need. I'll hold you responsible if they find yet another excuse for a delay.'

Paesano now turned to Nick.

'If you can spare a little time thinking outside your trousers, you can do some work for a change and contact Bruno Horsfeld. I want you to update him on all the Green Mines' financials before you make the necessary arrangements to fly him over. I want to discuss the bigger picture. He'll know what I mean, so you needn't bother yourself about things which don't concern you.'

Then, as if reading Nick's mind, 'I don't care if you think I am asking you to act as a travel agent. You'll do exactly as I please and you'll do it well enough to please me. Oh, and Nick, need I say this? Never go missing in action again or you're out the door.'

Shorty might have been very pleased Nick was being so comprehensively put down, but Paesano reserved a little venom for him too.

'Shorty, our Indian janitor seems to have lost his nerve in this crisis. I'd thought he was quick enough and smart enough to be useful to me in the longer term … now I have serious doubts. Make sure he gets on top of his job pronto, otherwise you can both get out!'

When Shorty, with Nick in tow, turned to leave, he was pulled up by Paesano.

'There have been complaints to the police on the gate at Kyalami. It seems the neighbours are sick of your gun practice so you can stop it now.'

Shorty and Nick were united in fury about the Boss as they left through the back garage alley. And they left an impatient man behind them.

Later during the day, tired of sitting on his hands, Paesano made a serious error of judgement. He did some simple research and soon discovered Major Brand's first name. He decided to put things on a more personal footing and to call him. After a long wait, punctuated by several departmental transfers, Paesano was finally put through to Brand's personal assistant. Even having to communicate at Brand's level was way below his perceived dignity. He kept his composure.

'Good afternoon Major, its Dieter Paesano here ... No, no. Call me Dieter. And may I call you Koos? ... Good. Well, Koos, I'm wondering if you have the results from the autopsy on my guard yet?'

Brand apologised for his tardiness and both knew he didn't mean it. He explained.

'As it turns out, the bullet fragmented on impact which explains the mess made of the poor fellow's face and skull. This has hampered us as our forensic people are still unsure which of at least two types of guns used by the assailants, killed him. After my people conducted a more diligent search, they found sufficient cartridge cases to match the shots heard by witnesses. We know all the gun types but none are registered, including your guards'.'

He knew he had scored another cheap shot at Paesano's

expense. Brand strung him out a little longer. This was just a minor matter to his new 'friend'. Paesano's concern wouldn't be about his own guard, rather he would be desperate to know the identity of the person found executed and lying in the grass outside the big gates.

'We got a very quick response from the embassy in Pretoria about the other deceased. Because the paperwork found on the body was all in order, they gave us much of what we need and I must say it is interesting to learn where the victim hails from. Do you have any guesses, Dieter?'

He didn't expect a reply nor was one forthcoming. After a suitably aggravating pause, Brand continued, 'The Columbian Consul certainly knows a lot about this man. Unfortunately, we can't release his name until the family has been informed. I expect to get that go-ahead tomorrow. I'll give you a call if I can. In the meantime, have a pleasant evening, Dieter.'

Actually, the scant information about the executed man's identity was more useful to Paesano than Brand could have known. And it tied into Shorty's earlier identification of the getaway car. First, Brand's revelation allowed him to grasp the execution and the IP work were separate issues. Second, the somewhat casual disclosure of the dead man's nationality was useful to Paesano. It made him think back to his South American past. Apart from an early paternal lesson that wealth could bring immunity from the law, his mother's way of spoiling the youngster was to encourage and fund him to travel widely in South America.

'I want you to know this continent well; there are so many opportunities for someone with your quick mind. Don't even bother about the lands of your forefathers in Europe.'

But he had taken on a set of ruthless mentors and it was almost inevitable his shady network had grown rapidly across several countries including Columbia. There was a lot of money to be made as a courier of both currency and drugs. There were friends with dubious credentials to be found everywhere and even back then it was Bruno Horsfeld who arranged his funding. He recalled laying down some fundamental rules for Bruno.

'I want to control funding of the supply side of the drug trade rather than the distribution end. That is just too messy and you know I've never been a user myself and I'm not starting now; it's just too easy to be sucked in. As for those pathetic front-end distributors … who cares?'

He now knew how it was possible to acquire wealth while leaving major risk-taking to others. Thinking back to those early years, he recognised his real skill lay in being able to organise others to do his dirty work. He knew from personal experience that direct involvement was both irrational and highly risky. He scratched unconsciously at the back of his hand as memories of those early days flooded back, but he cleared his mind to the present.

Now he was both a player in the drugs trade, which was a heavy user of weapons, and also funding the supply of small arms, an equation which appealed to his ordered mind. As Jonathon Franklin had been discovering, Paesano's cover as a somewhat dodgy mining tycoon with strong political and bureaucratic connections was ideally positioned in South Africa. There, gun ownership was prevalent at all levels in society: domestic, sporting, security, criminal or otherwise.

SEVENTEEN

Paesano wasn't the only one reviewing his priorities. Even as the two thugs drove away from the Parktown mansion, Shorty was trying to put his tasks into order. At the ever-present risk of offending the Boss, he decided to concentrate on the arrangements for the full trial of the IP, saying to Nick, 'The Wolhuter nonsense can wait and so can checking on the guards.'

And he tried to get Nick more involved in the trial as they headed for Kyalami Drive. Although he sounded conciliatory there was an order implicit in his next comment.

'You gotta better understand the basic nuts and bolts of this IP thing. You should hear what Curie and Dupain have to say. And come see the lab. We may need to doctor it for our own needs later. An explosion would do.'

And he gave a little snort at his own macabre humour, but was unsurprised by Nick's condescending response.

'No way, man. I've got better things to do than listen to those wankers, even if it is only getting Horsfeld over here in a hurry. I have absolutely no fucking idea whether he has a handle on the Green Mines finances, so drop me at the office and take my car back to Kyalami Drive. I'll update all those numbers and give Horsfeld a call.'

When they pulled up at the office, Nick couldn't help delivering another putdown.

'I'm happy to leave all the scientific crap to the boffins and I don't plan to get involved with your possible fireworks display in the lab. You shouldn't even bother trying to understand that stuff, not with your lack of education. And my law degree won't help you either.'

In front of the still sizeable media stake-out at the office and to Nick's clear annoyance, Shorty skidded the tyres and deliberately gunned the precious car away squealing and leaving the smell of burning rubber. This brought unneeded attention to Nick and he had a hard time forcing his way through the skirmishing media mob.

Shorty used the trip out to Kyalami Drive to make a mental inventory of Richard's requirements. He had decided to use one of Green Mines' dormant operations for the trials. This site had been closed for years so he'd told a senior engineer to look over the set-up and the ensuing report wasn't too bad. Given the status of the plant, the engineer had been thorough enough and was pleased about his assessment.

'The main shed, water supply, piping and the small flotation tank are in surprisingly good condition; however, the power supply and some pumps are really sub-standard.'

Using a squad of mine workers including a couple of technicians, the engineer had set up but not yet connected the equipment needed to run the trial. Shorty had been able to procure enough of Richard's specified feedstock to run at least five iterations. This was all essentially low-value discard material from several different sites, and was currently being ground to fine flour using small crushers brought in from another mine. The only missing elements were the assessment metering and feed-back controls now on urgent order.

Organising this procurement had completely exhausted Shorty's understanding of what was actually happening in the test program, and convinced him he had to find out more from the scientists. Despite Nick's belief to the contrary, he was extremely intelligent and a quick learner.

As Jonathon Franklin had learnt, Shorty's formal schooling had ended at age eight in Soweto township, when he'd started a course of criminal education which resulted in long spells in gaol. Shorty used every spare moment in prison to further educate himself, reading widely and seeking help from any visiting do-gooder. Increasing wisdom did not take him away from his crooked path as he was a repeat offender until well into his thirties.

The nature of his education must have had spin-offs. He became adept enough to be convicted of only a small proportion of the crimes he'd committed or managed. His last and longest sentence followed a serious intergang war which left several participants on both sides as casualties. As the clear leader of one gang and a widely deserved reputation for violence and extortion, Shorty was convicted of the criminal manslaughter of two of his enemies. Given his already well-established record, he was sentenced to a very long term, time perhaps to reflect on finding a better use for his talents.

Shorty's reputation and forceful character were endorsed by others, and Paesano used his leverage in high places to secure an early release. Ironically, this process, interpreted as support for convict rehabilitation, earned accolades for both Paesano and his glamorous first wife, although it was quite likely praise for her was more for her good looks than her good works.

Behind this charitable cover, Paesano immediately put Shorty into training for much more sophisticated criminality. He had been delighted to find the big man had a deeply inquiring mind and was never satisfied with half a story. He needed to bring things together.

Richard was astonished when the lumbering giant he had dismissed as a stolid thug strode into the lab and announced Richard was going to tell him exactly how the trial would work.

'Make sure you put it simply. I want to know how this stuff can ever make money by getting valuable metals from rubbish others won't touch.'

He clearly wasn't about to discuss the shooting at Kyalami Drive and Richard was left in the dark regarding anything outside the IP trial. Shorty was on a steep learning curve and they needed to cover all five components of the linear process.

'I can do all the basics in a few minutes, Shorty. First, there's an external crushing and milling machine which finely divides the feedstock into a sort of mineral flour. In the plant there will be a continuous dry mixing area. Then we have a testing chamber to determine the ratio of minerals in the feed. Here we have my so-called 'black box' computer program which automatically adjusts the mix of biological additives and flotation chemicals to maximise the value of the final products.'

He felt he was waving his hands about more than was needed, but pressed on.

'This information goes to control a simple mixer which

feeds the flotation tank, bringing the minerals to the surface in the form of bubbles which are skimmed off into a final testing chamber. Data is then fed back to the black box to adjust the mix of chemicals, the bubbles are stripped of their minerals to make the concentrate and the chemicals get recycled. There now, how's that for a concise explanation, Shorty?'

He looked down at his Rolex.

'Sixty-five seconds!'

The big man just grunted. Rather than being flummoxed, Shorty's interest had been considerably aroused and he began asking surprising questions. They took turns to answer him. They explained various nuances of the process and even managed to convey how all this differed from conventional flotation and leaching processes. Shorty paid relentless attention, and from time to time asked for explanations of what he called big words. Impressed about the man's capacity to quickly catch on, Richard was very careful not to demean him in any way.

In all, the scientists spent nearly an hour explaining their work and were astonished by Shorty's quick command of the concepts. They particularly noted the shrewd way he directed his questions towards commercial outcomes. He plainly saw the importance of a good crushing plant and although he skirted around the statistical side, he could see managing variability was the key to a cost-effective outcome. He was deeply interested in safety aspects and asked why gases were needed in early stages of the process. He was genuinely pleased to see where the equipment he had ordered for them fitted in. By the end of this session, Shorty seemed to have grasped the basics of the process they were finalising.

'So this is the joining of the two different methods you keep talking about, using the computer to balance out all the different feedstock stuff with all those different chemicals. It's a bit risky but not like the vinegar and baking soda which my mother used to clean things for the madam when I was a kid. I think it's very clever.'

Understandably, perhaps triggered by the mention of those cleaning materials, he felt a terrible pang. Fifty years ago, his mother, single and battling to keep him robust and clothed, had worked as a cleaner in a large house like those in Kyalami Drive. She had been buxom and cuddly, but became ill and skinny. At the age of seven he was farmed out to an 'Aunty' and his mother vanished from his life for ever.

Unaware of Shorty's momentary pang of anguish, the scientists were baffled by his abrupt change of mood. With his newfound knowledge, Shorty had quickly cottoned onto their delaying subterfuge. He pointedly asked for an explanation.

'You people are much further ahead than Mr Paesano believes. What the devil do you think you are up to?'

Margrit responded, speaking nervously.

'You've seen how difficult it is to manage the range of inputs and we haven't yet even seen the set-up of the trial site. I've only just finished making the chemicals we need in quantity, and we need time to get the process into balance. After all, you've yet to send us the assessment metering and controls for calibration. Yes, you're right, we've built in a safety factor, but those other two will never understand the real reason for this, nor have the patience to learn.'

At this point, Margrit tried a different tack and became ingratiating,

'As you well know, Mr Paesano is all big picture and doesn't want to be bothered with finer details, and Nick has no interest at all in any of this. Now you've got a good understanding of the complexity of all we're doing, you surely must see a safety factor is critical to ensure this IP is the success we all want it to be.'

This flattery clearly got her nowhere. Shorty's eyes narrowed and he reverted to his bullying ways. Then he dropped the bombshell.

'I can't see why this whole … b-b-bloody show isn't ready to start in a couple of days, so move your arses. It'll take me that time to round up a decent crew. Get everything tidied up here ASAP. I'm sending a truck out for your biological stuff the day after tomorrow and we'll all meet at an old mine site to set up the plant. Nick will pick you up in the big car as he hasn't anything important to do. And remember what Mr Paesano said about gossiping at the plant. It's not on!'

This last exchange set the scientists' pulses racing. There was no doubt they were technically ready for the set-up phase. The chance to proceed at a measured pace and deal calmly with the murky intangibles which were bound to cause problems, had been stripped away from them.

Margrit had been manufacturing the biological chemicals for weeks and storing them in the garage complex. Richard had successfully modified all his algorithms; he had tested them through his powerful computer and data files back in Kent under Winston's oversight. However, the house phone line was not a very efficient data link and caused lengthy delays. And the pressure mounted everywhere.

EIGHTEEN

While all of this had been happening at Kyalami Drive, Nick was pleased with the progress he was making in the office. Paesano had always demanded the complex financials were kept right up to date. This was never an easy task given the number of undisciplined participants involved and the volatile nature of cross- funding taking place. Green Mines' financial staff numbers in the office were far larger than the technical and operational support in the various properties and joint ventures. In fact, Nick prided himself in knowing more about the status of their businesses than the players themselves.

Nick was able to pull together everything on Green Mines' financial standing within the day and he emailed it to Paesano for verification. After a few subsequent adjustments it was encrypted and transmitted to Horsfeld for consolidation. He contacted Horsfeld again, and took pleasure in peremptorily telling him to get on the first plane to Johannesburg. Typically, arrogant and fundamentally lazy, he avoided making the bookings himself. A failing which he was soon to regret when he again became the subject of Paesano's seething sarcasm and fury.

'Ah, so it's the slack Senior Personal Assistant himself, is it? Please correct me if I'm wrong. I was under the impression I told you to deal with every arrangement for Bruno. Now I hear he's late and I know exactly why. Do you think you could give me your version, please?'

Of course, there could be no response and he had to endure another tongue-lashing.

'Listen to me, Nick, I don't know what's going on these days but I do know you no longer even seem to know which way is up. I used to think you were smart … a valuable asset. Now Shorty tells me you were completely bamboozled by those eggheads out at Kyalami Drive. It only took him about an hour to get to the bottom of their little tricks. I have to tell you your whole presence here is wearing thin and I'm starting to feel you're sucking me into your whirlpool of incompetence. You might want to stop and think about how I might handle that. And while you're deep in thought, Nick, you'd better be thinking about a heartfelt apology to Mr Horsfeld.'

Just as Nick was ejected from Paesano's study, Brand was making his way to a pre-arranged meeting with his new 'friend', Paesano. Engaging in good-natured banter with the dwindling media throng at the gate, he found it easy to access the Parktown mansion. The atmosphere was tense and Brand got straight to the point.

'I can now give you the name of the deceased man, Dieter. He has been positively identified as Senor Miguel Santos.'

He paused to watch Paesano's reaction and, for a split second, saw by a flicker in his eyes that this usually cool customer was at war with his inner demons. In that split second, Paesano was cursing himself for his initial lack of interest in this part of his puzzle. This was no amateurish stoush in a drug ring battle as he had at first found it convenient to believe. Things were taking a worrying turn and suddenly the diameter and speed of his vortex of problems were increasing.

In fact, as Will and Koos had just been learning from their Interpol connections, Miguel Santos was considered to be one of the leading operators in weapons trading throughout Central Africa. More to the point, he'd had a strong and long-standing connection with Paesano, albeit purely business-oriented and never on a personal level. This stretched as far back as their common South American backgrounds and on to their shared years as mercenaries in Africa.

Paesano knew Santos had absolutely no operating involvement or direct financial investment in drug distribution. However, he had, in more recent times, negotiated considerable working capital support from two of Paesano's off-shore companies. These had been set up by Bruno Horsfeld to fund a morass of illegal activities, including money laundering focused around the gold sector.

Paesano felt no actual remorse for the death of Santos. Koos sensing this momentary consternation didn't hesitate to take advantage and bored straight in, asking a string of questions.

'So, you appear to know something about this fellow, Dieter? I would, of course, like to know the nature of your association … Also I'll need you to tell me such things as when you were last in communication … and what he was doing here in South Africa … I'm keen to know as well, whether this revelation has led you to feel personally under threat in any way… Has anyone, other than the press, of course, tried to contact you lately?'

Instead of being disconcerting, this tirade had actually given

Paesano time to compose himself and he was now fully alert as he began to respond to some of the matters raised by Koos. He realised he would have to carefully steer these responses between fact and fiction without being aware of exactly how much the policeman already knew.

'Well, yes. I did meet him in Rwanda and as young men we shared pretty tough times. For a while afterwards we'd meet up occasionally, but I was never aware of him coming to this country.'

Brand interrupted him at this point.

'Does it strike you as at all strange that an old comrade wouldn't even go to the trouble of giving you a call?'

Paesano was glib in response.

'Certainly not, Koos, it's been years since we were close.'

Paesano was breathing a little more easily as a nodding Koos appeared to accept it all without asking further questions.

Moving on, Paesano could honestly say he hadn't recently received any untoward communications and there had been no hint of extortion. In the hope of getting more information in return, he openly confessed he had found the actual murder to be truly threatening. Koos, however, who was wanting to keep him on a string, did not get to reveal anything about the other material found on Santos' body, or of its physical condition. He decided to bring the meeting to a close and to do it in style.

'I don't have the time to take a full statement now, Dieter.'

There was a slight pause and he went on.

'Let's wait until your Mr Horsfeld gets in from B.A. It may well be he'll know something more about this Columbian connection.'

Brand was politely escorted from the room and Paesano sat in stunned silence, his mind a maelstrom of alarm and doubt. How on earth did Brand know about Bruno's visit? Did he still think the murder was all about drugs? Was this an internal leak or an extension of police inquiries?

Then he recalled Nick had phoned Bruno directly. So had that loose-lipped egotist again overstepped the boundaries? While Nick had been essential in holding together the legal complexities of his South African interests, he knew nothing about the other investments. He was perpetually indiscreet and, like Bruno, not beyond Paesano's suspicion.

Two days later, Nick in the somewhat demeaning role of chauffeur, was waiting for Bruno as the 'Arrivals/*Aankoms*' door discharged its crop of First-Class passengers from Buenos Aires.

He took control of the moment by loftily apologising for messing up Bruno's travel details and managed to imply some minion had let him down. During the first part of the journey to Parktown where Paesano was keeping well away from the press, Nick tried to prod Bruno into revealing his opinion of the group's consolidated finances. However, it quickly became obvious the South American was in no mood to talk about anything, least of all delving into such a sensitive matter with a man who seemed so untrustworthy.

For his part, Bruno Horsfeld had a poor understanding of the Green Mines operation other than the dubious repatriation of cash which he moved here and there only on strict instructions. His biggest worry was that Paesano's stockpile of investments had steadily diminished as his gambling in the gold industry had increased.

Bruno had only met the Nick and Shorty duo a couple of times and was wary of their roles in Green Mines. Of most concern was Nick's personal involvement in money laundering and Shorty's heavy-handed approach to resolving commercial disputes.

Still, as Franklin had been discovering before his death, all the local corporate misdeeds of Green Mines were far less concerning to the authorities than was the more sophisticated international criminal stuff. This was starting to trouble Bruno.

While Bruno was concerned about protecting his boss' business affairs, he guessed Paesano was concerned about him. And he was right. Never one to trust, he had made a mental note to do a thorough audit of his long-serving South American employee. Was he following the very strict investment guidelines handed down and was he exclusively Paesano's man? He would know within days, but he certainly wasn't comfortable just waiting.

In fact, Bruno was brooding over the very bad news he would shortly have to deliver. Knowing his leader's impeccable cunning, he knew he had to be open and honest and let everything spill out, but he continued to worry about the devious man behind the wheel. Nick must surely have a stranglehold on his boss. Why else would the man's convoluted contractual arrangements and side agreements have remained unchecked, and how could his hedging positions have been allowed to exist for so long? While he was unable to trace the accounts being used, Bruno suspected a Swiss connection. There would surely be plenty to discuss.

Considering they had known each other from school days over forty years ago, they had not met for some eight months because of Paesano's growing involvement as a Gold Bug. His icy, barely perceptible nod of welcome set the tone for the rest of the meeting. There were no pleasantries as Paesano was wordlessly presented with the files for the separate business investments. He pointedly snatched back from Nick the copy of Bruno's consolidation report before he had a chance to look at it. His next words were an order, cutting Nick out of any discussion on the matter.

'I want you to concentrate on the Green Mines books and tell us the destination of the investment funds from every joint venture. I am getting continual and aggravating questions from the idiots relating to our agreements.'

Bruno first had to sit through this grilling of Nick about the Green Mines figures, even though he had already discovered a major cash flow problem for the entire business. This interrogation made it quite clear Paesano had done more than just endorse the numbers which had been sent to him for approval. He was relentless in his questioning of an increasingly uncomfortable Nick, and summed up the situation tersely.

'It seems to me you have siphoned many millions to Swiss hedge funds to safeguard Green Mines from our failed joint venture with SMGT, which may have been all very well but for the fact Green Mines could lose all the money if the positions are closed out now. You are not, nor have you ever been, authorised to do these sorts of deals, and I can't make head or tail of which accounts are being used. Now Bruno is here, he'll be able to clarify it for me but you can get out of this room ...'

He raised his voice threateningly as he pointed Nick towards the door.

'Be warned, I'll want a much better explanation of the money trail and I'll want it fast!'

Again, Nick could only manage his stock-contrite response. He was now in a real quandary because he didn't know how far Bruno had been able to take his investigation before leaving Buenos Aires in such a hurry.

Bruno now expected it was his turn to face a furious tirade. Unusually, Paesano had become subdued; certain now it was the highly complex 'investment' and money laundering side of his interests which were causing the trouble. With Miguel Santos murdered and some as yet unexpressed personal threat looming, he realised he should have attended to all of this earlier, not allowing himself to be so distracted by Green Mines' issues.

In particular, his focus had been on wrenching as much as he could out of his investors through the potential of the IP project and without that distraction, he would surely have put a stop to the whole frightful situation. So, with his venom partially dissipated and again scratching the back of his hand, he attended closely to Bruno's long, rushed tale.

'Dieter, as you know, I've spent a vast part of my life serving you to the best of my ability and everything I've done has been in your interests.'

Paesano's expression was unreadable and he stared stonily as Bruno blurted on.

'Lately, you've been very busy over here worrying about Green Mines and all those problems with your mining investors, so I've tried to take some of the burden off you from South America. I admit I've at times exceeded my authority. I know you've said in the arms business you didn't want to deal directly in funding military weapons to terrorists and mercenaries. It was your directive that we should only provide funding to those distributing arms in the civil criminal sector and preferably those having minimal connections in the drug trade. So that's where our other investments now are.'

He paused, not quite knowing exactly how to drop his bombshell, which allowed Paesano to interject in his clipped, angry way.

'Yes, Bruno. Naturally I'm interested to hear where this wandering story is headed, so please get on with it.'

Bruno swallowed quite audibly and his tightened palms became damp.

'Quite recently, I was approached by Señor Miguel Santos. You'll remember him from your Rwanda days. Anyway, he said you owed him and asked whether we would provide short-term financial accommodation for a big shipment of military arms to Central Africa. I assumed it had something to do with where you both worked all those years ago.'

Typically, Paesano's expression did not alter on hearing Santos named in relation to a possible recent transaction. He decided to let Bruno go on, testing the truth of his explanation. It was a long explanation, nervously delivered.

'Dieter, it was only to be for a short time and since you had told me there was success for funding beyond the IP trial, I believed money was available here in South Africa. The money which had been raised from the Gold Bugs, as you call them, should have been more than sufficient, so I was shocked after Nick told me you had already earmarked it for a financial deal in Switzerland. He provided me some account details and at face value it looks like all the transactions are matched. However, there are agency commissions I haven't been able to trace yet, and most puzzling of all are recent activities in accounts which have lain dormant for years.'

Paesano didn't react to any of this although Nick had far exceeded his mandate by diverting these funds. As for the possibility of a side deal benefitting Nick, he would let the little weasel trap himself. He remained absolutely impassive as Bruno's next burst of comments closed the loop in his long-winded, nervous way.

'When I told Santos I couldn't give him our support he became furious and we had a very colourful argument followed by a lot of bickering. He said he was in serious trouble with his customers as he had once before let them down. I, of course, told him it was hardly our problem. He said he'd already promised them finance and the armaments were on the way. I told him he'd made a big mistake by acting without approval. I was amazed when he said he'd go to South Africa and personally settle the matter, rather than try to deal with a pathetic underling like me. I told him you would never agree to see him, let alone offer help, he told me to go to the devil and he was going anyway.'

He finished breathless.

'Believe me, it was the last I heard from him, so I think I saw him off like a dog.'

Only then did Paesano respond and what he said chilled the sweating Bruno to the bone.

'Well, as it happens, Señor Santos did come to South Africa but made no contact. Now he's lying in the police morgue and I can tell you there's not much left of his head.'

As he gave Bruno more gruesome detail, he went pale.

'Santos is dead? What's going to happen now? Is this payback? These terrorists, guerrillas, mercenaries, whatever you want to call them, are worse than other criminals. They trade in death.'

Once again, there was a cold silence and Bruno was left to reflect on his own position. It wasn't a particularly pleasant reflection, as it suddenly dawned on him that he was probably lucky to still be alive himself, and if Paesano even suspected he'd been double-crossed he would soon be dead anyway.

Sympathy did not come easily to Paesano and he certainly showed none for Bruno even if he was only an intermediary, or at worst, a part instigator of this mess. He now knew the threat was directed at him and he was a lot clearer about where it was coming from. He did not know what form the actual demand might take. Anyway, he was finished for the present.

'I'll get Nick to take you out to the secure house at Kyalami Drive. You'll be staying there with the scientists. I don't want you to say anything at all to them, nor to Nick for that matter, about this botched armaments deal. You'll meet them before they start the trial run of their system at the mine and as far as they are concerned, you're here to discuss further financing for the launch of the IP. There is no point in sticking your nose into their operational stuff.'

Paesano signalled his dismissal by flicking through the papers on his desk.

NINETEEN

Bruno was deeply concerned as he made his way to the car because he had no sense of where Paesano's anger was taking him. His own errors were bad enough, mitigated because they were made with good intentions. On the other hand, if Nick was siphoning off a secret commission and deemed to be working in his own interests, it would be viewed as both treason and highway robbery and the consequences would be dire. Despite Paesano's scarcely veiled threats, Nick seemed to be quite jaunty during the drive. Perhaps he really was so naïve he thought he could outwit him. Bruno knew better.

Once at the estate, Nick went through his routine, showy tour of the house, ignoring Bruno's reminder he had stayed there before. It seemed the charade was a way of Nick avoiding nasty reality so he could escape to the diversions of his newest, young girlfriend. Bruno went straight to his suite and kept out of the way until the next morning after things had settled a bit.

Shorty, arriving early and not feeling on top of things, started to berate everyone in sight, despite the scientists having made good progress getting ready for the trial.

'Don't you know two weeks have passed since the Agreement was signed? Mr Paesano's questions are driving me mad.'

He also gave Winston a vindictive earbashing in the foyer.

'Why in God's name haven't they all finished eating? Tell those ... b-b-bloody scientists to throw it down and get their stuff together fast. And where is the womaniser, Denning? We can do without him.'

As they hurried off towards their suites, Richard told an aggrieved Shorty he needed time to download more data and openly asked Winston to provide an external data line. Winston, becoming officious after Shorty's tirade, said, 'I will supervise you.'

And Shorty bellowed, 'No you ... b-b-bloody well won't, you idle, little fucker, you're gunna help us load.'

Shorty, now in full flight as project manager, commandeered everyone except Margrit and Bruno to help load drums and sacks of powder from the garage into the two vans, and to wash down some of the mixing tanks. All this took time and the task was complicated by many loud instructions and corrections from Shorty who really was not cut out to manage anything.

He was simply a driving force. At one point, he ordered all the duplicate equipment from Margrit's laboratory into the overfilled vans. The equipment had to be removed and the vans repacked. Nobody even sniggered at this wasted effort. This distraction, and especially Winston's involvement in the loading, provided the much-needed opportunity for Margrit to contact Will Wolhuter.

Openly using the external line in the foyer under her cover of data verification, which Shorty seemed to accept, by pure luck Margrit reached Will's mobile phone. It was quickly answered and he was startled when Margrit told him urgently,

'It's me, Will, please listen. An English scientist, Richard Curie, and I are in great danger. We are being held against our will by Dieter Paesano at his secure house in Kyalami Drive. Some killing has already taken place. We can use Richard's private email address to tell you more.'

She then spelled out Richard's contact details.

'I don't think I can phone out like this again because everything is almost always monitored and we can't trust Winston Naidoo. He knows Richard works on business emails late at night so it is not unusual for him to check his correspondence then. He doesn't know about that private address … must go … someone coming.'

She hung up just before Winston reached the foyer. To play out the subterfuge, she spent another ten minutes at the computer, hoping beyond hope Winston, still smarting from Paesano's insults transmitted through an abrasive Shorty, would be too distracted to examine the external call register. Everything now rested on the way Will would handle this plea for help.

Shorty was being more careful than before as he finalised the arrangements for departure. He put Richard's computer and Margrit's files on the passenger seat while the two scientists slid into the back of the big Mercedes. Richard unobtrusively tested his door handle as Shorty eased his bulk behind the steering wheel, but the baby lock was still on.

The vans and a second car containing extra Parktown guards joined them. However, Nick was nowhere to be seen and Shorty said, 'Probably sleeping in with some young tart. He'll catch it from Mr Paesano!'

Conveniently the media pack had dispersed back to their offices expecting to at last learn more about the identity of the murder victim. Brand, having also lost some interest in the murder case itself as the bigger picture was evolving, had recalled the police from Kyalami Drive, an order he was later to regret.

Silence prevailed in the Mercedes and there was now a palpable sense of excitement in the scientists. A successful trial would reward years of research, negotiation and small-scale experimentation, and both scientists were cautiously confident. What should have been straightforward enough was clouded by the need to gain time under Shorty's increased scrutiny.

Simple things had to be made convoluted and this, as they were well aware, increased the chances of mucking it up. For his part, Shorty was his usual enigmatic self, silently plotting the steps he might need to take if problems occurred and the trial was a failure. There had to be something distinctively different about the way the scientists might be eliminated.

He turned the car down a poorly maintained road, threading his way past high security fences and large, rusty, rundown corrugated iron buildings. Eventually after an uncomfortably bumpy drive, he pulled up in front of a pair of large gates.

Richard saw on the fence a newly painted sign which seemed incongruous in the general wasteland of this industrial area. It read 'Groenwater Mine' and underneath in smaller font, stated this was a Green Mines' property, entry strictly prohibited. He asked Shorty, 'Groen?'

Shorty replied, 'Groen ... green. Bad joke, really. Only thing green around here is the water oozing from those slimes dams.'

Shorty hooted loudly and two guards sauntered out of the guard house, saw the car and instantly stiffened up, rushing to let him in. The Mercedes led the convoy through the security gates and the scientists were deposited at the main shed. Shorty, as brusque as ever, wanted action and he almost snorted as he addressed Richard in a strange, formal manner.

'Dr Curie, you go test all the control stuff we talked about and install the meters in those boxes.'

He waved vaguely in the direction of the vans.

'As for you, Dupain, go make sure all your precious bloody chemicals are in order and double-check … and remember, absolutely no talking about anything other than the IP project.'

As she moved into her work space, Margrit vaguely recognised the foreman and, despite her instructions, attempted to engage him in friendly conversation. Her overture was met with such stony silence she realised the workers would also have been given the same strict instructions. While the foreman made a noisy show of moving the workers into position, Margrit used the distraction to craftily re-label a couple of large, sealed bottles of additive in the hope even this small act might buy them time later.

Shorty was by now so locked in command mode he lost all sense of delegation. He decided the big gas bottles were too dangerous for others to handle, and anyway he was keen to demonstrate he had the strength of at least two struggling workers. His shaven head glistened with sweat as he positioned the bottles and connected them to the flotation tank control valves.

His drive to get things done created another problem, for

when Richard did a double check, he detected a minor leak and a small flame at a control valve junction. Well knowing the volatility of the gas, he quickly ordered a complete shut-down, which certainly averted a major explosion. He remonstrated with Shorty, taking something of a risk.

'If the system is fully operational and if you have a gas leak like this, it only takes seven seconds after start-up for the main pumps to kick in automatically. The only way to stop the process is to shut off the main power supply over there, high up on the wall. Do you want me to design another safety measure? Otherwise, you put the whole place in danger.'

Shorty dismissed his concern out of hand and shook his ample fist in Richard's face.

'If you think you are gunna get away with any more delays you are dead wrong.'

He brusquely ordered one of the mechanics, 'Just fix the … b-b-bloody doings quickly!'

Next, the foreman bravely stepped in and tried to raise health and safety concerns. He was unceremoniously pushed aside.

'Your guys are being paid good money here so you can put up with a bit of danger. Be more awake, that's all the pansy Occupational Health & Safety Regulations needed around here.'

Richard now began an initial practice run using water instead of ore. Sitting at the control panel, Shorty loomed over his left shoulder while he started to finetune product flows and Margrit took measurements across the whole process. Somehow, they managed to outfox Shorty by dragging this procedure out much longer than was really required. Eventually,

Shorty became suspicious and responded in the way he knew best.

'Stop playing games you pathetic eggheads. Start the real thing,'

And he ordered several dangerous moves paying scant attention to the gas bottles and ignoring the careless way the gang was handling the piles of ore while working as fast as they could. With his newfound knowledge, Shorty told them all he knew and where they could take shortcuts.

With no breaks for hours, the workers were making simple errors. These further infuriated the big man who took it out on the foreman, questioning his competence in a loud and colourful rant. The lines were cleared, the crusher started, and the fine-milling machine run up. At last, the workers had something useful to do, loading the first sample into the receiving bin. Then the foreman was able to demonstrate his skills and Shorty, for the first time, was effectively relegated to the background.

Initially, the whole process seemed to integrate smoothly. It was noted the power load was much higher than estimated, and a larger than predicted demand occurred. As they began to monitor gold yields, these were somewhat lower than predicted, and Richard was unable to optimise the output. Again, the lines were cleared and a different ore sample tried. The result was the same.

Richard was becoming seriously concerned. Shorty was now breathing foully over his shoulder and it was harder to slow things down. He suddenly stepped away to take a call from the Boss who was demanding yet another progress report. Margrit quietly indicated she had switched two additives. Richard deftly corrected his controls and the next sample produced much higher yields and a visible trace of gold. They were still proceeding too quickly, so Richard took the risk of giving Shorty bad news.

'The control meters you chose are too sensitive. This means four algorithms have to be reworked and some of the additives must be adjusted. We can only do this work in Margrit's laboratory.'

As might be expected, Shorty exploded, but was forced to agree to this further delay even though he had been giving Paesano inflated progress reviews throughout the day. However, he did hold in his hand a sample bottle containing a serious show of gold. The project had started to deliver!

Leaving the foreman to supervise washing down the lines, Shorty angrily bundled the two scientists and their equipment into the back of the car and took them on a wild ride to Kyalami Drive. At one point, Richard recalled the brush with the cyclist on his first day of this nightmare, and, during another fearsome overtaking manouvere, Margrit reached across and grabbed his hand. A tiny delay in opening the big gate generated prolific swearing from Shorty who then virtually frog-marched the scientists into the house. He was pulled up by the presence of Bruno in the foyer, but even if Paesano had not then ordered him to proceed immediately back to Parktown, there was no way on earth he was about to give Bruno any feedback on the trial. He glowered at the scientists.

'I've seen more of this city than a courier service. The test program is gunna be completed tomorrow and you jerks had better be sure it is a success. No more stuffing around, see.'

He rushed off and the others were left looking at each other in trepidation. As soon as it was safe to do so, Margrit reassured Richard, saying quietly there was nothing a little more re-labelling couldn't fix. He said his algorithms would also work very well once the measuring equipment was de-tuned for sensitivity. They had nothing else to do, and reassured they agreed to meet again at the spa after a quick dinner. Richard really looked forward to that time together given the pressure of the day and the tense mood of the house.

TWENTY

iding his time, Richard went back to the foyer and asked Winston for a data line to make his regular evening email checks. This was an established practice and since it hadn't yielded anything juicy, Winston had become a bit slack in his monitoring duties.

Tucked unobtrusively among a number of bland messages and replies, Richard was able to slip a brief note to Wolhuter telling him about the continuation of the trial at the Groenwater Mine. Clearly Will was doing a better job than Winston, constantly monitoring his emails. There was a quick, suitably bland response from him.

R. Please delay delivery U.2. one day W.

After some thought, Richard fired back.

W. Difficult set up. Connect 9 morning R.

Richard thought the 'Intelligence' Colonel Wolhuter might find this all-amateurish rubbish, but they were taking a chance anyway. What was worse, Wolhuter now wanted him to fabricate a twenty-four-hour delay and Richard had to hope in the haste and confusion of the morning departure, he could hang onto his mobile phone for a nine o'clock connection.

This was the topic of the evening's hushed conversation in

the spa. Excitedly, after some time, Margrit had a breakthrough when she traced back the procedures and recalled each step in her mind.

'There is a weak point in the system; those heavily overloaded transformers. I'll distract the foreman and you see if you can reduce the overload settings for the crushers. If Shorty starts to push things as he undoubtedly will, then too much loading will crash that antique power supply. We can just hope Shorty gets a call from Paesano … he seems to phone hourly.'

It was risky, but if successful should give them a day's breathing space. They knew they were grasping at straws and there were too many unknowns in the whole plan. In the meantime, Richard suggested they download all their data, results and operating procedures onto memory sticks as a safety precaution.

Sitting back to mull over the quandary and its myriad of likely consequences, Richard thought how pleasant it would be in normal circumstances to be relaxing with this attractive, intelligent woman watching the huge, flooding moon rising beyond the reddish dust clouds. He reached across and took her hand for a moment and Margrit responded with a look and smile which helped to settle his anxiety. For just a moment she too felt comforted through their growing openness. Perhaps they might be stronger now to deal with Will's unexplained delay.

Their discussion ranged over several topics and somehow seemed to come back to Dieter Paesano again and again. What had activated his criminality and his brutality? Richard wanted to know how he had damaged his hand. Margrit said it had happened in Central Africa.

'He never shared the details. He also told me when he was much younger he had been caught trying to take over another man's territory in Botswana. He dismissed it as simply a business misunderstanding. And, he showed me huge weals on his back due to a colossal flogging.'

Seeing a look of distaste on Richard's face at this double revelation, she tried to lighten the tone and said teasingly, 'Oh come on, Richard, you've been married. Couples do actually get undressed you know ... or perhaps ...'

He flushed slightly and decided he didn't want to know anything more about Paesano's physical condition.

But he did want to know more about her and taking advantage of her change of mood, he quite blatantly asked a number of questions, now a listener rather than a talker. She told him her parents were conservative and great believers in education. She had as many degrees as Richard, thanks to their support over a long time.

'However, they were very staid and said I was too rash and headstrong. They said I needed to concentrate on a career. They certainly did not like Claude or any of my boyfriends and they really despised Dieter. They said I was acting like a teenager attracted to money. This wasn't true, as you know. Anyway, we fell out in a serious way. Even my divorce didn't patch things up and I decided to concentrate on research here in South Africa for a few years.'

Richard found this an ideal opening to pry further and settle something which had interested him from the start. Risking offence, he asked how old she was.

'Oh, I'm just forty-six ... '

Noting his astonishment, she added with a devilish grin, 'Going on thirty-seven. It's what I tell everyone. It is so much more fun to overstate the position.' Richard reckoned even at thirty-seven she looked younger than her years.

Then in a completely unexpected change of mood, he saw tears in her eyes. She swallowed down an inaudible sob and stepped out of the spa. The terrors of the past few days had become too much to bear. Without looking back, she walked awkwardly to her suite. Richard really wanted to comfort her and was about to follow, but remembered the snooping Winston and his array of monitors.

Next day Winston decided to show the two thugs a recording of this interlude. Shorty's response reflected his aggressive nature.

'Looks like they've had a fight.'

Nick, as lewd as ever, commented.

'No way could it be made into a porn movie.'

They agreed it would be stupid to show the segment to Paesano and told Winston to keep an eye on more important things.

'... like the bloody gates.'

It might have been a relief for the scientists to know their growing closeness was being dismissed as unimportant. But Paesano, growing apoplectic with continuing delays, had many more issues on his plate than the proof of the intellectual property.

Unknowingly, he too was becoming obsessed by Gold Bug fever, and was infuriated when late in the afternoon Shorty turned up to report slow progress. With the gold sample actually in Paesano's hand, success seemed so near. He was getting closer to ending the chorus of doubt from his increasingly querulous investors, but the trial had stalled.

With Shorty sidetracked by other serious matters to do with violence and Nick on the nose, Winston now became the aggressive controller at the house and revelled in the chance to give instructions to everyone. He stopped short at Bruno because he didn't quite know what authority he had as a director. To the others, he made things quite clear.

'Tomorrow I am wanting you to be at the mine before seven and we won't have the messing around business like this morning. I will draw up a timetable and checklist tonight and you will be following it to the letter. The Boss will be pleased if we are being efficient and everything is under control.'

Paesano had never been known to show his pleasure and he was certainly not feeling much in control at that very moment. Having shouted at Winston Naidoo on the phone, he sat hunched forward, hands slightly clenched and his forearms resting on the desk, looking at the scar on the back of his hand. He was astute enough to recognise his power was weakening every day. Key issues churned over in his mind.

He began with the scientists. He considered them a necessary short-term encumbrance, a means to an end. He despised Curie as an arrogant English boffin having no commercial savvy. As for his ex-wife, apart from her bio-metallurgical discoveries, Paesano considered her to be as irrelevant in the scheme of things as she had been in their short marriage of his convenience. How come these two inconsequential boffins were causing him so much trouble? It had never been his intention to pay them for their IP and who would miss them anyway?

His mind turned to Nick, the architect of the shabby Agreement. There was no doubt the show-pony with his brilliant, twisted, contract-drafting skills, had been very useful on so many occasions. A significant number of companies and small financiers had fallen victim to his lethal legal sword, and Paesano had been the happy beneficiary of these victories. Recently, Nick had been showing unwelcome signs of independence, even hinting he had come into some money from his family. This was a fabrication. His philandering and boastful fornicating had reached new depths and he had just purchased an expensive, new car. Nick was unknowingly knotting his own noose.

Never one to have any faith in human nature, even he found it difficult to question Bruno's loyalty. This was not by chance either, as he had made sure Bruno was connected as if by an invisible leash almost from childhood. Bruno had become his lynchpin in managing investments channelled through Luxembourg. Making doubly sure of that loyalty, Paesano had provided Bruno with a generous share in these.

'Bruno, it may surprise you but money is not the first thing on my mind. I want you to stay focused on my interests which are also your interests now.'

And, always aware of risk, he had devised with Bruno, a detailed escape plan.

'I want you to be ready to liquidate most of the international portfolio at short notice. Forget about Green Mines and as for that stuff the scientists are doing, as long as it is properly documented, we will find a buyer somewhere. When we next go to Europe we must finalise those new identity papers and I don't care if they cost millions as long as we find a couple of safe havens. At worst we can get plastic surgery done in Switzerland.'

These arrangements had been well tested on some of his mysterious international trips. Sadly, the recent retirement of the eternally corrupt Brigadier Oosthuizen would require a tweaking of the plan at the South African end.

As for Shorty, Paesano reckoned a bag of money and a few days' notice would allow him to make his escape if things went wrong. If he had to exercise his own escape plan, he truly believed Shorty could look after himself even if he was the last man standing. In the meantime there was plenty for him to do, and much of it was work well suited to his vicious nature.

High on the 'to do' list for Shorty had been the matter of tracking down Colonel Wolhuter to clear up his involvement with SMGT. Somehow this role seemed to have led the man to poke around Green Mines' business. Was this a screen for something broader? One of Paesano's moles in SMGT had muddied things by reporting Wolhuter was seldom on the premises and when he was he seemed to spend more time in the finance department than anywhere else.

Curiously, the mole had also reported Nick talking casually to a head office executive, Ms Martine Monard, who managed the department. Still, Paesano thought it could simply have been another of his Casanova-styled escapades and grumbled about this to Shorty.

Shorty, with plenty to do, felt Wolhuter could wait because he was now fixated on oversight of the trial run at Groenwater Mine. Paesano had made it very clear to him he wouldn't be hoodwinked any further.

'Ready or not, I am preparing to present the IP fundamentals to our investors. I've started to round them up for a presentation even if we only have window dressing.'

This hugely distressed Shorty who was beginning to see

practical success on the horizon. He promised to increase the pressure and pleaded for more time but the Boss was adamant, telling him, 'I don't care about academic integrity and as for the companies and securities regulators I've got around them before. Just tell those two boffins if they can't make the IP work properly in time, you'll be the ringmaster to ensure they pull off my bluff with investors.'

This only strengthened Shorty's resolve to make sure the trial worked and bluffing wouldn't be needed. The Boss seemed to be standing away from direct involvement in the IP project to concentrate on financial matters. This didn't stop him from continually seeking updates on the IP trial.

'I'll be calling you every hour and I want good news each time.'

Paesano had ample evidence things were not being handled perfectly in his international financial portfolio either and he spent considerable time with Bruno digging into the contracts and transactions.

But there was another quite separate matter occupying his mind and which had really set him on edge. It was the murder of Miguel Santos without any accompanying threat. There was a slim connection to Santos, but only on the financial side and not through the physical operations of Green Mines or the IP. So who wanted what?

Bruno had stepped way out of line in first encouraging Santos and later denying him financial support for his arms-dealing rackets. This problem was in the first league and seriously frightening. He swallowed back an unpleasant taste. Who was it and what did they want?

Just as an aside to all his problems, he felt Koos Brand, the investigating Major in both the Franklin and Santos cases, seemed to becoming more aware of the wider international dimensions.

Had Paesano known how quickly the investigators were closing in on his treasure trove, he might even then have begun to activate his escape plans. However, he was increasingly smitten by the Gold Bug and as much as the scientists and Shorty he wanted to see a successful outcome of the IP project. But fate was already conspiring against him and a serious threat was looming on the broader international front.

TWENTY-TWO

When this threat came, it did so in an unusual and frightening way. Early the next day, Will Wolhuter was in his office catching up with overnight messages and planning his next moves following the urgent email from Richard Curie. Suddenly, Martine Monard the normally obstructionist and uncooperative SMGT finance executive, barged into his office and closed the door. Stunned by her rude entrance, Will was surprised by her extremely flustered and drawn look, given she was invariably impeccably presented.

'Good Lord, Mme. Monard. Are you alright?'

She looked at him with an unfocused stare and gasped out.

'I have just made a rushed trip from Luxembourg and I came directly here to see you with this.'

She waved an A4, padded envelope in front of him as if by way of an explanation.

'How can I help you, Mme. Monard?'

She thrust herself into a chair in front of his desk.

'Please, Will, call me Martine. It's all about this. It was left by a courier at the Luxembourg office. It's not actually addressed to anyone. The courier gave specific instructions to hand it over to me.'

Will was still drawing a blank.

'So why haven't you opened it?'

Martine pointed to a scrawl on the front of the envelope

'Because it says here, 'Col. W Wolhuter is to be handed this item unopened and he is to personally deliver it to Mr D Paesano of Green Mines. It is to be unsealed in the presence of Mr Paesano with Mme. M Monard as a witness.' It goes on to say it's a matter of top security and must be given absolute priority.'

Something in Martine's demeanor suggested she knew or suspected more. There had to be an implied personal threat in there somewhere and yet she was presenting him with a sealed envelope. He fleetingly toyed with the idea of delaying his next step until he'd had the material X-rayed, but was far too keen to enter Paesano's lair and meet this psychopath face to face.

'Look, go and sort yourself out and I'll see what I can do to get in touch with this Paesano and set up a meeting ASAP.' The flummoxed Martine left for her office and early as it was, he winkled Paesano's number from Brand and made a call. Thinking he may have had to do some sweet-talking to get through the mansion door, he laid out bait for Paesano.

'... I'm also told in these instructions the matter will be of great interest to you financially.'

No bait was needed as Paesano was very keen to meet Will at his Parktown mansion as soon as Shorty returned from Groenwater Mine.

In making arrangements for a four o'clock meeting, Will had to put a lot of pressure on the Swiss finance executive to accompany him. Her resistance reinforced his growing belief Monard was not just a courier.

'We have to remember whoever sent this parcel channeled it directly through you and the instructions clearly state you are to be present as a witness. Paesano has a foul reputation, but what have you got to be worried about? And your English is better than mine.'

He phoned Brand again to tell him about this development and to ask for discreet cover.

'I don't yet know where this is heading, Koos. The instructions haven't come from SMGT. It will be critical to find out exactly what's in the package though, do you agree?'

The matter was picking up quite a bit of momentum and he already had a lot on his plate.

'I'll arrange backup for you man, make sure to call me as soon as you're out of the mansion. Then let's meet so you can debrief me both on this meeting and also on your contact with Dr Curie.'

Will and Martine arrived at Parktown for the meeting just as Shorty turned up and all were shown to Paesano's office. Paesano was surprised to see Will was accompanied by a woman and as Will made the introductions, Paesano glared at Mme. Monard. Even in her anxious state, Will thought she looked like one tough nut. Throughout the introductions Paesano hadn't risen from his chair, so Will promptly sat down opposite him. They were both quite short men standing and this action nullified Paesano's normal rude dominance.

Suitably piqued, he motioned to the other two to sit down as well. As this was happening, Shorty was staring at Will and now remembered the stocky man and his small black VW at the airport a week or so before. Will smiled thinly at him.

'Ah, Mr Mpane. I remember you driving away from the airport one morning. I'm sure you'll be pleased to know the cyclist is now out of hospital. Lucky for you, the police are too hard-pressed to care much about that incident. No one died and they certainly ignored my complaint.'

Shorty swallowed back any reaction.

The two principals tried to outstare each other as they made their own assessments. As usual Paesano had no time for pleasantries or small talk and it was clear to Will he wanted to get over with it. The devil was in Will that afternoon and before handing over the envelope he was condescending.

'Bad business out at Kyalami Drive eh, Mr Paesano?'

He even managed to make the 'Mr' sound patronising and Shorty stiffened in his chair at the offence to the Boss. Surprisingly, Paesano ignored Will's innuendo and slit open the package using a long, slender, gold, paper knife. He sat stock-still for a moment as if gathering strength. Then, ignoring a small package quickly plucked out several typed pages and began to read. He hadn't got very far when he stopped and, his face thunderous, thrust a couple of pages at Will.

'It says you must read it too.'

Will scanned the content. He saw it was written fluently, typed in single space and neatly filled each page. On first glance, he saw nothing more than a statement of facts followed by a straightforward demand. He decided to read it aloud for Martine's interest and for Shorty's edification and, reading ahead, he was able to introduce telling pauses, designed to aggravate Paesano and add to the tension.

<u>Attention:</u>

Mr W Wolhuter (SMGT), Mr D Paesano (GM) and Ms M Monard (as witness).

<u>*These are known facts:*</u>

Your two organisations have been exposed through information gleaned with great difficulty from the late Miguel Santos. The companies were engaged in joint ventures which closed some years ago after a serious disagreement. Since then, they have:

- *frequently milked investors through risky capital raising for high tech IP*
- *continued to bank separately in Luxembourg in a money laundering conduit*
- *laundered a great deal of investor money into a number of tax havens*
- *made fixed investments and also secured legitimate but weak mining businesses*
- *used the balance to underwrite illegal weapons and drug trading throughout Central Africa*
- *not seen fit to amend their separate operations.*

From time to time, the companies provided finance for Miguel Santos in his own role of direct dealing in large quantities of weapons for national conflicts. You did not want to know where the weapons were used and wanted to remain at arm's length. Recently, your two companies let Senor Santos down in these dealings. He, in turn, let our syndicate down at a significant cost in cancelled orders.

Demand for restitution:

At this stage our syndicate requires immediate financial restitution and is not seeking further retribution. Our claim for compensation is exactly as outlined below. This is not a matter for negotiation. The amount assessed purely on a business basis, is $US36 million.

1. The syndicate is only interested in the total sum.

2. How the burden is shared is to be decided between you.

3. Any forfeiture will incur penalties beyond a 'Santos-style' solution.

4. Forfeiture will include exposure of all the highly illicit operations.

The syndicate would far prefer you personally and your companies continue to maintain viability

The restitution process:

This will occur in two stages. Your first step is to indicate within a two-day acceptance period, beginning after your meeting, whether it is the intention of both companies to proceed.

Given a history of connivance at the most senior levels in both companies, our syndicate must receive the full sum required within ten days, inclusive of the acceptance period.

Mr W Wolhuter, the bearer of this letter, is to act as the exclusive conduit and will receive further instructions regarding the manner of payment.

No regulatory or legal authorities are to be involved. This matter extends well beyond your own countries' interests.

As an encouragement to you all, you will find a small

Despite an externally calm appearance, Will was stunned by the content of the letter. He and Brand had been making good progress in tracking down Green Mines' international funding arrangements, and this exposé didn't actually add much to what they already knew of the company's shady dealings. What floored him was the way in which SMGT had been implicated and made to look equally corrupt. If true it might have something to do with the collapse of the Joint Venture. He recognised the whole issue was far bigger than he had thought. The threat was explicit and the damages pitched at a level not designed to ruin the companies, but would certainly rein them in.

If Will had managed to appear impassive, the same could not be said for Paesano. At first he seemed stunned and then his anger kicked in and Will watched in silence as pale turned to florid. The tyrant suddenly grabbed the envelope, clumsily shook out a small object wrapped in brown paper and tore it open. Inside was a rolled-up, clear, plastic, zip-lock bag and everyone leant forward as he flattened it out. On first inspection it looked like a very old gherkin and there was a mild stench of antiseptic. Then Shorty spotted a fingernail at one end. Even he shuddered as he muttered

'My God, a finger. No wonder he was wearing a glove.'

Everyone else reacted differently to this grisly present. Paesano's face again registered shock, drained of colour and he looked away, shaking his head in disgust. To Will he seemed to take a 'big picture' approach. He seemed to readily accept the guilty verdict. And there was an obvious need for negotiation with SMGT, which Paesano wouldn't relish at all, especially as a hefty portion of the blame for this mistake seemed to be levelled at him.

Martine's last vestige of calm had evaporated and Will thought she was about to vomit. This business had turned into a monster. If this major payment were to go ahead, she, as international treasury manager for SMGT, would be in the thick of it. Will wondered what might be dragged out of the cupboard to implicate her.

Will was simply disconcerted. The rotten finger itself didn't particularly worry him as he'd seen the same, and worse, before. He was a bit annoyed Koos hadn't told him more while reporting Santos' beating and execution, but there was so much other evidence of torture it was a small enough oversight. He thought of the ruthless nature of the people who had orchestrated this whole macabre performance, and wondered how far they would go to get their way.

A more immediate problem for Will was the impending discussion within SMGT and how high up the executive ladder he would have to carry this demand. This was not a transparent organisation and he had felt from the outset the senior management team was less than ethical, as several of his risk investigations had been inexplicably thwarted.

Without any farewell, Will stood and nodded to Martine, signalling she should get up and leave too. Thinking quickly, he claimed the finger and turned to Paesano.

'You might expect another call from the police.'

Paesano's head snapped up and he said tersely, 'You saw what the note said about alerting the authorities.'

Will just shrugged his shoulders and moved towards the door.

'I don't know what you intend to do, because this seems to be bigger than you. You're lucky you don't have to get approval from anyone else. I'll have a lot of talking to do with the right people at SMGT. You know the top people there far better than I do. I can bet this will shock even them.'

Will's drive back to deliver the now subdued and obviously frightened Martine to her office began in silence. After a while he decided to revisit his unfinished business in her finance department.

'As we have time at our disposal, Martine, perhaps you'd be kind enough to explain why SMGT has held open those bank accounts which relate to the failed joint venture with Green Mines.'

Her response was too quick, too glib.

'Both sides had to agree and my predecessor in Treasury couldn't get anyone at Green Mines to clean up the problem. That's why the bank accounts just sit there.'

His next question was a little more direct.

'Martine, you were only seconded to South Africa a couple of years ago. How come you are now a signatory on what are, after all, dormant accounts?'

Again, her instant and perhaps rehearsed response, 'I don't like to have loose ends in my department.'

Will, an expert in conducting interrogations, now opted for a long, pregnant pause as he passed a couple of trucks and sensed Martine bristling beside him. Eventually, he resumed his questioning.

'And who is the Green Mines signatory?'

This time Martine paused, guessing where this was heading and crafting the best response she could, said, 'He is GM's lawyer, I think. Nicholas Michael Denning to give him his full signatory name. He appeared one day to see about fixing the matter, and after lively discussion we decided to hold the accounts open in the event good relations could be re-established between the two sides.'

She probably expected him to be way out of his depth in this area of financial risk management. After all, he'd been sniffing around the Treasury Department in the last two weeks deliberately asking a number of very naïve questions. Even in the midst of her troubles, she smiled wanly as she recalled the curt and condescending way she'd handled him. Then she was caught off-guard.

'So, if there are banking transactions using these accounts, you both have to sign.'

It was a statement, not a question, one which deserved nothing more than a nodded response. For some reason, Martine chose to complicate things by adding an explanation.

'I don't believe there is any money in the accounts.'

Will appeared almost disinterested.

'But they could still be used as a conduit for very large in-and-out transactions? If the two companies felt they had to pay out a huge ransom, these accounts could be a useful pipeline?'

She nodded and that was the end of it.

As the delivery boy, Will had done his job and now he had to get the executives at the top of SMGT to quickly understand the implications of this fiendishly-delivered demand. They would either handle it on their own or be a great deal more open. He now began double-guessing how the company heavyweights would respond.

For a business which relied so much on favourable PR, any exposure which trashed their reputation could lead them to shut up shop and withdraw from the country, thereby losing an attractive source of risky investment funding.

In reality he knew the note and the finger didn't amount to enough to make a connection between murder and the laundering of money. If the SMGT top brass saw it this way, then they might make a hard-nosed response and pay nothing. After waiting for things to cool off, SMGT would then carry on business as usual.

If the restitution demand had been all financial, this ploy might have worked. However, the demand had implied a 'Santos solution' as the alternative. As already demonstrated, Mafia-like action was easy and this surely would be an over-riding incentive for SMGT to settle.

Will was relieved Koos Brand could be trusted to support him. He'd immediately decided he would ignore the syndicate's warning about not alerting the authorities, but he did restrict this to his good friend. He knew Koos was discreet and did not go off rashly chasing thin leads. He had already explained to Will how political and bureaucratic pressures could easily be applied to curtail a weak investigation.

For his part, Koos did make one important immediate

decision which, because it exceeded his delegated level, he had to clear with Brigadier Mfuleni.

'Sir, we need to put pressure on these guys. Could I have permission to undertake phone taps and watches on the SMGT Offices, the Green Mines Office, Parktown, Groenwater, and especially Kyalami Drive?'

He handed over the up-to-date paperwork. Then with a sense of irony and in the hope of identifying a connection between them, he assigned Sergeant Ben Mgeni to tail Shorty Mpane if he could. His sergeant was not bright enough to dream up creative solutions by himself, but he did seem to be enjoying a better standard of living lately. His constables didn't call him 'Bentt Mgeni' behind his back without good reason. Had they been questioned in confidence, they might have even suggested an unhealthy relationship between their boss and the poisonous Mr Mpane.

TWENTY-THREE

There was a moment's silence in the Parktown room after Will and Martine left. Paesano was a mere shadow of himself, unable to focus on anything in particular, while Shorty just seethed. The big man's understanding was limited to the local context and its problems. Suddenly, he was being overwhelmed by the full international story. He wondered if his boss would ever enlighten him, but it was perhaps better for him to remain ignorant.

They heard a car starting in the driveway below and instinctively moved over to the window to watch. As the black VW passed through the gates Shorty burst out.

'Now I've seen the … b-b-bastard … sorry, Mr Paesano … I'll fix him as soon as he tries anything. I could do him tonight!'

Paesano seemed to snap out of his reverie.

'Don't be so stupid man, just look.'

He pointed as the VW pulled up in front of two cars parked on the roadside. Will got out, and Paesano was not surprised when the unmistakable burly figure of Brand stepped from the second car. They spoke briefly before driving off.

Things were hotting up and Shorty really needed to do something to break out of the ominous mood in the room.

'Alright, Boss. I'm gunna get back to Groenwater, but I've got some bad news for you. The old machinery at Groenwater is busted and we need another day to fix it up.'

He gave some further detail omitting the fact that he had pushed the cobbled-together system far too hard, but certainly not hard enough to burn out a major pump, the power supply and eventually, to shut down the whole trial. He felt in his bones the bloody Englishman had once again fooled him while he was being distracted by Paesano's instructions.

'Believe me, Boss, I am sorry, really sorry.'

The boss was strangely subdued for a moment. He slowly turned to face Shorty.

'So, you're sorry, are you, Mpane? You've been made to look stupid all over again by a scientific freak and you've single-handedly managed to damage my whole project, and here you come cap in hand, saying sorry. Now, tell me exactly what's happening out there.'

With hard fury in his voice, he was unrelenting in getting to the bottom of things. The tale was indeed a sorry one and for the normally taciturn Shorty, a long one.

'I've got electricians all over the plant trying to replace machinery and cables. They've agreed to work all night. Even so, the show won't run before late morning. Now you've called me back here, I've had to leave the foreman in charge and I don't know how far I can trust the bastard. I had to suck up to him to supervise the doings overnight. That cretin'll pay for his cheek after this is over.'

He paused looking to see how Paesano was taking this news, but he remained stony-faced and Shorty went on.

'I took the scientists back to Kyalami Drive and told Naidoo he'd be dead meat if there was the slightest security breach.'

Paesano only grunted angrily and then summed matters up for him.

'Another day lost. Those two can forget about the contract. There's no way they're getting any money out of me after this delay. They must be kept under the closest control because you tell me they are closing in on a solution.'

To mollify him, Shorty handed over the sample bottle showing a flash of gold which really raised his interest.

'This is more like it. Still, I'll have to put off those puerile investors again and I'll look like a fool, which you know I detest.'

Shorty was in a hurry to concur.

'I'm with you there, Boss. When we no longer need those jerks I'm gunna fix them up proper. No one makes a fool out of me, either.'

Once again Paesano pulled him up.

'Be very careful, Shorty.'

Then as he turned to leave, Paesano changed everything once more.

'I want to see you later this evening at Kyalami Drive, Shorty. I'll get Nick to take me there in his new car. You just think about dealing with the cocky wretch.'

To say the poisonous Mr Mpane's day had so far been abysmal would be to understate the obvious. Ignoring Paesano's orders to moderate his aggressive driving habits, he veritably tore back out towards the mine-site and took vengeful pleasure when, glancing back, he saw the ponderous car driven by the foolish Mgeni making heavy weather of keeping up.

During the trip he tried to replay the events of the damned meeting, but all he could conjure up was the ludicrous shrivelled finger and a sense of helplessness as his boss was plunged deeper and deeper into trouble. Shorty did not do helplessness well, and had an overwhelming desire to damage someone to relieve his pent-up aggression. Fortunately, there was no one within arm's reach.

He recalled his day had started well enough, but it hadn't taken long to go downhill. He had arrived at Groenwater this morning to note Winston had done a surprisingly good job of managing the transport from Kyalami Drive. In a way, this peeved him and he had no intention of lavishing praise on the smarmy little Indian when he next visited Kyalami Drive. He didn't even contemplate Winston's success was helped by the fact he himself hadn't been there to stuff things up in his haste.

Then he had received the first call from Paesano who wanted to express his concern about Nick's recent behaviour. Paesano told him Bruno had called to say he had identified the signatories on one of the dormant bank accounts.

Paesano had ordered Shorty back to the mansion for a face-to-face chat. What was the boss thinking? How was he supposed to supervise the critical trial if he had to attend yet another useless meeting, for Christ's sake?

Shorty knew immediately things weren't good for Nick and even though he detested this rival for Paesano's trust, it did not mean he necessarily wanted to provide the ultimate solution for Nick's wrong doings. He also knew instinctively a paranoid Paesano was becoming suspicious of everyone around him and it was only a matter of time before an order to fix the problems came his way. As if this wasn't enough, he had been instructed to find out more about a woman Nick had been meeting at SMGT and he could hardly contain his annoyance at this extra demand. He grudgingly accepted Paesano didn't give a damn about his feelings and this added fuel to his worsening temper.

Unfortunately for all concerned, Shorty's return to Groenwater Mine had happened around 10 a.m. just as Richard and Margrit were finalising the start-up procedure. Needless to say, his temper had been gradually mounting to explode into a petulant tantrum which he didn't bother to control. He turned on the scientists and roared.

'Didn't the fucking Indian tell you to wait for me?'

Richard and Margrit looked at him blankly as he went on.

'Don't stare at me like … b-b-baboons. I don't trust you arseholes one bit. I bet you've played Naidoo for the fool he is, so guess what? You're gunna start everything from zero. Now you'll need to work harder than you ever have in your pathetic little lives because we're gunna finish this thing today. Has this got through your thick skulls?'

Not reading the mood at all well, the foreman of the maintenance gang boldly butted in to suggest Shorty was taking serious risks in such a cobbled-together plant. His bravery was rewarded by a long, scowling stare and a shouted order for Richard to start the crushing and milling machines together as a load test. There was a distinct dimming of the main shed lights as the extra start-up load came onto the system.

Things soon settled down somewhat, but the Amp Meter still indicated close to a *'red-line'* reading, even though the motors were working well below maximum capacity without any ore being processed. Shorty was initially alarmed until he realised he had once again been too impetuous, but since nothing had blown, he began looking very pleased with himself. The foreman walked off in disgust.

TWENTY-FOUR

The first bit of luck came their way when Richard was handed an opportunity to execute his sabotage plan, courtesy of Paesano himself. The Boss, still in Parktown, seemed unable to refrain from contacting his right-hand man, and around midday Shorty was once again distracted by his ringing phone. The noisy machines meant he had to go behind a wall to hear and be heard, and Richard took the chance to adjust the main pump controller so as to start it in a dry condition. Under a full ore load, this would quickly cause a catastrophic system failure. As he reached for the panel, a sixth sense warned him to pull back and he did so just as Shorty reappeared.

'Mr Paesano wants a full report on a successful outcome by the end of the day ... and what in hell are you up to, Curie?'

Richard had a long list in his hand and he waved it about saying he was just going through a routine check. Shorty peered at the control panel and glanced down the list in what he thought would be a knowing way. Then, surprisingly, he moved away again to examine the additive tanks which had been set up by Margrit.

This time Richard was able to use the distraction more successfully. He managed to adjust the algorithms for the pump controllers, estimating this change could provide about five minutes of continuous operating under full load, before the crusher and milling motors began to slow down. If Shorty tried to increase power, as was likely, the motors would probably burn out and the cause of the problem would not be located without the cooperation of the foreman, who seemed to want '… nothing more to do with the big, rude bastard.'

Soon after Shorty returned, his phone rang again. The call was yet again from the Boss and he raised his hand and ordered everything to be stopped for a ten-minute break. Clearly, he was not leaving that damned Curie unsupervised with the machines running as he had before. Shorty walked some way off to avoid being overheard and Richard nipped out to the toilet block and hurriedly phoned Wolhuter. Given the pressure he was feeling, it was a pretty unsatisfactory discussion. After a terse greeting, Will Wolhuter's hasty message was no comfort to Richard.

'The police and I have uncovered a vast international conspiracy, involving SMGT and Green Mines. Our country is being robbed and infected by corruption. You'll have to hang on longer. There will be discreet protection for you at the house. The plant's a bigger problem because it's so spread out and too risky. Whatever you do, try to stick together. Now, have you managed to create a delay for your project?'

Richard was dismayed to hear of this new complexity. It made things even unhealthier for Margrit and him, but Will seemed to be trying his best so he finished on a positive note.

'Probably by the end of the afternoon. I'll email tonight.'

He stopped the call as he could hear some stirring near the

control board and hurried back. Shorty, looking somewhat distracted, reappeared just as Richard was approaching the panel. At the end of his long call, Paesano had been quite specific in telling him, 'If Nick has cheated me you'll have to fix him up, and the same goes for those two eggheads. I'm fed up with them.'

Disconcerted for a moment, he avoided looking at the scientists and made another cursory examination of the control board without knowing why. Then he fixed Richard with one of his chilling stares, and in a tone which had become even icier, again asked, 'What have you been up to?'

This time he didn't even wait for a reply.

'Needed a crap, did you? I can understand why you're shitting yourself.'

The whole trial was restarted. It was clear to Richard that Shorty had become less than happy about the foreman's attitude, and in order to keep an eye on everything, told Richard to monitor the control panel as the testing program now began in earnest.

Initially there were runs of only a couple of minutes each as different ore samples were tried and additives changed. This did not appear to affect the power supply, although there was a *'red line'* moment and a distinct dimming of lights as Shorty tried to override a pipe-cleaning procedure. The foreman was incensed and one of his men only escaped serious, high-pressure injury by a whisker because Richard was able to shut down a section in time. Shorty's response was predictably bland. He may have been slightly embarrassed but there would be no apology. After all, his estimate of the value of human life was never over-generous.

The test proceeded without further interruptions. The pressure was really on the scientists as Shorty alternately loomed over Richard at the control board and interfered with Margrit's additive processes. Be damned if he'd be hoodwinked this time! He showed growing confidence he would be able to operate things himself with just a little more hands-on experience.

The analysis of each run took time and he perceived a growing sense of excitement in the scientists, enough to tell him the results would be far better than the day before. And excited they were, but Richard's joy was tempered by his knowledge of the disaster that loomed if his fiddling worked and if Shorty took over to force the pace. He was scared for himself and even more concerned for Margrit if things spiralled even further out of control.

By early afternoon, the testing was ready for a full-scale continuous run. Richard laid bait.

'So, we'll start carefully by running the softest rock sample through the crusher first?'

As expected, an exasperated Shorty rose to the occasion.

'No way, you coward, I make those sorts of decisions! Go for the hard material and if you don't like it, piss off. I've watched you two long enough to know I can now control the show if I need to. I won't have you messing it up.'

The first load of ore was loaded into the crusher and everything proceeded well. Almost according to a script, it didn't take long for Shorty to increase the tempo and apply more power. Richard watched eagerly as the needle began to approach the *'red line'* on the dial, and after a few minutes the motors on both the crusher and milling machine began to slow down. Shorty opted for his natural solution to this situation and applied more power.

Suddenly the lights dimmed and an ear-splitting explosion plunged all in the shed into darkness except for the glow of the burning motors and the smell of tar and rubber from the now red-hot cables. It was a disaster, initiated by Richard and consummated by Shorty himself.

This debacle was first met with eerie silence and everyone was in a state of shock. The only exception was Richard, who was prepared for the spectacular outcome and mostly pleased about it, as well as with the pandemonium which began to rage in the semi-dark. At Shorty's bellowed command, security guards bounded into the shed while two workers reeled in agony and others were dousing some small flames. Richard moved over to Margrit who was visibly shaking, and whispered to calm her.

'Don't worry too much. I caused it. Keep out of the way as much as you can. I've got no idea what the thug's reaction will be.'

It didn't take long to find out. The foreman stormed at Shorty and shouted in frustration.

'You idiot. I told you not to rush it and now two more of my people have been burnt. Well, bugger you, I'm taking them all off the job right now.'

Shorty's response was swift, and in character. He let fly with a hefty, right round-arm knocking the foreman flat.

'The rest of you … b-b-bastards stay right where you are. If anyone even thinks of moving you'll find out my guards hit as hard as me.'

He stood stock still, obviously deep in thought. He knew once again he'd over-reacted and it dawned on him that he would need these men to make the repairs and get things operating again to complete the trial. He certainly didn't want Paesano to find out it was he who had so spectacularly ruined it all.

The foreman groaned as he came to. In a surprising move Shorty reached down and quite gently helped him to his feet, then actually made him if not an apology, certainly an explanation.

'I've been under a lot of stress lately and this last shock was too much for me, so I reacted too fast.'

He stood up straight and forced a contrite reaction to his outburst. He didn't actually apologise.

'If you and your people can get this show on the road again quickly, I'll see you all get a very large … b-b-bonus.'

In offering this he had to swallow his disgust. The foreman, still groggy, was able to shrewdly milk this changed situation for all it was worth, and eventually agreed to such a staggering sum of money even the injured were clamouring to get back to work. Soon they set about assessing the damage, including a most cursory look at the control board which they could see was completely untouched. As the workers went about their job and the afternoon wore on, a fuming Shorty turned to the scientists.

'If any of this is your doing, you should know you're dead meat, experiment or not. As I said before, I've watched enough to know how to work this stuff to produce the right results, so you pathetic leeches are no longer indispensable. Now I'm gunna get a guard to take you back to Kyalami Drive while I get things organised here. It'll take hours. I'm gunna give the Boss my very accurate account of exactly what happened! Get it? Get the message?'

Then the phone had rung and Shorty had been ordered back to what had turned out to be such a disastrous four o'clock meeting with the enigmatic Wolhuter. Oh, yes. It had been a bad day indeed.

TWENTY-FIVE

While things had been going so spectacularly pear-shaped at Groenwater and the meeting with Wolhuter had caused him so much angst, Paesano was still planning his night. Knowing he may well need an alibi for later on, he brazenly inspected the police from a brightly-lit window and ostentatiously drew the curtains making sure a chink of light was visible to the watchers below.

Around ten o'clock, he called Nick to come around to Parktown immediately. He wanted Nick to go to Kyalami with himself as a hidden passenger. Sure enough, it was only a matter of crouching down in Nick's new car as it left. The incompetent police on duty were duped into logging the driver, as the car's sole occupant.

Ominously, not one word was exchanged between the two during the drive. This was not necessarily an unusual state of affairs, but on this trip Paesano was lost in his anger, and Nick was desperately trying to convince himself things weren't really as bad as they seemed. The arrival at Kyalami Drive was managed by repeating the same simple trick, and the police barely awake, lazily logged only the driver. The gates closed and Nick edged the car into the shadows cast by the moon.

Wordless, the two headed for the house. Once safely in the foyer, Paesano strode past Winston as if he wasn't there and hissed at Nick.

'You wait here until Shorty gets back from Groenwater.'

When he at last acknowledged Winston, it was through a harsh instruction.

'You! You go tell Bruno I'll see him in the dining room, then fetch the two boffins and tell them to wait in here.'

At this Nick seemed to recover some of his arrogance, saying flippantly, 'You'll only need to go to her suite to find those two lovebirds.'

The only response he got was a withering look of distaste from Paesano who savagely slammed the dining room door behind him. Bruno appeared and went straight in, looking confused and dishevelled, as though he hadn't fully recovered from his jetlag. His hasty, pressured examination of the newly discovered banking information had not helped his state either and he nodded warily at his long-time boss. The scowl on Paesano's face was enough to warn him off starting a conversation. Eventually the interrogation began.

'What answers have you got for me? Who is involved and how much is involved?'

Bruno was about to sit down and thought better of it.

'I'm still working on the second bank account, but in total it seems about five million Rand is involved and there are no residual balances in either account. I was thinking about speaking to an old contact at SMGT in Luxembourg but maybe we need the full story first ...'

Here he was abruptly cut off by Paesano's raised voice.

'I don't need any more of your futile cross-checks. I only need to know who could access those accounts.'

Shaken by this ill-concealed venom, Bruno stammered out an answer.

'It's really only Nick Denning and a fellow … Martin Mon …'

Paesano cut him off, snarling, 'Fellow? I know all about a woman! Her name is Martine, you fool, Martine Monard. Couldn't you even get that right? She's a further complication and I've already got Shorty on her case. You're a bit slack in your banking investigation, aren't you?'

Thoroughly confused and now growing more alarmed, Bruno had no idea what else might be known, so he remained silent. This only served to further anger his boss who launched into another tirade about Bruno's total incompetence, and he particularly focused on the awful mess involving Miguel Santos. Eventually, he ran out of steam and got back to the business at hand.

'As soon as Shorty gets here, I'm getting to the bottom of Denning's ugly pranks. I want you to shut up and let traitor Nick dig his own grave while I question him. The pig has patently stolen money from me in the same way he's diddled others in the past; and the worst thing about it is the idiot thinks he can get out of it. He's mixed up with at least one of my enemies and who knows what he's been telling SMGT about The Curie Dupain process. Luckily he knows nothing about science because the little thief hasn't any scruples.'

Even in his dire predicament, it flashed through Bruno's mind that coming from Paesano this was a bit rich.

There was a knock on the door and Paesano switched off his tirade. Shorty, dressed in work clothes and a jacket from his day at the mine, led Nick and the scientists into the room. They huddled together, uncertain about what would happen next. There had been no opportunity to eat and the stress made them particularly queasy. Paesano didn't waste a minute before launching straight into Nick as the others flinched.

'Does the name Martine mean anything to you?'

Nick was obviously quite unprepared for the direction of this attack and his discomfort showed.

'I believe it does, Mr Paesano. A Martine Mardon or something like that?'

He stammered on.

'A foreigner … possibly French, I think … we tidied up some old joint venture arrangements a while ago.'

He paused, his gaze averted, not at all sure where things were heading with the Boss.

'It's Martine Monard, you treacherous weasel, and I've already had the pleasure of meeting her.'

Paesano's sharp retort hung in the air for a long moment. Eventually Nick seemed to recover some of his poise.

'Yeah, that's the one … Martine Monard. There was nothing in those old accounts, you know; we just wanted to clear things up.'

As much as he tried to sound calm, Nick was obviously a bundle of nerves now and Paesano, casually glancing at papers in front of him, let him squirm. Then deep in thought he softly repeated.

'MD … MD?'

He slowly fixed Nick with an ugly grimace, and with controlled hostility, resumed his grilling. He continued on unrelentingly for the next twenty minutes, looking at Bruno from time to time for confirmation of the points he was making.

'Now, all those big hedging transactions you've been banging on about … are they still in profit?'

This question released the pressure a little and Nick was puppy-like in his desire to please.

'Oh yes, Mr Paesano, I checked them all today and we are well ahead'.

Perhaps Nick may even have dared to believe he had once more slipped past his boss' understanding of money market mechanisms. Like a master yachtsman, Paesano changed tack again at precisely the right moment.

'How much does it cost us to use those financial tools? Do we use a commission agent or something?'

Surer of himself now, Nick fudged his reply, slyly answering only the first part of the question.

'I've cut a good deal with our brokers, Mr Paesano, and because of the large number of transactions, we're getting it at about half market rate.'

Paesano was relentless.

'And how much commission in total has been charged since we started this arrangement? It doesn't seem to me like much of a challenge to shift my money around.'

Nick, all too well aware of the amount, blustered on.

'I need to check because I have been concentrating on the big-picture transactions themselves rather than the commissions.'

Paesano snarled.

'It's a simple question and I want it answered! How much commission has been paid?'

Nick's head was spinning and he mumbled.

'Err … its something like nine million Rand over two years.'

He began to scrabble around in his brief case. This revelation certainly startled the scientists who wondered about the comparatively low value placed on their complex IP, but Paesano appeared to take it in his stride. Then, icily, Paesano set about expanding the unanswered second part of his earlier question.

'This firm I'm hearing about, this MD Finance, would you care to tell me who owns it?'

There was silence from Nick but Paesano didn't let up.

'Oh, and while you're thinking up an answer to this very difficult question, perhaps you'll also come up with an explanation of how come the commissions are being paid through those old JV bank accounts? You know the ones, those which have nothing in them?'

Suddenly, Paesano leapt up from his chair and moved threateningly towards Nick.

'Answer me, you little pig. It's you and the Swiss woman? MD indeed. More like Monard Denning incorporated. Pathetic, really.'

This sudden switch to physical menace had never happened before and proved too much for Nick who collapsed, unasked, into a chair. With his voice trembling, Nick tried both to answer and to plead.

'I'm so sorry, Mr Paesano. It was her idea … and it isn't a big sum of money in the overall scheme of things. I've made you lots of money and virtually all of it has gone to Green Mines. Please forgive me, Mr Paesano. I can repay it all or most of it anyway. I'll sell the car.'

He looked up into a face totally devoid of expression. There was no point at all in saying any more. Paesano had enough of apologies and, now back in control of himself, calmly addressed his underling.

'You have stolen from me, and as you of all people should understand, no one gets away with that. Get a sheet of paper and a pen from your briefcase.'

Nick hurried to oblige, fumbling badly.

'Now, write this,' and he slowly dictated in clipped tones to the trembling Nick.

Mr Dieter Paesano. I wish to deeply apologise for my continuing criminal behaviour despite all the support and trust you and others have given me. I recognise this behaviour is ingrained in me and I know of no way to make amends. If I could, I would seek to compensate you and all others who have tried to help me, but there is not enough money and money is not enough. It is all the property of other people. I can make no claim for the future as I have none. Nicholas Michael Denning.

As he finished his shaky writing, Nick dropped the pen and stood up. He straightened himself and tried to look his boss in the eye, relieved to have finished this awful deed in front of the others. There was no relief, as Paesano's fury now rose again and he roared at Nick.

'Hand your gun to Shorty.'

At this, Richard, who was standing directly behind the big man in the line of fire, nearly panicked. He imagined a desperate Nick might now actually choose to use the weapon. He needn't have worried as Shorty's towering presence and Paesano's all-encompassing authority were far too much for any bravado. Shorty, as usual wearing his gloves, was blank-faced as he calmly took the gun by its silencer, wiped it carefully, and very deliberately placed it into the side pocket of his reefer jacket. Paesano's whisper was cold and measured and everyone in the room absorbed each word.

'I'm now finished with this toad. Take him down to the cabana. Use one of the guards if you need to but do what you know you have to do.'

He picked up the hand-written admission of guilt and shook it in front of Nick's face as he thrust it at Shorty.

'Take this and leave it there with him.'

In that moment, Richard saw the final demolition of the bully boy who had caused him so much grief so long ago at school. He caught Margrit's eye and in an instant she knew intuitively how this had impacted on him.

Suddenly Nick seemed to realise what all this meant. The self-styled hero of the Angola Border Wars jumped up and tried to grab at the paper. Shorty was quicker and stuffed it into his jacket pocket. The tussle, if it could be called a tussle, was short-lived.

The inevitability of his death came at him with full force and he screamed with outrage and fear before Shorty clamped his mouth and bodily lifting him up, took him through the glass doors down towards the cabana.

The others were frantic but powerless. They could hardly look at one another and all were close to vomiting in their fear.

Paesano seemed emotionless, idly playing with the big revolver which Shorty had left on the table. No one was going anywhere.

Richard, Margrit and Bruno had watched things unfold with rapidly increasing horror. If they had been able to look outside, they would have seen silhouetted in the moonlight, a puppeteer and his dummy, stumbling away. As it was, only Nick's diminishing incoherent ranting marked their progress. Away in the distance, a door closed solidly. There was nothing but the sounds of the night.

The atmosphere in the dining room was surreal. Paesano, his breath heaving and unconsciously rubbing the scar on his hand, seemed totally focused on the floor in front of him. Bruno looked briefly at his long-time comrade and was about to say something. He changed his mind quickly, and set his gaze on the door, through which he knew in his stomach only one person would soon return. Richard and Margrit stood close together, revolted by Paesano's vicious hand-scratching and certainly not prepared to risk a look at each other, or anyone else.

In fact, it was barely any time at all before Shorty sauntered back in and, apart from a brief nod towards Paesano and the vestige of a cruel smile on his face, it was if nothing untoward had actually happened. Margrit stifled a gasp as she noticed the spray of fresh blood on the right-hand side of the thug's jacket; the others didn't need visual evidence.

Although he hadn't necessarily been looking forward to this one, killing came easily to the big man and he had felt only scorn for the wretched little poser who had tried to put him down at every opportunity. He looked across at Nick's briefcase and decided to leave it untouched, documents and all, near the chair. This had to look like suicide and, knowing Nick's easy way with confidential papers, it was a bit of a risk because there could well be snippets in those documents incriminating others. He didn't really care now.

In taut silence Bruno and the scientists tried to come to terms with the callous ease of this execution. The covert threat to them was now well and truly out in the open and they began to worry about what might follow. Eventually it was Paesano who broke the spell.

'No one messes with me and a suicide is a suicide … as you will all do well to note. It's all too bad really. Anyway, none of you liked the wretch.'

Scarcely pausing for a breath he went on.

'Shorty will take me home soon in the Mercedes and you all will do well to remember I haven't been here for days. You've seen enough to clearly understand what I'm saying. There is little point in talking to the police. I can assure you they will be making up their own minds, although I would have preferred to help them if my old friend, Oosthuizen, had only still been in place.'

Then, looking up at the security camera, Paesano spoke directly to Winston.

'I know you've been watching from the foyer, you little jerk. Shorty's coming for you now.'

Knowing Winston had nowhere to go, Shorty took his time and the others heard a small squeal of terror from him as the big man strode across to the foyer.

TWENTY-SIX

After a brief pause, sounds of disturbance came from the foyer and as Paesano sat passively, the others tried in vain to block them out. The angry muttering, sharp commands and an occasional distant plaintive cry were not uncommon in this building. Several dull thuds and a couple of gasping sounds which could only be body blows were unusual.

With this proximity to violence, somehow more acute even than Nick's execution, Margrit gave a deep sob and swallowed as heavy footsteps approached the dining room door. In burst Shorty frog-marching a terrified and bloodied Winston towards them. Behind him came another man, rather dirty and dishevelled, their driver from the mine. Shorty savagely hurled Winston at the wall.

'What shall I do with this little ... b-b-bastard, Boss? He thinks he's already a dead man, so is he for the cabana too?'

Paesano's emotionless response was barely audible.

'We can work it out later. We certainly can't afford any more suicides and anyway we might need him and Horsfeld as security. Let's go. I'm sick of the lot of them.'

As the two of them turned to go, Margrit took a step towards Winston but was pulled up short by the glare of the guard.

'Stay where is, Señora,' he rasped in vaguely comprehensible English. Desperate to avoid any more trouble, Winston gasped out, 'I'm alright, Dr Dupain. Just let me get my breath back.'

The guard followed his masters into the foyer. Winston lifted his head, surprisingly somehow trying to lighten the moment and coughed out, 'Aren't you the lucky ones? He's my replacement.'

After another pause, Winston gingerly began flexing his arms and legs before stumbling across a chair. This time, Margrit was able to gently help him up as they waited to hear what had happened. Despite the warmth of the night, she couldn't suppress another shudder as she came to grips with their frightening situation.

After their new guard at last settled behind his desk in the foyer, Winston's story was quietly told.

'Shorty came into the foyer. He started to rant at me, punched me, pulling me out and pushed me so I was falling over the chairs and there he was shouting about how many of Mr Paesano's dining room conferences I had heard. Then he was wanting to know whether I met Wolhuter at SMGT. Then he was going on about the newspaper people. Then he slapped me hard and punched me a few more times and asked me what I thought my chances were of staying alive.'

After a long pause, he added hesitantly, 'It was all the usual Shorty stuff but it was very strange. He did all this without instructions from the Boss. It's like he has taken over and I really believe he was working out how to kill me.'

So Winston, as duplicitous as he had been, was now bound tightly to them because of his fatal nosiness. Like a fellow conspirator, he turned on the scientists and gave them a clear warning.

'I know you two were planning to delay things.'

Margrit couldn't help make guilty eye contact with Richard as he went on.

'Indeed that's all finished now. The guard is getting solid instructions. Earlier, this foreign freak was telling me a lot more guards were being brought in. So, there goes any chance of escape'.

Winston looked at all three.

'Now we are in the same boat, even you, Mr Horsfeld. You can be betting the monster, Shorty, is dreaming up a scheme to kill us. Until then, Kyalami Drive is our prison'.

Bruno now recognised his necessary alliance with these unfortunates, and poured out his understanding of the Santos execution and the background to the gun battle. He told them that Paesano was trying to mobilise a very large sum of money and Bruno's only slight value was that he knew how to get at the investments.

One detail had especially traumatised them all. Nick had not been an external enemy, so none of them could expect any mercy. Bruno knowing Dieter far better than even Margrit did, was keen to share his burden.

'Dieter is a totally vindictive psychopath. I know how much hostage-taking and killing he has arranged over the years to get his way, and now he has staked way too much on the success of your project. The pressure on him is enormous. He sees things are starting to unravel around him and he's got financiers and potential customers on his back crying out for progress and success. Worse yet, there are two or three very dangerous criminal syndicates beginning to feel he is letting them down.'

He stopped to let it all sink in and looked slowly at each in turn.

'Think about Denning. As things get worse for Dieter, they'll get much worse for us. I know he sees me as the cause of some of his troubles, so all these years of friendship and loyalty won't mean a thing. One mistake is enough.'

He then looked directly at the Indian.

'And you stepped way over the mark, Mr Naidoo. How did you ever think you could get away playing games in Dieter's league? As for you two … ,' he said, nodding towards Richard and Margrit, 'even if your project is the success Dieter hopes for, you know far too much to ever be able to leave. None of us will ever get out of here alive.'

Bruno finished talking and they chimed in together until Margrit held up her hand to calm them all down.

'We should remember one thing. Despite Shorty's nonsense about being able to work the project without Richard and me, Dieter can't harm us until he has successfully demonstrated our work to his backers. He needs you too, Bruno, at least until you've sorted out his financial messes. I believe he's likely to use at least one of us as a hostage if he is put under pressure.'

Margrit had been looking hard at Winston as she was speaking, and now addressed him directly.

'Can't you see, Winston, if he does go for the hostage bit, it would most likely be you?'

Winston immediately became defensive.

'What do you mean? Why did you say that? I'm only a junior

worker and while I've worked for him for a long time, I've got no value at all now.'

Margrit tried to be as gentle as she could.

'This is my point exactly, Winston. He needs the rest of us to work through our different issues but he needs nothing else from you.'

After her blunt appraisal things went silent again. Eventually she quietly wound up the conversation.

'We all need time to ourselves to think things over. The way I see it, we've got until Shorty gets back and I think it'll be mid-morning before he picks us up. We'll need to get together again so we can share any ideas. Agreed?'

Nothing was said as Bruno got up and went out towards his suite, Winston limped slowly off to his quarters under the eye of the new foyer guard, and Margrit and Richard wandered separately towards the pool.

Richard made room for her on the bench. The balmy night provided such a contrast to the chilling horror of their past few hours and they tried hard not to look at the cabana, standing so starkly in the brilliant moonlight.

'Things aren't too good, are they?'

He didn't wait for her reply.

'Listen, I'm sure Winston and Bruno don't know we've made contact with your friend, Wolhuter. I'm not at all sure we can trust those two, but there could be a way out for us. I'll bet the ignorant Columbian in the foyer knows nothing about computers and Shorty has already told him I've got more to do. I'll work openly in the living room tonight revising our project controls. Our new guard won't expect other people to be working at this hour. With luck I can secretly let Wolhuter know how critical things are for us.'

Margrit saw that this was probably only a bit of bravado on his part, more to cover his own unease than anything. At last, when she stood up, he said very softly, 'You know I'd rather be going with you now.'

Her response was a restrained squeeze on his shoulder.

'That would be wonderful, but you've got to do all you can to get us out of this hell-hole. And Richard, you must know our own escape, if it ever happens, will make things even worse for the other two.'

Richard ruefully watched her walk away and the uncharacteristic slump of her shoulders was enough to galvanise him into action. He moved quickly to retrieve the computer from his suite and bustled back into the dining room. As he noisily set up his computer, he deftly connected it to the external line. There was no telephone involved, which baffled the guard when he stormed in.

'What you do? You make it up trouble?'

Richard didn't even glance up as he waved at the laptop and scattered pages.

'I told you before I have to work on this before the morning. You go talk to Mr Mpane.'

The guard looked at the incomprehensible mess.

'No telephone talk outside. Capito? You not talk to anyone outside, see?'

He stomped back into the foyer to focus again on his monitor screens, keeping a watchful eye on Richard.

After a bare ten minutes of this subterfuge, Richard made contact with Will. Using the same amateurish technique as before he sent a message in several parts. In this coded staccato fashion, he was able to convey to Will there had been an execution, the full-scale trial would continue at Groenwater in the morning, there were now four of them under direct threat at Kyalami Drive, and a hostage situation might soon arise at the house.

A response came back promptly and it did nothing to boost Richard's confidence.

R. Expect contact 2 on return trip. W.

There was precious little to make of it and it offered no help to Winston nor to Bruno who wouldn't be making the trip to Groenwater. Still, he hoped it was a plan, and there hadn't been one before.

There was no breakfast. The idea of getting together to talk more about their plight may have sounded good on the night, but it was soon clear this wasn't going to happen and there was actually relief when Shorty appeared early and promptly ordered Bruno into a security van to be driven to Parktown. He bundled the scientists into the Mercedes and drove off, leaving Winston alone with the guards.

Shorty was quite oblivious to the looming problem of the cabana and pursued his own agenda. After a whole night spent in finding more guards for his small, private army, the big man was non-communicative but almost jaunty as he sped off recklessly. He clearly thought his worst day was behind him. How wrong can anyone be?

There is no doubt had either Shorty or Paesano been on top of their game, the next events would have been handled very differently. Perhaps there were excuses for Shorty. Nick's execution was sprung on him at a time when his mind was so thoroughly preoccupied with the test at the mine. He'd failed to properly set the scene for a clean, orchestrated discovery of the 'suicide's' corpse. On the other hand, Paesano should have ensured the event was mapped all the way. It never crossed his mind to closely supervise the big man.

The discovery of the corpse by the gardeners, who arrived on the scene before anyone had a chance to waylay them, massively disrupted the day. There had been a burst of unseasonably hot weather over the past few days. By chance the gardeners broke routine to clean up around the tennis court which hadn't been used for months. They had a shocking surprise. Drawn by a swarm of blowflies and a dank smell in the cabana, they discovered a slumped corpse. They stumbled backwards in shock, one retching. His colleague looking more closely, gulped, 'It's that Denning boss.'

Without another look, the gardeners fled for help. Instead of heading for the foyer they rushed to the gate, calling for assistance from the police stationed there. The gardeners had been so roughly treated by the new squad of thuggish security guards there was no way they would seek help from them. As a result, Shorty, already attending to his priority at the mine site, had lost control of the situation.

As soon as the babbling gardeners alerted them, the police outside decided to activate their standing warrant. They called Major Brand, informed him of the situation and got his permission. They moved onto the property and were led towards the cabana. With a third body now found at the property, Major Brand headed quickly to the scene.

Immediately, Winston's ugly replacement had phoned Shorty at the mine, and in a convoluted discussion, suggested he might like to come and see what was going on. The big man responded quickly. He bundled the scientists back into the car and rushed off to Kyalami Drive. This was not an easy trip on the back road he had chosen and it took time. Hot on Shorty's tail, in a manner of speaking, was Sergeant Mgeni who was finding it very hard to match his terrifying driving.

Needless to say there was soon a lot of activity and several conflicts of interest at Kyalami Drive. Major Brand had arrived. He drove into the property through the now unmanned security gates and headed straight across the lawns for the chaos down at the cabana. Not long after, Shorty carrying his two very frightened passengers roared in.

Sergeant Mgeni, who was trying to follow him, pulled up at the front gate and spent some time figuring out whether to head for his boss at the cabana, or hang back and keep an eye on Shorty as ordered. Shorty, hoping to keep a low profile, said to his prisoners.

'There is no way I'm hanging around here and I don't want those cops talking to you two. I'm gunna get my story straight first. We're driving back to the Groenwater so you two eggheads can finish your urgent business.'

He drove slowly back toward the gate, doing all he could to avoid attracting attention, but the sergeant stepped forward, his arm raised. Shorty was more than a bit peeved.

'Going somewhere, Mr Mpane?'

Shorty wound down his window and said sarcastically, 'Good morning, Sergeant Mgeni. You didn't waste your time getting here, eh? As it turns out I've just been told by your people I'm not needed, so I'm heading off with my friends to get on with another important job.'

The sergeant looked doubtful, guessing he had not been anywhere near the Major, but Shorty spoke with authority.

'Look, Ben, we can tidy things up later. From what I'm hearing, it's most certainly suicide and not murder. I can see your boss is a very busy man.'

He shook hands in an awkward way and the sergeant suddenly smiled and stepped back smartly.

'Once again I agree with you, man. Off you go then.'

As Shorty drove slowly out of the gate, Richard looked back to see the smiling officer take out his wallet and add something to it. The sergeant now decided he had better stand guard at the entrance as there were bound to be more visitors. Then one of the gardeners hurried towards him, pointing to a figure slinking along the fenceline towards the gates.

'Hey, Mr Policeman, that fellow is one of the bosses here. It looks like he's trying to get away.'

At last the sergeant had something he could actually handle and he barked at the would-be fugitive. Winston's past overbearing officiousness with the staff had caught up with him; he might otherwise have disappeared entirely.

Down at the cabana, Major Brand was suspicious. If this was anywhere else, the evidence around him would indeed point to a classic suicide, but he was dubious of everything at Kyalami Drive. First, there was something odd about the corpse's awkward angle, and he could not quite nail it. Also, the crumpled suicide note found on the floor was rather too contrived and the last line, *I can make no claim for the future as I have none,* smacked of theatrics.

Keen to get as far away as he could from the fussing forensic team and from the growing stench, Brand moved up to the house and listened in for a while as his sergeant took some rather bland statements from addled staff members. When the sergeant beckoned Winston over and told the Major this man had tried to do a 'runner', his curiosity was aroused. He asked, 'Who are you, man?'

After a short pause, he got his reply.

'I'm only being the janitor here, sir.'

Brand dwelt on this for a moment, but the sergeant said nothing.

'Well, why would you want to leave here with so much happening?'

There was another short pause.

'Why shouldn't I? As if anyone would want to know what the janitor thinks. Besides, I am wanting to go into the city and tell Mr Paesano personally.'

The Major just smiled evilly.

'Come on, man, things haven't changed so much around here, eh? Since when has Mr Paesano needed to get his information in person from a janitor and doing it on foot?'

Winston was nothing if not quick-witted with his response.

'I am getting on well with Mr Paesano. He and I are often talking about things and, besides, everyone else around here is either too busy or can't even speak English.'

The Major had another question,

'Tell me, man, did you think it was strange Mr Denning's car was left here overnight?'

He just told the officer he was in his quarters because he

had a nasty bump to his head which was plainly obvious to Brand.

The Major gave the impression it wasn't worth his time asking any more questions and did two astonishing things; he apologised for detaining him and promptly arranged for one of his men to drop the flabbergasted Indian in the city. As terrified as he was, Winston maintained great composure as he sat in the police van and even gave a brief nod to one of the new guards at the gate.

The driver was of lowly rank and Winston didn't feel the need for much chatter. Later, the man was able to recall snatches such as Winston's request to be dropped in the city so he could tell the office staff what had happened.

Of course it was not Winston's intention to do anything of the sort. He was now on his own and a potential hostage if caught by Paesano's people. He went straight to his bank and set up a fresh account using the forwarding address of an old friend in Durban, 600 km away. He saw this only as a holding move while he sorted things out.

His paranoia ramped up and he even began to wish the police had detained him. He didn't know for certain how far Shorty's reach extended, but he knew the thug wouldn't want another potential witness on the loose. A whole new identity was a must (expensive but not unattainable.) However, those plans were soon to be cut short thanks to the tail Major Brand had belatedly placed on Winston Naidoo.

TWENTY-EIGHT

Looking around the now empty foyer at Kyalami Drive, it dawned on the Major he hadn't seen the infamous Mr Mpane at all. From what he had been led to believe, the big, black man was always to be found wherever there was trouble in Paesano's world.

'Sergeant, how come you're here but M. Mpane is not?' A look which was a mixture of horror and discomfort briefly crossed Mgeni's face and he hesitated before offering up a lie.

'I'm sorry, Major. I heard what had happened on the radio, so I decided I'd be more value to you here than being stuck out at Groenwater with nothing to do.'

Brand was livid at this response.

'You did what? Who makes the decisions in this outfit, man?'

The sergeant was flustered realising how likely he was to get ensnared.

'You do, sir. It's just Shor … err … Mr Mpane is occupied all the time with those scientists.'

This was the last thing the Major needed.

'I don't like your attitude, sergeant, and I'm surely starting to question your loyalties. I'll discuss this with you in my office before you go off duty tonight. In the meantime, get your big, black arse out to the mine-site and God help you if your insubordination has lost us any advantage there'.

Having seen his sergeant off and in the absence of anyone else worthy of questioning, the Major decided to take a self-guided tour of the house. He was intrigued to find such an extravagant laboratory set up and his first reaction was to think he was looking at a sophisticated drug manufacturing operation. Then he remembered the scientific project which had to do with the Paesano's Gold Bug fetish.

He returned through the dining room and noticed a very expensive briefcase. He picked it up and saw stamped in gold the initials, NMD. *At last,* he thought, *I may find something to go on with and at least Will might find it useful.*

Understandably, Brand had now almost convinced himself suicide was one explanation. He wasn't about to find anything which would help him dethrone Paesano and he was becoming bored about the whole Denning affair. It was an obvious and pretty much deserved end for someone who had been caught out short-changing his boss and probably an array of other heavies. When the pressure was piled on, Denning like so many of his ilk, had taken the easy way out.

Reluctantly Brand picked up the briefcase and headed for his car, his thoughts captured by Will's recent talk of international skullduggery complicated any plans to free the hostages. His attention had sharpened as soon as he heard the word 'hostage' but given his officers were already spread too thinly, he had to face reality and leave the unstitching of the problem to Will.

TWENTY-NINE

Will had been keeping Brand informed whenever his investigations touched on the vortex swirling around Paesano, but it was only after the grisly threat had been made to both GM and SMGT that a broader picture started to emerge. The syndicate was arrogant enough to believe they could bypass authority as had happened in the past. With a heavy heart, Will sat down to compile a brief synopsis for Brand which included Richard's message. Then he started to make the rounds of his trusted and influential contacts across the intelligence world. Continually in his mind was the dilemma surrounding the two scientists.

Will decided to focus on the Franklin episode, believing there was more to be learnt from any records in Mrs Franklin's possession which might have escaped Brigadier Oosthuizen's destruction. A widower himself, he'd decided to tackle this in a forthright, sensitive way. He phoned her to ask for a few minutes of her time to clear up a couple of questions regarding her husband's death, explaining he was a private investigator. She was happy to oblige if this would resolve the innuendo arising from the inquest.

'The police told me while their investigating section was

overloaded, they could put some junior officers on protection duty. I must say the only thing they've done is to create a nuisance. There isn't anything about me that's a threat to anyone.'

Will expressed real sympathy and the upshot was she agreed to give him any assistance she could if it would help to reveal the truth.

After he'd taken Martine back to her office following the grisly meeting with Paesano, Will visited Mrs Franklin. As he pulled up outside her 'secure' house, he couldn't help notice the protectors Brand had provided didn't exactly look like the sharpest knives in the drawer. He also noted the house in its quiet cul-de-sac was new, substantial and well-kept. This appeared a little unusual for the young widow of a journalist who was specialising in areas unlikely to be great revenue-raisers for a newspaper. However, she was very open.

'Please understand, Colonel, I'm not looking for more compensation. The newspaper has been very generous and there was a huge anonymous donation made. The card said it was, *In the hope you will not be bothered any further.* This gift enabled me to buy the house.'

She paused and looked straight at him.

'After being such good friends, the editor and the rest of staff just cut me off. They seem to think Jon's death was his own fault. I'm getting quite desperate to get my story told and the kids will want the truth one day, not lies from the press. The police are no better. Why do I need those people watching everything I do?'

As Brand hoped would happen, Will had struck a real chord with Mrs Franklin, who spoke passionately about Jonathon's work and his high ideals. It wasn't just a one-sided conversation either, as he felt comfortable talking about his life and work, which was unusual for this unassuming man. Eventually he got up to leave and with trust established, she said, 'Wait a minute. There's something you might like to see.'

She brought out an envelope which contained three computer discs.

'You can borrow these if you like. The police said Jon's briefcase and laptop were burnt in the accident, but he always kept a backup at home. After I moved here, all his other records and our computer vanished in transit. Conveniently, I'd say. As I was unpacking his books recently, this fell out of his big Oxford dictionary. I can't make sense of it at all, but it should be something for the authorities if only they would take interest. You surely will have more luck.'

After skimming through the files, Will was blown away by the treasure trove he had been given. This was financial misbehaviour on a vast scale, covering a wide range of schemes which included money laundering, arms dealing and extortion. It implicated people in business, politics and bureaucracy in several countries.

One drawback was Franklin had not identified his sources in these records. However, he had meticulously laid out his modus operandi for seeking out those sources over a significant period of time. So, while the material would not stand up in court as unsubstantiated evidence, it did provide a wonderful array of inter-connected leads which would be a boon for any investigator. Because the linkages were so pervasive and at such a high level, Will was dubious about whom to brief concerning this windfall. Luckily there was enough incriminating information to know whom to avoid.

Early in his investigation, Franklin had chanced upon the initial covert association between Green Mines and SMGT. He had also uncovered the 'working relationship' between Nick Denning and Martine Monard, alluded to in Paesano's office when Will had delivered the nasty parcel. Now it was all spelled out.

What was clear to Will was the hierarchy of their relationship. Denning had been very much the junior partner. The threads from their petty collusion had led way past them and well upwards in their respective organisations. Will realised much of his consulting work for SMGT had been regularly thwarted by the very group Franklin had so cleverly identified.

Clearly these issues were far bigger than a one-man band could hope to handle. Reluctant to take the matter directly to the perennially blind South African authorities, Will decided it was critical to first activate his international connections, which he did in a series of calls which took him well past midnight. It was then he received Richard's cryptic four-part message and was plunged into an ethical dilemma.

Back at his office, Brand was given Will's brief written report which had also been forwarded to his Brigadier. Will knew one sentence would stimulate Brand into a change of focus: *Received, from one of the house guests, garbled and poorly coded message about murder looking like suicide.* He also knew that the balance of the report covered matters which lay well outside even Brigadier Mfuleni's ambit of responsibility.

Should he focus exclusively on this real chance of squashing the biggest accumulation of criminality he had ever come across, or should his first priority be helping the rescue of those hapless individuals? With grave ethical misgivings, Will elected to delay the rescue, at least until he had advised the highest level intelligence and fiscal authorities about his discoveries. He was relying heavily on his exemplary credentials to get things moving quickly.

It was, alas, not quickly enough for poor Mrs Franklin. Before dawn, her house was comprehensively fire-bombed. As she had inferred, the so-called protection proved worse than useless as the officers were only woken by the roar of the fire. At least they had helped save the family. They told Will they had been confused about the whole attack.

'Colonel, there were two, not one, petrol bombs. How were we to know there might not have been another? We took cover at first. Besides, we had to break down the door to get the lady and her kids out.'

Will was devastated. Could he have been followed to the 'secure' house after dropping Martine off? Because Green Mines was now desperate to avoid public scrutiny and because Shorty, the hit man, was so tied up at Groenwater, Will was inclined to dismiss any Green Mines involvement. He knew arson was one of Shorty Mpane's tools of trade, if not his trade-mark, but had he anything to be gained by destroying the house?

THIRTY

Shorty Mpane knew nothing of this when he arrived at Groenwater with the scientists on his first trip of the day, well before the gardeners at the house found Nick's body. He was astonished to see a huge crowd of men milling about the locked gates. Somehow the news of his generous bonus scheme had leaked out and in a community where unemployment was endemic, even a remote chance of well-paid work was irresistible.

The original team had managed to assemble together in a solid block nearest the gate and had already been involved in a few skirmishes as they battled to hold their ground against the pressure of the 'outsiders'. It wasn't so much the horde of workers which bothered Shorty as the sight of the small crew of Brand's watching police and a group of reinforcements. This much scrutiny was not at all what Shorty wanted.

With the police valiantly trying to impose a sense of order at the entrance, it was some time before a seething Shorty was able to drive the Mercedes in and the legitimate work gang was admitted. Margrit and Richard were subjected to close and hostile inspection as the car inched its way through the crowd of disgruntled men, who were venting their frustration in a barrage of noisy and obscene invective.

The whole episode at the mine gates had delayed the start of the day's test, and just as Shorty was coming to terms with the problem in his usual blustering manner, his guard's panicked call informed him the police were already in the cabana about to examine Nick's body.

Shorty's fatigue, his raging temper, and his realisation of his own incompetence, addled his thought processes. Consequently, he had made a snap decision to rush back to the house at a terrifying pace through peak-hour traffic with the two frightened scientists on board and Sergeant Mgeni battling to keep up. It was only after he was through the entrance gates and could see the figure of Major Brand near the cabana, he realised his stupidity and retreated as quickly as possible, courtesy of Ben Mgeni's greased palm.

Shorty was now fixated on the test, so the bizarre news that Winston had been freed and was actually being driven away from Kyalami Drive in a police van was just another irritation. He drove recklessly back to Groenwater. Like Paesano, and to some extent the scientists, he was becoming consumed by the Gold Bug and was excited by the prospect of a successful test outcome. After all, he had expended an enormous amount of nervous energy on the project and his involvement was at a personal and intellectual level he had never before experienced.

The Mercedes arrived and the work gang sprang into life as he once again took control. He gave the scientists back their laptops and, treating Margrit like a Grade C stenographer, yelled out his instructions.

'You make sure to note down every step taken after I start up. And I mean every step. I want a record of all the measurements on those controls. We'll run it through twice and I'm gunna use your stuff as a check. Your records had … b-b-bloody better be complete and easy to follow because the test will only be a success if I can run this whole doings by myself.'

Then he turned on the foreman.

'I want your slack shits to be wide awake and work quickly to keep things in order around here. Keep them clear of those gas bottles, too. We don't want any more of yesterday's nonsense.'

He found it convenient to forget the nonsense was entirely of his own making, and still suspicious of Richard's role in the stuff-ups, reserved a last blast for him too.

'Stand where you can see what I'm doing and keep telling me if I'm on the right track. I don't want you touching anything, you sly … b-b-bastard, Curie. And I'll keep an eye on your girlfriend. Don't trust her at all!'

He pushed her across next to Richard who firmly took her hand and then to general relief, Shorty's mobile again burst into life. It was Paesano in full flight and his opening tirade could be clearly heard.

'What the devil is going on out at Kyalami Drive? I have just been told there's a problem! Why haven't you called me?'

Shorty scrambled to turn down the volume and replied in his most subservient tone.

'I'm sorry, Mr Paesano, things have been frantic.'

As if anything would mollify the irate tyrant who was furious at this insubordination.

'Get over here at once, the test can wait.'

Shorty was clearly distraught.

'But Mr Paesano, we're just starting the whole show up.

Can't we deal with this over the phone?'

The Boss was by now apoplectic.

'Of course, we can't, you idiot. Have you forgotten the police just happen to be able to hack into these things? I've received another small present like the one we got yesterday, so lock up those boffins and tell the gang to have breakfast or something. I don't care what you say; get back here so we can sort this problem out once and for all.'

So once more the test was to be delayed. Shorty was beside himself with equal doses of anger and frustration as he wordlessly herded the scientists into a small, dirty laboratory and once again grabbed their laptops.

'There'll be no more sending those email things to anyone behind my back, and don't think you can bluff those guys about a need to do some work for the test. You told me it's all set up.'

He locked the door and a mere flick of his head indicated the guards should marshal the workers into another space. In a flash, Shorty was gone.

THIRTY-ONE

In their small isolation cell, Margrit was now quite buoyant and tried to raise Richard's spirits.

'Do you see there's now one big plus here? We're not as isolated as before. Our laptops may have been confiscated again, but in his panic to get back to his precious boss the imbecile didn't think to frisk us; we've got our phones and they're not blocked here.'

Richard listened at the door while she dialled Will's number. She quietly brought the investigator up to speed with their current circumstances and told him all about the execution. To round things out, she also described Winston Naidoo's unusual escape and voiced her opinion that Major Brand had lost the plot. Will was initially annoyed and quickly refuted this accusation, although he did concede his friend often cut corners due to a lack of resources. He began to fill them in.

'Koos Brand has already given me a sketchy account but at first he was of the opinion Denning committed suicide. I'll get this message to him and get him to apply sharper forensic attention to the body and the crime scene. I'll also suggest he rounds up Naidoo again as a matter of urgency. He'll be a vital corroborating witness.'

After a brief pause to collect his ideas, Will continued,

'Believe me, not too many people will care how our Mr Denning died. He's left his slimy snail trail all over the place, but he was certainly no big player. The real plus is if we can pin his death on Paesano. However, if Paesano gets away it'll mean you two will be in particularly dire straits.'

Margrit told him plaintively that this was a bit rich as they were already in mortal danger. Richard joined in, his cheek brushing hers as they spoke very quietly into the shared phone.

'Will, right now we couldn't care less about Dieter; that monster, Shorty, is preparing to kill us soon!'

Will changed direction and started up again

'I don't know what's what with the newcomer Horsfeld from Buenos Aires either; he seems to have gone missing this morning. There's too much happening too quickly and until we've gathered up all the strands, I'm reluctant to have Mpane arrested. Doing so would upset my prime aim of nailing Paesano's money-laundering and arms dealing arrangements. I'm dead sure he's a key player internationally and of interest to my friends at Interpol.'

She made it plain that this wasn't exactly what she needed to hear right then. Feeling somewhat guilty, he decided to pay more attention to their predicament.

'I am getting straight on to Brand now to set up a rescue, most likely out at Kyalami Drive, because where you are now at the mine is too much of a jumble.'

They were somewhat mollified by this assurance and when the call ended, they suddenly realised how physically close they had been to each other. In the gloom of the tiny room, Margrit could feel his warmth as they pulled apart to look at each other and her heart hammered.

THIRTY-TWO

A kerfuffle at the gate announced the return of their tormentor and Margrit quickly hid her phone. Listening carefully, the scientists could hear only Shorty's usual shouting at the guards and realised Paesano must have stayed away, even from this much vaunted final trial. Knowing nothing about the recent seismic shift in Paesano's world, Richard wondered why Shorty was alone, but Margrit was quickly able to put the matter into perspective.

'Think about it, Richard. Dieter has only attended two meetings during the entire course of our work. He doesn't like the physical stuff, he doesn't need to see the test in real time, and it's his style to keep all personal contact to a minimum. So, he can dispassionately order up retribution if he is crossed in any way.'

Margrit and Richard were handed their computers to complete the final set-up. Neither the guards nor Shorty knew the small, black memory-stick plugged into the side of her machine would enable Margrit to copy every instruction. As dire as their predicament was, both scientists still sought an advantage for themselves.

The first adjusted trial run worked well. Richard had pleaded with Shorty to take things slowly and methodically while Margrit battled through her documentation. He called out minor adjustments which the big man implemented, and after a while there was a consistent run of product which Margrit sampled and tested, carefully recording all inputs and outputs. However, the final balance of elements didn't match Richard's algorithms despite the sensitivity having been reduced considerably. Shorty had to reluctantly agree to a re-run and even his speech was more coherent, free from his stutter.

'This time I can see you are not stuffing me around, but hurry up with the wash down. It can't be so important. In real life things aren't bloody perfect. I'll want a full run on my own after this one and I'm already running late.'

As time moved on, he kept glancing at his watch, trying to allow enough time to get to Wolhuter's cursed meeting in the city. When the second run was ready to start, Richard pointed out to Shorty the changes he had suggested would enable the process to be operated using the automatic controls without intervention. The only response he got was a return to growling anger.

'Oh yeah? Listen you, I'll do exactly as I please now I have the hang of it. Piss off and stand over there out of the way.'

Richard backed off smartly and stood close to Margrit.

The run started smoothly enough and the workers were hard-pressed to keep up the raw material supply. This was not enough for Shorty who, impatient as ever, intervened to increase the operating tempo. Inevitably, the old motors rebelled and the entire process spluttered to a premature halt. Luckily the electricians were still on site, but there was no way the trial could be restarted and finished before Shorty had to leave for Will Wolhuter's meeting.

'I'm gunna meet this guy for the first time and when I come back, I'll run this whole thing by myself. I won't need you anymore, so one of these guys will take you back to Kyalami Drive and I'll decide later just what I'm gunna do with you. Dieter has already told me the way you've … b-b-buggered us about and created those delays which means your Agreement no longer holds. As far as he is concerned, Green Mines now owns all this stuff and you two losers are simply in the way.'

Shorty still had no grasp of the bigger picture and he was becoming increasingly frustrated by Paesano's lack of action on several fronts. He turned his attention to his guards and simply ignored the Boss' specific instructions. To one he said, 'Get a driver to collect that creep, Horsfeld, from the city and bring him out here. Then he can go back to Kyalami Drive with these two as well. I don't care how much work he says he has to do, I want him safely tucked away back at the house.'

He spoke as abruptly as ever to Margrit.

'Gimme your computer. Are all the instructions in there? You'd better show me how to start the damn thing.'

At this point, Richard gave a realistic imitation of dry retching and doubled up dramatically. With Shorty diverted, Margrit deftly slipped the memory stick out of the computer into the palm of her hand. Richard had maintained his charade and had even contrived to become alarmingly red-faced, much to Shorty's disdain.

'Shut up, you gobbler! I'll soon give you something to puke about, you little wimp.'

He rushed over to the Mercedes and nearly took the gate out as he drove off to yet another meeting with his interfering boss.

Locked back in the little laboratory for as long as it took Horsfeld to be collected, Margrit and Richard were once again left to ponder. Richard confidently told the disbelieving Margrit, 'If we come out of this in reasonable shape, we'll get justice through scientific recognition and also material reward. Not only is this a breakthrough in thinking, but will soon have been thoroughly tested. I have sent every single change to my algorithms back to my computer in Kent. All this corroborating evidence of an actual operating outcome will go down well with those big mining companies who have ever so politely spurned me in the past.'

They knew in the short term at least they would be safe as Shorty would be gone for some hours. Then Margrit realised a major problem.

'If Shorty is out of action because of this meeting, Will can't be contacted either. I just hope he has been able to talk to that Major. Otherwise how on earth can we be rescued this afternoon?'

'Agreed, Margrit. It's unfair and irresponsible to delay our rescue, but perhaps ours is a very narrow perspective.'

They tried again and again to update their would-be saviour, but of course he wasn't taking any calls. As convener of this crucial meeting he had, as Paesano soon found out, given a 'no-phones' directive and was certainly not about to take any himself. A really scared and frustrated couple could do no more than leave a detailed message before they were taken off to Kyalami Drive.

THIRTY-THREE

Will Wolhuter had carefully selected a small, discreet meeting room in a secure building well away from the business offices of both parties. Furthermore, he had arranged for Brand to bug the place, despite feeling neither side would give anything away which could implicate them criminally. He was sure that this would be a serious, but nonetheless bland, business meeting with himself in the dual roles of chairman and 'delivery boy'.

The sides arrived at the meeting place more or less at the same time and crammed in. From the start, Will felt sure the two principals knew each other well. Regardless, each studiously ignored the other and they were impassive when Martine Monard formally introduced her boss to Paesano.

'Mr Paesano, I would like you to meet Herr Schneider who has delayed his return to Head Office to hear what you have to say on this matter.'

Will saw Paesano stiffen at the hint of being patronized. 'And I would certainly like to hear what he has to say.'

They sat down without shaking hands. This was not an auspicious start and there was a long, heavy pause before Will exercised his role as chairman to calm things down, and addressed the two principals.

'I have taken the liberty of preparing an agenda on the assumption we are dealing with commercial arrangements between the two of you and also with the complainant syndicate. I see no need to discuss the background to that arrangement.'

Will paused and looked at Schneider and Paesano in turn, seeking agreement on his approach, but he only met blank stares.

'Alright then. The agenda is quite simple and rests on commercial principles which I will pose as questions. First, is this demanding counter-party genuine? Second, is there a justifiable complaint about lack of performance by both of you? Third, is the amount of compensation realistic? Fourth, can you two parties agree on the division of compensation, whatever the total agreed sum may be? And finally, what is the best mechanism for ensuring both parties execute and deliver their share?'

Will could see Shorty was the only person in the room completely unused to the formalities required for such a meeting. He needn't have concerned himself about his lack of experience because the whole meeting took place exactly as Will planned.

'Could you please keep away from the detail as we don't have much time.'

Will was surprised how quickly the meeting proceeded with Schneider and Paesano sticking tightly to the agenda. Martine didn't say a word and didn't even take a note. Although she did blanch when both principals tacitly agreed there had been inexcusable incompetence and petty thievery in each organisation.

The first two agenda items were dealt with in short order. An actual syndicate did exist, but there was no discussion about its possible membership or the shadowy nature of its operations. There was mention in passing of the unusual way it had chosen to deliver its threatening messages and how it had created and enforced its own brand of law through a troika without a defined principal.

The second item on the agenda was dealt with easily because each boss admitted tardiness in satisfying urgent funding needs, which had seriously affected the various arms of the syndicate. They only alluded to the syndicate's enforcement and discipline methods as being 'severe' and passed over the Santos affair rapidly.

There was no doubt the question about the quantum of payment demanded was harder to resolve as it required both parties to 'show a bit of leg' and expose some of their operational procedures. Will deftly drew out each position and tucked it away in his mind for future use. Their assessments of the damage incurred were remarkably similar. As Schneider put it, 'This is hugely overstated by the syndicate.'

Paesano readily agreed.

'We should regard this merely as an ambit claim.'

They even agreed on a counter-offer under half of the original claim, clearly substantiated by a few facts which inadvertently slipped out in the heat of the discussion. This demonstrated SMGT was struggling to hide its financial position from its shareholders. Again, Will tucked these revelations away, knowing this information would help Interpol as its investigation spread further into the syndicate itself.

When the division of costs was raised, Paesano nearly sent the whole thing hurtling off the rails. His unrestrained competitiveness kicked in as he had to negotiate with his former foe and he immediately took the stance that he should pay a significantly smaller proportion of the total. He clearly had no grounds for this position and it took all of Will's negotiating skill to bring the split back to fifty/fifty.

'There are no winners in this, Mr Paesano. Can't you see we have to get back to them quickly and not spend time bickering about the finetuning? How can it be entertained that either side will stick to any agreement you make if you conduct yourself like this?'

With sullen, bad grace, Paesano eventually gave in on the matter and the agreement was drafted then and there, but Will still wondered what the chances might be of him sticking to it. Was there honour among thieves? They all realised this would be unenforceable as a legal document anyway, but would certainly do as a Heads of Agreement.

On the final agenda point a revision was made. It was decided the parties would wait on a response before deciding on payment arrangements and security compliance. These matters would be of no interest to the syndicate and would not delay delivery of their proposition. Having constructed their response, the participants knew there was nothing more they could do but wait for Will to hear from the syndicate.

Schneider started to leave and he looked at Paesano, muttering, 'You have something which rightfully belongs to us.'

Paesano stared hard at his Swiss rival.

'Well come and get it then.'

To which Schneider had quickly barked, 'We might just do that!'

The exchange was over in a flash which left Will wondering whether it referred to the stuff which had been keeping the scientists so busy at the old mine site and in the laboratory at the secure house. Were commissions the only matters shared in the collusion between Mme. Monard and the late Nick Denning, and had disloyalty played some part in his death?

To Will it clearly looked like a murderous execution and not a remorseful suicide. From the icy nature of the final exchanges, there must be a lot at stake for Green Mines and SMGT in this IP matter, even if it was a sideshow to Will's interest in their international money-laundering. Things were rapidly developing too fast on both fronts and there was simply too much to worry about, but worry he did.

On returning to his office, Will had found the distraught message from Richard. While it was difficult for Will to keep tabs on the movements of the scientists, he had anticipated being able to free them on their way back to Kyalami Drive. Now he knew that they and Horsfeld were already there and facing real danger. Troubled by this, he asked Brand to strengthen the force outside the property even at the expense of reducing the watch at the mine.

He also asked for a quick update and learned a car driven by one of Shorty's guards and containing one passenger had driven from the city office into the mine shed. And then, with Drs. Curie and Dupain and an extra guard on board, the car had left for Kyalami Drive.

Brand told him, 'Mpane's next journeys have been harder to

track. We know he took Paesano to Parktown after that meeting of yours, but then he made a strange trip to Kyalami Drive via Groenwater. He broke the speed limit most of the way. He didn't stop anywhere for long before he returned to Parktown with that Horsfeld from Buenos Aires. We nearly lost track of him before he went back to the mine alone.'

Brand said Mpane was working in the main shed, but the police there couldn't make out what he was up to. Will told Brand he would need to spend more time on the extortion threat at the expense of the murder investigation.

'Earlier this afternoon, someone got to me on my private line. I have no idea how, but it certainly shows the reach of this syndicate.'

He recounted the last words of the brief call from a foreigner.

'No more talk! You know deal! Go tell again. We call to you the next tomorrow not the tomorrow and not bother find call … this phone put now in water drain!'

Brand could understand this presented Will with a difficult problem; how to get action from the principals. So Will began another round of calls. Schneider was particularly put out because he had to again delay his flight. He was insistent that the counter-offer to the syndicate be negotiated well before the 'day after tomorrow.' However, he was not a delegator and wanted to attend in person.

'We must all meet tomorrow to frame a precise counter-offer with non-disclosure guarantees.'

Will was flabbergasted.

'I am only the messenger, the man in the middle, but with all due respect what makes you think you have any negotiating power left?'

Schneider replied.

'I am running out of patience and your boss, Paesano, isn't helping.'

Will answered curtly.

'Mr Paesano is not my boss and nor are you, but I'll see what I can do.'

Having received a similar response from Paesano, Will grasped the steely determination of these two feisty characters. He worried about the price and terms they would finally offer and how he could stitch them together in a final arrangement.

Despite these demands, Will was still maintaining contact with his international counterparts on a more secure line. He passed on to them all he had learned about syndicate connections at the negotiation meeting and the way they worked. Because all these conversations took time, it was quite late before he could turn his attention back to discussing the rescue plans with Koos. It was likely to be another very long night.

THIRTY-FOUR

On the way back to the Parktown mansion from the city meeting chaired by Will Wolhuter, Paesano had continued in his sullen mood and, changing his mind, was now furious about Shorty sending Bruno to Kyalami Drive.

'I need to talk to him about our funds and you didn't even ask me. I am not going out there. You go fetch him!'

Shorty knew the evaporation of Green Mines' finances was another complication. It affected his hostage problem and the payments to the workforce as well as his own guards. He briefly mulled over a complex scenario involving his trademark 'fire' in a dramatic manner. Was it too soon to include the scientists and could he use the laboratory in some way?

Finance was a matter which he had been stoically trying to raise with Paesano. He now knew Green Mines didn't even have the funds to pay the work gang at Groenwater their original wages, let alone the flamboyant additional sum he had negotiated to get him over the crisis brought about by the breakdown. The first response from the Boss had been a cold stare.

'I am telling you the bottomless pit of money has actually bottomed out. I've been doing all I can and now it's your turn. You can tell your old gang to rustle up some funds. I don't care how … anyway they've never seemed to be too fussy about pressing people.'

Quite out of character because he had never felt the need to explain anything to anyone, he outlined the position to Shorty.

'Thanks to the meddling of friend, Horsfeld, and the excesses of the idiot, Denning, I can't readily access funds I have diverted from Green Mines overseas. My last hope is that Bruno, working in the city office, will find some money to release. But even if we can release the short-term overseas funds, I won't have enough for the syndicate yet. So success at Groenwater is now critical!'

For the sixth time that day, Shorty was on the road and now his mood matched Paesano's. Would he ever be able to wrap up a final trial at Groenwater? All was quiet at the old mine with four of Shorty's guards inside the compound and a much reduced force of police beyond the perimeter. Once Shorty had departed after his earlier whirlwind stopover, none of the guards had seemed to take his duties too seriously.

During this flying visit, Shorty had given terse instructions to the foreman.

'See sufficient batches of raw material are prepared for another test, and then clock your gang off.'

Since there had been no sign of the much vaunted bonus payment, there was much grumbling and some reluctance from the workers to carry out those orders. Yet they had finished and were well clear of the place when, to the astonishment of the remaining guards and the half-alert police, Shorty having delivered Horsfeld to Paesano, re-appeared just before dark.

To his guards, it was immediately apparent Shorty was in a

bad way. They couldn't know Paesano's continuing demands had rendered him virtually sleepless for days and the stress of the trials and building up his own small, private army, had got to him. Little did they recognise the need to be very careful about what they said and did. They were soon enlightened.

'Okay you lot, enough of your slack-arsing around. You and I are about to accomplish what those sleazy eggheads have been stuffing around with all this time.'

He grabbed Margrit's computer, found her notes and set to work with gusto. It seemed he had been a good student, and despite his incurable haste, was surprisingly thorough in the start-up procedures.

In no time at all he was swearing and sweating as he dashed from crusher to settlement tanks to the product analysis area and back again in the gloomy shed. He was relentless in shouting instructions to his hapless guards who showed signs of exhaustion as they stripped down to their vests and loaded the bins. There was no way they were about to slacken off though, such was the frenetic pace of the operation. Shorty had soon removed his own jacket and flung it onto the control panel desk. Outside, the police who couldn't see into the shed were astonished by all the noise.

Shorty would never be a perfectionist and despite trying hard to slow down and work at a more even pace, he omitted one vital step. There were only three manually-operated, chemical-supply valves in the otherwise automated process, and in the gloom he managed to leave one of these open and this simple error very quickly polluted the product bins. It was only during the final analysis phase that Shorty noticed the fatal flaw and by then there was no going back. The whole test was once again a failure.

He was now wholly convinced the process would work next time around and fully aware there was no one else to blame. He didn't even swear at the guards. Without bothering to pack up or say anything at all to anyone, he simply climbed wearily into the Mercedes and was off home, knowing tomorrow would be the big day, even though a complete clean-up and resetting of controls would take up most of it. He had reached a point where he really didn't care what Paesano thought, didn't even bother to call him, and was content to let the people at Kyalami Drive stew until the morrow.

THIRTY-FIVE

While Shorty had reached a point where he didn't care about anyone else, he would have been amazed to know how many others were thinking about him. Major Brand, at last aware of the desperate messages Dr Curie had sent to Will Wolhuter, was finally forced to face up to murder rather than suicide in the Nick Denning incident. To Brand's great consternation it was clear Shorty Mpane, with a legendary reputation for violence, had not even been interviewed by the bent Sergeant Mgeni. It was now certain Mpane had been at Kyalami Drive at the time Denning died and had slipped away well before the body was found.

Paesano's possible presence at the scene was now also an open question. In the transcripts, Dr Curie had clearly named him the judge and Mpane the executioner. The house and mansion staff, superficially interviewed earlier, had offered unsolicited comments and believed their boss hadn't left Parktown in days. Despite corroborating police logs, Brand thought their statements were somewhat contrived and protective and was determined to interview each of them again.

There was no doubt Major Brand was deeply troubled. How could he justify the claim that a murder had taken place based solely on a garbled message from a man, so distraught as to perhaps be beyond reason? Although the autopsy had detailed an unusual corpse position inconsistent with a self-inflicted shot, it didn't specifically rule out suicide. It had also been graphic in describing recent bruising on Denning's arms but couldn't factually relate this to the death event.

The suicide note was compared to the papers in the brief case and was clearly but shakily written by Denning himself. Then there was the problem of a total lack of fingerprints, Denning's or anyone else's, on the weapon. Denning was not wearing gloves when his body was found, so had a murderer worn them or wiped the gun clean after the act?

Why hadn't he personally interviewed all present at the death scene rather than rely on the slack, crooked bastard who had somehow become a sergeant in the force? He recalled his own discussion with Naidoo, whom he had soon realised was particularly shifty and seemed to have had much to hide. In retrospect, he should have come down on him much more heavily there and then instead of taking the creative but unorthodox step of releasing him and sending him into the city as bait for Paesano.

The corrupt fellow had changed his banking details and skulked around the main railway station before catching the night train to Durban. Perhaps he had hoped to vanish forever from the police and Paesano? Anyway, Brand had already put a stop to his little escapade and he'd had him arrested two hundred kilometres down the track. He was particularly looking forward to the coming interview.

From a professional point of view, Brand was eager to come

to terms with the matters eddying around Messrs. Paesano and Mpane. As he saw it, and despite initially making the wrong call, he was now almost convinced both Denning's demise and the fire-bombing of Mrs Franklin's home would eventually be attributed to Paesano. While the death and the fire had to be his two main priorities, he was as committed as Will was to get to the bottom of the over-arching issues of money-laundering and international criminal funding. With these matters front of mind he had cautioned Will to be alert.

'There is a real risk one of our investigations will move too far ahead of the other. The whole lot might be jeopardised if those villains melt away to safe havens. We just don't know who to trust at the top until we have a watertight case and have threaded through the connections.'

Will responded, outlining one of his concerns.

'Koos, we don't know what's happening at Groenwater and whether we can organise a rescue there.'

'Look, man, my patrol out at the mine tells me Shorty Mpane has been there and has been active inside the main building. He has now gone. I know it's late but why don't we go and have a bit of a look around the place and see if we can find out what he's up to?'

There was a pause at the other end of the line.

'Normally, I'd never go along with such a crazy idea, Koos, if there wasn't any possibility of finding a way to spring the scientists from the mine site. Let's face it, we're neither of us scientists so how in the hell will we know what Mpane and his friends have got brewing in there? Maybe it's even drugs.'

Brand was ready.

'I'm way ahead of you. I've had a bit of a trawl through our recent records and found a mining technician who's facing time for falsifying mining results. I've already been in touch and made a vague promise of some leniency if he'll help us out. All I have to do now is drag him out of bed and collect him on the way.'

In the early hours of the morning, the three pulled up quietly next to the police vehicle stationed outside the Groenwater gate. Happily for the officers on watch, they were wide awake and responded quickly to the arrival of their superior. After assuring the Major there were no longer guard dogs inside the perimeter, it didn't take long for one of them to adeptly pick the two padlocks. On the other side, Shorty's two guards were nearly comatose with exhaustion, having celebrated Shorty's departure by resorting to a small personal drug cache. The trio was able to slip deftly into the main building and the technician was very quick in his appraisal. He told them the set-up was not particularly complicated or different from most.

'This is a test process for an unusual concentrator. The equipment is mainly very old, but there's a modern control system that I wouldn't try to run in a bloody fit. It looks as though it has recently been operating as you'll see from the mess and the chemical spills. That's all I can tell you so I'm waiting outside. I really don't want to be here.'

The two investigators continued to quietly poke about the plant by torchlight. As they approached the control desk, Will noticed the huge jacket Shorty had flung there.

'I'm sure this belongs to Mpane, I saw him wearing it this afternoon. Gives you an idea of how big the bloody brute is, eh? You wouldn't buy this one off the rack.'

Koos paused for a moment.

'There was a lot of blood and stuff around Denning's body so I reckon forensics could have a field day with this. Just look at the thing; it's filthy and must have picked up a lot of dirt after the body was shifted about, alive and dead. Phew, it doesn't half reek either.'

They kept on the move, but weren't able to discern much else of value and quickly came to agree, given the jumble around the plant, that it was by no means an ideal place to stage a rescue. Their job done, they picked up the big jacket, let themselves out, thanked the officers for their help, collected the technician and quietly drove off. But, showing even two highly trained professionals can make mistakes, they overlooked Margrit's computer.

The police settled back down for a long, boring night on this dreary road in the squalid rundown industrial precinct, its ugliness actually accentuated by the light of a huge waning moon. After about an hour, boredom became the least of their problems when a dark, unlit SUV slid smoothly up to the police van. Thinking it was Major Brand returning, the two incumbents casually clambered out, ready to help their boss in another of his unorthodox manouveres. They were totally unprepared for the attack which followed and were easily overcome, tied up and soundlessly gagged by several camouflaged assailants.

The thugs climbed back into the SUV which proceeded to smash through the gate so noisily that Shorty's guards, despite their recent indulgences, were woken and staggered out to be confronted by a gang of skilled, alert attackers. After a brief scuffle, these guards were trussed up as tightly as the police beyond the perimeter. When they were recognised as members of Shorty's old gang, they were subjected to renewed kicking and beating as vengeance for past gangland battles and necklacings in Soweto. The violence only ceased after the gang leader called them off and reminded them there was work to be done. The guards were dragged into the small room which had housed Margrit and Richard.

There was a real breakthrough after Margrit's computer was discovered by the gang and was placed, almost reverentially, into the SUV. Later after they were freed, the police were adamant the gang had been quite careless in talking about the money they had been offered and the focus of their actions pointed to SMGT. These intruders clearly had to be hirelings of Herr Schneider, who had been keen to establish the status of the IP project and, if necessary, to regain ownership of whatever could be deemed to belong to SMGT.

The only hitch came when some of the team members tried to remove the control panel without success and did damage by attacking it with a hammer. Had they been more knowledgeable, they would have paid more attention to the power supply which, like the measuring equipment tucked away in the small laboratory, was dismissed as being old and unimportant. But they did pick up a tray full of sample bottles. After once again kicking Shorty's two guards into insensibility and giving the bound-up police a derisory insult, the gang departed in their overloaded van.

If the gang was well pleased with its night's work, Herr Schneider was not. After the booty was delivered to SMGT early in the morning, there was much backslapping and congratulations. However, he didn't take long to realise without the relevant formulae, the complex bio-metallurgical additives would take weeks to analyse and replicate. Then there was the matter of the final product which, as Shorty had also quickly learned, was completely polluted by his lack of attention to the manual valves.

And the high hopes of learning all about everything from Margrit's computer were quickly dashed. The operating instructions were certainly there in glorious detail, but without Richard's control algorithms that was all they were—simply operating instructions and nothing more. Schneider needed much more, particularly as the sample bottles were some indication of success.

In the final wash-up, the last act of the fateful night at Groenwater had been a real fiasco and a very expensive one. Apart from the satisfaction enjoyed by the gang in exacting retribution on Shorty's people, the only achievement was to stir up a hornet's nest involving both the police and the much-feared Paesano. It would certainly make Will's job much harder as he tried for mutual cooperation to put together a response to the syndicate's demands.

THIRTY-SIX

Shorty arrived back at the plant in the morning to work out how much damage had been caused by his muddled, forceful efforts and was astonished to see a fresh squad of police milling about. By then they had released the two men in the police van, but told the big man they hadn't yet been able to get much in the way of lucid information from them. Realising what must have happened, Shorty stormed into the main shed to search for Margrit's computer and his own jacket, totally disinterested in the fate of his guards.

His frantic quest took him to the small laboratory and he quickly crashed the locked door, but instead of computer or jacket, he saw the floor was bloodied and so were his two semi-coherent guards, huddled together. Angry rather than sympathetic, he roughly removed their gags, stood them up and berated them.

'You idle dickheads! Do you think I hired you to sit around and smoke dope? Could it be I may actually have expected you to be alert and protect the property? Now listen carefully, bird-brains. If you value your pathetic little lives you'll tell the police you were mugged in the dark and you saw bugger-all.'

Then he pushed the hapless pair out of the building, and

changing his tone completely, suggested the police '… might like to question the poor fellows.'

After a brief chat, Shorty was able to piece together a probable scenario. There had been two sets of visitors during the night, one entering with Major Brand's authority to examine the layout of the site and the second with the likely intent of finding details of the secret process itself. Remembering Herr Schneider's final comments at the negotiation meeting, Shorty was sure this group was arranged by SMGT, and he immediately rued the missing computer.

It was unfortunate it had fallen into the hands of their competitor and it was a real catastrophe in thwarting Shorty's plan to manage the entire process. It would mean starting again after the place had been cleaned up. Setting up a new computer would take time. The only positive was the electrician, who had by now turned up for work, was able to quickly confirm the wanton damage to the control panel was superficial and at a pinch it could be operated using minor replacement parts. Concern about the missing jacket was an issue, but definitely not one he was inclined to raise with the police. He did suggest they would be safer off the plant site while testing was going on and he locked them out.

Shorty addressed his now-depleted crew of workers. From the start he was accusatory and singled out the electrician and the foreman for his most vitriolic abuse. Given his vile temper, it was no wonder the crew was smaller now and only the more financially desperate remained while the rest had decided to cut their losses.

He finished up with a rumbled threat, 'If one of you thieving

... b-b-bastards has taken my coat, you'll find yourself in a ... b-b-bigger mess than my guards. I'll get other people to do this fucking work.'

The foreman looked on with thinly masked disdain. He knew there were no signs of prospective employees outside the gate. In the wider community a garbled rumour was already circulating about simmering gang warfare. He told Shorty, 'There are no fresh recruits interested.'

While knowing the whole trial process had been polluted by nothing more than his own hasty actions, Shorty went back to Parktown to brief Paesano on the night-time attack, describing the damage and rectification already in place.

'The only problem is a single flow valve was set the wrong way. I think one of those ring-ins you hired just did it by mistake with no trouble intended. Now there's nothing wrong with the plant, but I still need that witch, Dupain, to make sure the chemical stuff is in order. I would have dealt with her already, especially if I found out she's been fiddling with the additives. As for Curie, his work is all about numbers and measurements and is mostly stuff I can handle all by myself. Why don't you come and have a look?'

At this point Paesano broke into the monologue to raise his concerns, which to Shorty only demonstrated weakening resolve.

'I am sticking right here. Just you be extra careful about how you ... err ... remove these people. Capito? Things are changing with the police and I can't shut down every investigation as I did before. There are now far too many complications with them sniffing around everywhere ... even overseas. I can't understand why they haven't pushed harder with the fire at the widow's house, either. It wasn't us, unless of course you've been holding back on me …'

Shorty appeared so anxious to demonstrate his loyalty that Paesano's suspicions were only further aroused when he broke into the diatribe.

'Boss, I've never heard of her. I've got hardly enough workers to run the trial.'

Paesano scowled.

'And now there's Schneider and SMGT trying to pinch our ideas and that ugly syndicate trying to get money we haven't got right now. Horsfeld says we can get the money, but not for weeks and we certainly haven't got that much time. I suspect the police are closer to tying things together than any of us know and once they do, we're gonners. If by chance they don't crack it, there are other people after us everywhere.'

As Paesano rambled on he became increasingly agitated and persistently scratched at the scar on his hand. This really troubled Shorty who was unused to such indecisiveness.

'It might turn out we'll need those scientists as a bargaining point. They obviously know far too much for us ever to set them free as they would surely go straight to the police. I'm not sure yet what to do about Bruno. However, if you can ever catch the slimy, little Indian and get him …' he cleared his throat, '… put down, it would remove another link to Kyalami Drive. He obviously overheard everything …'

Paesano paused and Shorty was anxious to put an end to this self-pitying discourse when his boss started up again.

'Schneider must have our laptop. Why on earth would they

take your clothing as well? Surely the police can see Denning committed suicide and there's no need for forensic games. Why are the police watching all of our properties? Whose side are they on anyway?'

Then, another U-turn.

'That fellow, Wolhuter, seems to be in the thick of everything. Who does he actually work for? Schneider didn't seem to know him, yet he appears in their recent fundraising prospectuses. And only as a consultant? What's the story?'

At last Shorty was able to relax a bit as he recognised Paesano was merely thinking aloud and clarifying where the threats were coming from. But he had never before shared his concerns in this way. While threats themselves were not exactly a novelty, it was some time since his boss had been such a serious target, and never before had he been subjected to such a comprehensive and diverse attack.

Paesano seemed certain the police and their counterparts in other countries were trying to fit together a massive amount of evidence against the members of the syndicate. He believed individual cases of murder and mayhem were of lesser momentum, and were secondary to this main investigation. So a murder or two, the theft of ideas, or serious threats to life and property could be put on hold while the central game was played out and he implied as much to Shorty.

This was a very poor assessment of the situation, because Brand's investigation was quickly strengthening the case against Mpane, but he didn't have the wider information that Will was gathering so he called him and started with his analysis of Denning's death.

'The forensic analysis of the blood on Mpane's jacket has been proved to be Denning's. The bruises on the corpse's upper arms were undoubtedly caused by the grip of a very strong person with extraordinarily large hands, and the path of the bullet through the head was forensically inconsistent with blood splatters on the wall.'

It was all more than enough to enable Brand to arrest Mpane on suspicion of murder, but Will pleaded for a delay.

'Please wait until these wider crimes of money-laundering and the funding of arms and drug trading can be sheeted home. There is a web of international scoundrels at work and it puts our country at serious risk.'

This plea presented Brand with the same moral and professional dilemma being faced by Will. On the one hand, he was required to close down the murder case and, hopefully, some other deaths could be pinned on the amoral thug. At the same time though, he was aware of the ramifications of Will's work and the fact this wider reaching task could be compromised by acting too early against Mpane. He made his decision.

'I'll go along with this in the short term but we must set a deadline. My resources are thinly spread all over the place and my Brigadier is getting anxious. He's sure to be getting pressure from the top and I wouldn't be surprised if some of the big boys have more than fingers in the pie. As well, Mpane is almost programmed to commit murder again which I don't want on my conscience.'

'Many thanks, Koos, I just hope you can spare a couple of

people to watch Mpane. He seems to be irrational and all over the place and it wouldn't hurt to keep him under pressure.'

Brand said this could be dangerous if Mpane went viral, but he saw the point.

'Ah, man, I'll do my best with the rubbish I've got.'

Will was thankful for this, but later he wished Brand had put some of his brighter officers on the task. Shorty Mpane was never to be taken lightly and Will recalled in the past the Major had sometimes lacked attention to detail.

THIRTY-SEVEN

Despite Paesano's ranting and the long list of his other tasks, Shorty was absolutely determined to see the Groenwater trial succeed, even if this meant working on his own through the night. Late in the day while taking Bruno back to his house arrest at Kyalami Drive, he called in to the mine to check on the cleanup process and the control board repair. To his chagrin, he found things were progressing very slowly.

He noted a number of items had been moved about, including the big gas cylinders which were not yet reconnected and the electrician was waiting on parts for the control panel. The foreman had been unable to attract any additional workers and some of the more skilled members of his team had taken off, pay or no pay. There was a lot of work left to do and before he set off, Shorty gave one more demanding instruction.

'I'll be coming back here tonight and the show had ... b-b-bloody ... b-b-better be ready to go or your ... b-b-bonuses will be waiting for you in hell!'

Of course, he still had no idea how any of them would be paid given Paesano's recent somewhat enlightening explanation of Green Mines' cash position.

Shorty had always enjoyed driving and in better times he

had indulged himself in a high performance BMW. He now set about taking its performance to new levels and, with malicious satisfaction, saw he had almost shaken off his police tail. He slowed down knowing if the need arose, he would be easily able to lose a pursuit from incompetents like these.

On this trip, Shorty had more than enough time to reflect on Paesano's changing mood and his lessening confidence. He began to plan what he might do if things went haywire. He was now under no illusions the Boss would abandon him without a moment's thought if the time came. His one-time hero could, by silencing a few key witnesses, make him personally wear Nick's execution as an act of revenge and jealousy on his part.

Musings like this made Shorty even more determined to get on top of the IP and its operational instructions. He was bold enough to think once he'd done so he could find a way of selling the thing on his own account. That this was totally impractical completely escaped him, because selling these complex ideas was unlike a sophisticated arms or drugs deal relying on brutal stand-over tactics. After all, Paesano had left the entire oversight of the project to him and his earlier discussions with Margrit and Richard had provided him a fundamental appreciation of its commercial value.

He also knew enough about the evil side of human nature to be sure there would be opportunistic buyers out there, irrespective of who might hold the patents. Certainly, SMGT would be keen. As for loyalty to or from his boss, in this at least Shorty was nothing if not a realist.

The asinine way in which he tackled his next steps at Kyalami Drive obviously reflected on Shorty's state of exhaustion, and his audience of three house guests was astonished at the instructions he gave. He shouted at Margrit, 'You just use one of the other computers in your suite to remake all the stuff you recorded yesterday and it had better be … b-b-bloody right because I will check it against your machine later.'

Turning to Richard, his tone completely changed and he spoke almost as if he was again reading a part in an unrehearsed play. It was naivety in the extreme and Richard saw straight through his stilted presentation.

'Despite what has happened, Mr Paesano wants to ensure all your work is recognised and paid for.'

He cocked his head at Margrit, but addressed Richard more calmly.

'You can decide how much she gets and how much you gunna keep for yourself. I want you to make a … how do you say? Computer record … of all your formulas and stuff. I want it ready in a briefcase with a copy of all her work by tonight.'

Through all of this, no mention was made of Nick's execution. The implication seemed to be if they shut up it would all go away and as Paesano had said on that awful night, 'None of you liked him anyway.' Despite all he'd seen and heard, Richard couldn't believe Shorty's personal values were so warped he would assume money could buy their silence in such a terrible affair. Perhaps it was all some wicked game, but for the fact he was not one to play games. Now, looking poker-faced at Richard, he continued in a measured way.

'Mr Paesano is a man of principle and even though I personally think you've gone out of your way to delay the project, he wants to honour the Agreement.'

At this Richard, who had seen enough of Paesano in action to realise the absurdity of this statement, nearly choked and decided Shorty had either become deranged or was double-crossing Paesano. He now knew more than ever they must get out soon and he wondered what on earth Will was doing.

Shorty peremptorily dismissed the scientists to their suites and turned his attention to Bruno Horsfeld, who was also incapable of hiding his disbelief at what he was hearing. Like the big man, he felt Paesano was losing his edge. Having gone over the finances in detail with him, Bruno was convinced he had reached the end of the road in South Africa. Had Shorty come to the same conclusion and was he now seeking to protect his own welfare? He was brusque as he sought Bruno's cooperation.

'I have to pay the work gang at the mine. Dieter won't tell me, but I must know how much money we have … for now and for later as well. And while you're about it, what about my personal trust money? Is it safe?'

Bruno paled, knowing Nick had already sucked the trust dry. Not the sort of information to share with Shorty in his present mood. Bruno did not like the manic look in his tired, bloodshot eyes and quickly came to the conclusion loyalty to Paesano was one thing and a complete skin was another. He asked tentatively how much was needed. Without any hesitation, Shorty nominated a vast amount in Rand. It seemed enough to keep a small army in comfort for months. For Bruno the conversion from South African Rand to Swiss Francs was easy, but it was still a devil of a lot. Having gone through the syndicate demands and an analysis of the international cash position with Paesano an hour before, he knew quite well the problem. However, he was desperate to keep Shorty on side.

'I can access most of that sum in cash.'

'Perhaps I should have asked for more then?'

'There isn't any more in South Africa.'

'Then what about the overseas stuff I am just beginning to learn about?'

Bruno made a non-committal reply.

'I am trying to sort it out. Denning left this end in such a mess, particularly his financial trading.'

Shorty was fearful enough of Paesano even in his present disjointed state to know there was a limit to prying and let the matter drop. Of course, what Bruno didn't add was he had judiciously set aside a reasonable safety factor for Paesano and himself in the event things did start to go pear-shaped. This would mean activating their escape plan soon. Ironically he wouldn't be sure until the last minute whether he himself would be included. More than anyone else in his world Bruno knew how Paesano could hold a grudge.

THIRTY-EIGHT

Late in the afternoon, as he was making yet another trip to the mine, Shorty had mulled over the events of the past few days, feeling sure he was right in his assessment of the complex situation. He now knew all about the syndicate's threat and its demand for prompt payment of a huge sum of money. He could also see reasons for SMGT's profound interest in the stuff the scientists were doing and which now, through his intensive hands-on involvement, he had come to understand so well. What riled him was old gang warfare had been re-ignited and threatened to ruin the whole project when it was nearing the very cusp of success.

While he personally failed to understand the full ramifications of the money-laundering side of things, Shorty could easily sense its importance for Paesano. He could see the impending collapse of both sides of his business was driving the man to the brink, and the huge demand from the syndicate added another dimension to his troubles.

He had to confess to himself he rather admired the macabre touch of violence provided by the severed finger. It added credibility to the threat and he was maliciously pleased to see how it had traumatised the less-hardened onlookers. He also surmised Bruno may well have been able to recover sufficient funds to cover Paesano's proportion of the demand. But this could not come from Green Mines.

He thought it ironic that all the players in this bunfight, as powerful as they seemed, appeared to be fatally strapped for cash. Shorty recognised Paesano might choose to conserve his off-shore investments and do a runner from his troubles in South Africa. He was undoubtedly already withdrawing, allowing himself to get more and more distracted and letting self-doubt consume him. There was possibly an escape plan and if this was the path chosen by the Boss, it was almost certain he, Shorty, would be left high and dry. Even given his own immoral standards, he considered this to be grossly unfair.

His years of single-minded commitment to Paesano would, in the end, be deemed worthless. In frustration he thumped the steering wheel hard and roared at the windscreen.

'The bastard, the miserable, dirty bastard!'

In this frame of mind Shorty decided, once and for all, he would steal what he could of the IP value. His rationalisation stemmed from his deep disappointment over Paesano's obsession with the commercial side of the project, losing any interest in the technical aspects. His priorities had left Shorty in complete charge of the scientific side of things and he had invested far too much intellectual, nervous and physical energy in the project to see it fail because the Boss chose to turn away.

Given the ruthless nature of the syndicate and the time constraints, Shorty thought he might be able to negotiate the sale of the IP to SMGT. Furthermore, his own new-found operating experience gave him increased bargaining power.

Herr Schneider would then have leverage to convince the syndicate there was good reason to delay the payment of the demand until the full value of the IP could be realised. If Paesano did have the gall to vanish, then be buggered if Shorty would let him take the scientists' work with him.

There was no doubt this strategy of theft would also require the removal of the two scientists as contenders for the IP rights. How advantageous was that? Shorty was able to rationalise his thinking, recalling their role as witnesses to Nick's execution. Just that day, Bentt Mgeni had warned him that Major Brand wouldn't accept suicide as a reason for Denning's death, even if he was unsure about a murder motive.

Shorty had begun to fret over a lot of things which until now he had been ignoring and which could tie him to the execution. Why hadn't the police bothered to interview him? In the past, the police investigative process had almost inevitably been stymied by the old, corrupt Brigadier through Paesano's liberal oiling of palms. But why had he not been interviewed at all in this case? Then he remembered the disappearance of his jacket and this caused his big hands to clench the steering wheel and it sent an unusual shiver of fear down his spine.

There were some positives, though. The one guard, Christian, who was a witness to the killing was as close to Shorty as anyone could be, given his foul nature. He would never squeal and now Shorty could see his way clear to eliminate the two boffins. So, to clear the decks, he would only have to go after the shifty Indian and, if necessary, the enigmatic Argentinian, Horsfeld.

The number of victims didn't bother Shorty at all. He

had long recognised he had been born to kill and was totally impervious to those deaths. Stemming from his youthful experiences with necklacing in the townships, he had used fire as his tag. His gloved hands hid the scars of his first amateurish venture in this field and he was annoyed he hadn't taken the time to organise something pyrotechnical at the cabana on the night of Denning's death. He thought killing the scientists in the lab could be tackled more methodically and in his unconscionable way, he was beginning to look forward to those three or even four future slayings.

There was another thing which had been gnawing away at his increasingly fragile mental state. He was keenly aware Paesano had been cunning enough to maintain the illusion of personal distance from the events on that fateful night, which certainly wasn't enhancing Shorty's prospects. Despite the sizeable language barrier when the police had questioned Shorty's guards, they had no doubt been able to verify their logs which clearly showed Paesano had not left his mansion nor visited Kyalami Drive for days.

Conversely, the logs would reveal constant coming and going of the big man and would clearly put him at Kyalami Drive at the forensically determined time of Denning's death. Again, Shorty felt he had been gravely let down by his boss, and began to think vindictively about a way to bring Paesano squarely back into the picture.

THIRTY-NINE

Shorty had finished his angry musing just as he arrived at the mine. While the gate was opening, the remnants of the working party were pushing their sullen way out, scowling and muttering about their pay. He postured theatrically to the foreman.

'Tell 'em the wages are even now being made up in the city office and can be collected there in the morning.'

After this message was conveyed to the men, there was an angry outburst. Shorty doubted whether Bruno had found any spare cash and his instructions to the pay clerk could only be window dressing. There would be the mother of all ruckuses outside the nameless city building when these men who had been fobbed off, inconvenienced and brutalised, turned up to collect their dues.

Knowing he desperately needed their manual labour, Shorty tried to project a more conciliatory attitude. No amount of sweet-talking could get any of the departing workers to stay back and even the foreman was rebellious. Pleading other work commitments, he turned to go but then spun around.

'You'll find everything except the gas supply is back in place; all the piping is clean and tidy and the raw material bins are full.

Why don't you wait until tomorrow? If this lot does actually get paid, some of them might even come back. You won't need so many this time anyway.'

This was pushing his luck as far as he dared lest Shorty thought it a veiled criticism of his own understanding and competence. His cheek was still tender from the thumping he had been given a few days before.

A desperate Shorty turned his attention to the four replacement guards who had been brought across from the force at the Parktown mansion. They had been given specific instructions by Paesano and at first, had no inclination to focus on anything but their security duties. It took a combination of promises and thinly-veiled threats to inveigle them into reluctant cooperation. Twice Shorty had to take the demeaning step of pretending to phone his boss.

Communication was also a problem and if the situation was not so grim it would have been quite comical. Over the years, Shorty had picked up barely half a dozen words of Spanish from Paesano and this just about matched the guards' meagre grasp of English. There was a lot of *amigo, si, que?* and *rapido* but he had never bothered to learn the words for please or thank-you.

In his frustration, Shorty resorted to shouting a few commands in Zulu, thinking to convey his intent by speaking loudly and gesturing violently. In Apartheid times, he had seen this tactic used by English-speaking riot police with no real language skills, but while it may have worked for them it certainly didn't impress Paesano's guards.

As usual, he worked like a demon to get the plant set up, but a red moon was sinking towards the horizon before it was all complete. At this point, he realised he needed Margrit's operating instructions and Richard's algorithm settings before he could run the trial under his own steam. He groaned aloud as he contemplated yet another drive back to Kyalami Drive.

This trip was made at a more moderate pace and he didn't worry much about the very obvious but distant police tail he was carrying. He did find this style of surveillance a tad puzzling as his normal involvement with the law had been a lot more direct: immediate arrest and an almost-as-immediate release when Paesano's bribery kicked in.

To help pass the time, he made a call to his friend, the bent Sergeant, to learn the best news of his otherwise miserable day. Bentt casually let slip that Naidoo had just been taken into custody and he felt as though he had struck a minor jackpot. Now that he knew where the miserable little bugger was and was likely to be for some time, he could make a plan to silence him once and for all. A few brief calls were all it would take and he reached for his phone to get the ball rolling.

While he was making his phone calls, the scientists had completed their tasks and had copied everything for their own later use. This was done quite quickly and they had plenty of time beside the pool to share their worries about the looming finalisation of the trial and their own desperate situation. As usual, Richard did most of the talking.

'I can't understand what Will is up to. He keeps making promises to rescue us but nothing has happened. I really thought he cared for you.'

There was almost a note of jealousy in his anxiety and trying to allay his fears, Margrit reminded him Will had promised them freedom that very day. Richard was not prepared to be fobbed off and again there was an obvious touch of jealousy in his response.

'I know you think Will is all action, but we can't even use our mobiles to tell him how far the IP trial has progressed. It seems to me Shorty is happy although he's not quite on top of the operating side yet. I'm pretty sure he's not far from the point where he'll no longer have any need for us then what …?'

He left the question hanging before continuing, '… Luckily for us he's not computer savvy and we've got copies of the final procedures.'

Then he gestured at the poolside CCTV camera.

'While our new guard seems such a pal with Horsfeld, you can bet he's been watching us like a hawk. There's nothing more certain than the thug'll be reporting everything back to his master tomorrow.'

There was a very long pause and it was Margrit who broke the silence in a most unexpected way.

'I do believe in Will and I do so wish we were far away from all this horror and had real time of our own. Richard, I just long for you to hold me.'

She moved closer to him and oblivious to any concerns about the guard in the foyer they walked towards Margrit's room.

It was then they heard Shorty's car coming up the gravel drive. As he wasn't due until the morning, their hearts sank and they were unable to quell their mounting fear. The big man burst into the house, barked a short question to the guard, brushed past Bruno and marched out to the pool where Margrit and Richard were still standing close together. His appearance and actions more than hinted at derangement.

'Are you two taking me seriously? Is all my stuff done? Where's the brief case? How can you prove I have everything? Don't you think I've done enough testing to deserve my share? I'm gunna kill anyone who is trying to cheat me. Anyone!'

A rampaging bull with his own agenda and no concern at all for human life had usurped the long-standing loyalty to the clinically vicious Paesano, which had kept the old Shorty in check.

Nervously they followed Shorty to the dining room and pointed at the briefcase in the centre of the table. Next to the case they had placed a computer and printer expecting a need to demonstrate the range of material collected, but Shorty obviously wanted a briefer version. He started with Margrit's careful recording of the operations which had been captured on her computer. He couldn't let on he was relying on memory. As far as he could tell, the rewritten procedure seemed to be a fair version of the original. His attitude changed in an instant and he spoke thickly as though he had rehearsed it all.

'I didn't bring your old machine here but I think you have listened carefully to what I require. Paesano ... um ... Mr Paesano will be relieved it's so clear.'

Richard's material proved to be a much bigger problem since it was so mathematical and way beyond Shorty's grasp. The printouts, however, seemed to relate to the procedures he had followed earlier and in any event the control settings were unchanged at the mine. Despite the damage caused by the previous night's raid, it would be easy to establish if Richard had covered everything. Shorty seemed well satisfied and the two were for the moment relieved. He scooped up the material on the table and untidily shoved the whole lot into the briefcase.

In another complete change of mood, he scowled at Richard and ignored Margrit. Now he could tick Margrit off the list and Richard would only be needed for one final test.

'You come with me, you won't need anything else. All the mathematics should be here in the briefcase. You woman, …' now pointing at Margrit 'you'll stay here with Horsfeld. I'll soon see whether either of you have tried to cheat me. If I can't do the thing by myself, it is useless to me. But no one else wins either.'

It was now evident to both that Paesano was being completely cut out and Shorty had become savagely deranged. Their time was nearly up. If it hadn't been for their faith in Will Wolhuter, Richard felt he would have collapsed. He turned to Margrit and in his schoolboy French told her to stick to Horsfeld like glue.

Shorty spun around and lashing out at Richard, threw him off balance, knocking off his glasses.

'What didya say, you little wimp?'

Richard answered quickly, trying to avoid another blow.

'I said Horsfeld can't be trusted.'

Shorty growled in his fury.

'You won't speak some foreign lingo here. My guard can barely understand English and I've told him to keep a good eye on you, woman.'

This time he hit Richard in the mouth and drew blood. Richard stumbled to the floor and scrabbled around for his glasses. Shorty gave him a kick in the back which took his breath away, yet Richard was still able to exchange a glance of comfort with Margrit. She called out softly.

'*Je t'aime. Au revoir, mon cher.*'

Shorty spun around and shouting at Margrit, hit her full in the face.

'Didn't you hear me? No fucking French, bitch.'

Defiantly, she protested in pain.

'I only said, I love you … goodbye, my darling.' She rubbed her cheek. Shorty yelled again.

'Let this be your last warning.'

He dragged Richard out to the Mercedes and pushed him into the back.

'You just keep your bloody head down until we are right out of here, see!'

The car was logged out as carrying only the unmistakable Shorty. They hadn't travelled far before Shorty unaccountably burst into song and Richard, dire as things were, felt it was a remarkably good rendition of Elvis Presley. He then just stopped in mid-verse and bellowed at his prisoner.

'Bloody good, hey?'

Richard was now certain Shorty had reached a crisis point in his madness. As they drove on in icy silence, Richard wondered desperately what Will Wolhuter was up to.

FORTY

Like Shorty, Will had also being mulling over events and he too was finding the whole situation complex. The balancing act between the two prongs of their investigation, the murders and the international financial manipulation, were proving difficult. The sooner he was able to divest himself of the former, the sooner he could concentrate all his attention on the latter. Nevertheless, they were inter-connected matters with their origins in the perennial standoff between two highly corrupt entities, and the shadowy role of a vicious syndicate embedded in this manure pile.

Will was well aware of the growing ramifications of all this and now the international connections which Franklin had so painstakingly explored and exposed became really relevant. The two principals, Paesano and Schneider, were only one dimension among many and both had spread their wings across a range of activities. Apart from involvement in the international drug and weapons business, which had so upset the syndicate, the pair had conduits to other areas of criminality such as money-laundering for some directors of FIFA in the run-up to the World Cup. They were stepping on the toes of the syndicate in several different ways.

As could be expected with two megalomaniac rivals,

such alliances are only ever brief affairs. When their paths ultimately parted for good, it seemed to Will the more conservative Schneider stuck with money- laundering, while the opportunistic Paesano took an interest in other avenues of funding, the most exotic of which had been suggested by Shorty: the very rich trade of rhino-horn poaching near the Limpopo River. As a bonus, this poaching activity provided Paesano an entry into the Asian underworld with a nice little sideline in financing the movement of domestic servants from the Philippines to the Middle East. This was toe-stepping on the syndicate in a big way and ultimately became yet another thread of international investigation for Will Wolhuter.

He changed his mind again.

'Koos man, this fire-bombing of Mrs Franklin's house must be a serious warning from that syndicate. I know it looks like a Shorty crime, but the police logs tell me he was far too involved with the scientists to organise this attack. His old gang of thugs, like your police, is already too thinly spread.'

Will now thought about the scientists and their innovative processes. He had no idea what they were actually working on, but it seemed to be of great value to the outsiders who had organised the raid on Groenwater. To his eye there was nothing special about the ramshackle collection of tanks, pipes and meters which appeared to form the basis of their work and which certainly didn't seem to be worth a killing or two.

'I didn't think the stuff we saw at Groenwater was important, but I'm unsure whether the raid was an attempt at targeted theft or just a spoiling operation. In any case it certainly smells strongly of SMGT.'

Will was now properly aware his friend Margrit and her English colleague were in extreme danger, but earlier he had been inclined to think they were getting things out of perspective. Once his far more important crusade against the international operations of the syndicate was launched, Will would be able to extricate these very frightened people.

In the light of the early morning raid, he and Brand had factored in the likely reaction of the guards and Mpane to a rescue attempt at Kyalami Drive, and had agreed it was too risky at this stage. As Brand had been quick to point out, Mpane was a compulsive killer who once cornered would spare no one.

'Will, he is as good as convicted in the Denning case. The witnesses who had previously been cowed could certainly support our forensic evidence. That little Winston Naidoo has already spilled the beans. He provided us a very comprehensive statement before he hanged himself in his cell last night.'

Will was astonished.

'How on earth could it have happened, Koos?'

'Damn the sergeant who allotted witness protection duty to a newly-appointed constable. You can bet I'll be threading that one through; however, I don't think I can pin it on Mgeni. Now we have to get your two friends out of harm's way.'

Will was in no doubt an alternative plan to save the hostages was required. Logic told him if an uncontrolled gun battle was to be avoided, the rescue would be best attempted somewhere on the road between the house and the mine when the two scientists were together yet out of the reach of Shorty. This was decidedly fanciful given the close scrutiny being applied to the scientists and the endless and seemingly erratic trips

Shorty was making between the three different locations. To complicate matters, Brand called again.

'Will, Mpane has recently arrived at Kyalami Drive to deliver the Argentinian fellow, Horsfeld, and then left on his own. Where he might be heading is anyone's guess, but you're right about Horsfeld and the scientists being held as hostages in the house. Our problem is the search warrant has now expired because charges haven't been laid.'

Will's response was a strange mixture of disappointment in the uncompleted wider investigation, but relief action could now be taken to rescue the scientists.

'The cat will be well and truly out of the bag if a fresh application is made because the search process is meant to be open. There are enough squealers in the force to pass the message on to Paesano.'

To complicate things even further, Will had learnt two of the countries in the international round-up had yet to confirm their participation and therefore the huge investigative resource he had assembled was dormant.

Sometime later, Brand gave him an update.

'Mpane has returned to the mine site and driven straight into the main shed. Another car has travelled from the Parktown mansion to Kyalami Drive, with some of my better police on its tail. It's Denning's flash sports car which we returned after it was finished as evidence.'

With great satisfaction, he added, 'It's likely, although not confirmed, that the car is being driven by Paesano. It's his first trip out of Parktown in days. Maybe it's our chance to get them all in one place.'

Indeed, it was Paesano who had turned up unannounced at the secure house. Shorty's particularly unpleasant minders had been very tense and guarded when the big boss arrived, as they were unsure of his standing in the face of Shorty's recent and terrifyingly explicit instructions.

These instructions had been delivered in shouted English, the meaning of which was nonetheless abundantly clear to them. They had been told Horsfeld and Margrit had to stay put … or else! Now Paesano in explicit Spanish was just as viciously commanding them to release Horsfeld into his keeping. Completely ignoring Margrit, he re-enforced his instruction that the woman should be carefully watched until Mr Mpane returned to deal with her. He pushed Bruno into the car and drove quietly down towards the gate with headlamps off.

Perhaps the police who had tailed the BMW were as good as the Major had claimed, but they certainly hadn't anticipated Paesano's quick turnaround. They were stretching their legs after a long night's vigil and were casually recounting their experiences to the other police at the gate when it smoothly slid open and the BMW accelerated through. Despite a swift response, it didn't take the officers long to realise their quarry had evaded them and they shamefacedly alerted Brand. Severely chastened, he contacted Will.

'Dammit man, my police are so bloody hopeless. Paesano and a passenger have left the house and shaken off the tail. I now have a general alert out for that BMW.'

Will's response was enigmatic.

'Time's up! I have to tell all my contacts to proceed with arresting all the criminals associated in the syndicate, as

Paesano will compromise everything now that he is on the loose.'

What the police and Will had been unable to factor into their thinking was the sophistication of Paesano's long-developed escape plans and his subsequent ability to fade into an international jungle of obscurity. There was one positive in this gloomy development. A number of banks in several countries had responded quickly to freeze some accounts identified by Will's forensic team. There were any number of surprises.

'Colonel, we have just uncovered his investment in some rhino-horn poachers and their Asian customers.'

So Will wasn't too put out when Denning's much-loved BMW was found abandoned and looted on a little-used airstrip near the Limpopo River. The nearest villagers had been most unhelpful and only admitted to having heard a plane the day before. They claimed their neighbouring villagers were rascals who would kill all rhinos and steal anything.

Effectively, Dieter Paesano and Bruno Horsfeld had completely vanished leaving behind a widely distributed package of debt and worthless holdings in joint ventures. There were no fixed assets to support the liabilities. The vile Nick Denning had constructed a labyrinth of shady arrangements which Bruno had been unpicking before Nick was executed and those laundered funds would provide Paesano with a reasonable kick-start wherever he turned up. Will was sure it wouldn't be South Africa and, with his Interpol connections, he could ensure that several other havens would be denied to Paesano.

FORTY-ONE

As soon as Shorty had departed with Richard hidden in the silver Mercedes, the foyer guard taking his instructions literally ordered Margrit into the living room.

'Not touch … not move … just sits.'

These were the limits of his orders and probably his English. Shorty had been frustrated beyond measure by this language barrier and had called up more of his own gang members. This in turn had surprised the police at Kyalami supposedly watching the gate, especially after all the permanent house staff and gardeners had been peremptorily kicked out. The manic Argentinian guard had continued to control the foyer according to his boss' instructions, and in Shorty's absence, his people had nothing better to do than relax in the garden.

In her enforced isolation Margrit had plenty of time to reflect on her dilemma and her logical mind was in turmoil. She and Richard had always assumed they would be rescued together and Bruno and Winston might also be included, even if this complicated matters. Now Richard was with Shorty at Groenwater; her last glimpse of Winston being some time ago as he was surprisingly driven off in the police van; Bruno had just been taken away by Dieter; and here she was on her own under close scrutiny at the house, soon to face Shorty's music.

Questions churned through her mind: Would things go well for Richard at the mine and would he return? Could it be their rescue might be simpler now the other two were not in the picture? Had Winston really been able to dupe the police into setting him free? She had certainly expected more of Major Brand. What did Bruno's departure mean? Perhaps he was safe and even had residual value to his boss? If so, would his loyalties revert to his old friend, Dieter, and how might this all come back to haunt them further?

She thought Will and the police couldn't know her dear friend was heading to the mine with the madman. Time dragged on as she agonised over this and Margrit realised just how deeply she felt for Richard after all the trauma they had shared. Without thinking clearly, she suddenly cried out aloud.

'Why can't the police just act?'

With a low sob she sank further into the couch. The foyer guard was startled by this unseemly outburst and rushed in, shouting at her, 'Just sits … no talks … no cry… no police.'

After an hour or more, Margrit could see the guard getting edgy and despite Paesano's instructions, Margritwas forced to help him. The guard forced her to make a call to Shorty on the foyer phone just as he was pulling up at Groenwater.

Shorty began to grasp the gist of the problem and became increasingly agitated and incoherent. Irrationally he took it out on the foyer guard who couldn't understand any of the tirade thundering from the phone. His fury was then directed at Margrit.

'So, he's … b-b-buggered off, has he? And he's taken that Horsfeld parrot, has he? Now how am I supposed to get my money? How am I gunna pay those idle … b-b-bastards outside the town office? No wonder none of them are here to help me. Shit … Shit … SHIT!'

He drove into the main shed setting to work with a vengeance using all the guards. There was little Richard could do to help the infuriated thug, who turned on him.

'Well don't think I'm gunna stop this … b-b-bloody process again for anyone including that swine, Paesano.'

He lurched toward Richard, fist raised.

'It had … b-b-bloody… b-b-better work, Doctor Dickhead!'

And with that, he threw his phone into one of the chemical tanks and started to move the gas bottles back, muttering to himself as he began the process. Richard was now well and truly the target of his irrational anger.

'I don't need you here, you pathetic, gutless English piece of shit. I can do all of this myself, you know. So now it's time for you to … b-b-bugger off … b-b-back to the house.'

He turned to the nearby guard and spat out orders.

'All of you can get out of the shed; this is my show! Take this English ponce away.'

And to Richard he shouted, 'Leave the computer here you stuck-up nerd and get your head right down as you go. It's worked before with those dumb cops …'

He ranted on.

'After I get back, I'm gunna do some negotiating with you and your girlfriend, and you won't be getting much time to put your ideas to me as I'll be hell-bent on getting out of this mess.'

He simply ignored Richard's plea.

'Can't you leave her out of things?'

Shorty was raging now.

'Don't be fooled by this guard, either. He may not know his way around the English language, but he's a professional killer and he knows exactly what to do if you try him on. As for that other arsehole at the house who allowed Horsfeld to go with Paesano, I'll be fixing him up too.'

He ordered the driver to tie Richard's wrists as a further precaution against escape and watched with scant interest as the Mercedes pulled out of the shed and left the mine. It slowly passed the police contingent and the driver exchanged some ribald obscenities with them as they logged him out.

FORTY-TWO

Only Margrit knew Richard had been taken to the mine by Shorty, while the police believed they were still holed up together at the secure house, guarded by a replenished force of Shorty's ferocious gangsters. It was all most confusing, especially for Major Brand who was anxious to avoid any confrontation until absolutely necessary. The quandary was suddenly made a whole lot worse when Will rang through.

'Koos, the international cooperation has fallen apart. Two South American countries aren't ready to act, doubtless because of the strength of the damn drug cartels. As well, a large West African nation has a real problem with rebel-sponsored arms importation and has suddenly also backed off. I'll pull us out and forget about the lot of them.'

His friend now apologised for more bad news.

'Listen, Will, I am sorry but it now seems Paesano has certainly done a runner and we simply can't wait any longer to free those two hostages. Are you with me, man?'

At last Brand was determined to act. Without waiting for a warrant and as soon as Will reached the site, he ordered the police to storm the house in Kyalami Drive with a force large enough to make a sizeable dent in Brigadier Mfuleni's budget.

The new gates were hammered flat, the gang in the grounds offered no resistance at all and only the Argentinian made a pointless stand in the foyer. Margrit had rolled to the floor at the first sign of disturbance and was hidden from the initial exchange of shots.

During a second fusillade in which the foyer guard was killed, she was struck by a fragment of a ricocheting bullet, causing a bad flesh wound in her upper arm, but was able to tell her rescuers Richard had been taken away by Shorty. Brand quickly realised he needed to reinforce the police at Groenwater.

'As we speak, Dr Dupain, a rescue plan is being activated, but we have to be very careful because Mpane has become seriously deranged and we cannot predict his reaction. The surveillance police have not yet been able to see Richard Curie from their positions outside the fence and as Will and I found when we made a little visit to Groenwater the other night, the layout is complex and the place is full of rubbish.'

Will then cut in.

'Margrit, where is your colleague likely to be? As it is, we'll have to go in blind and this will give Mpane the chance to harm him.'

Margrit described the small laboratory where they had been held and the location of gas bottles and some volatile chemical bins. She was blunt in her warning.

'There are chemicals, explosives and gases all over the place and the worst thing you could do is to go in shooting like you did just now.'

Brand conveyed this to his small team at the mine, but the advice was to prove too late and futile. Shorty, who was already way beyond rationality, was focused simply on a successful test outcome under his own control. Anything else was immaterial because his personal satisfaction was knowing his cheating, white chief would not share in any bonanza.

Shorty grinned maniacally thinking that if someone didn't actually get at the pig, he would forever remain a frustrated Gold Bug. And to hell with smarmy scientists, SMGT, syndicates and interfering police, Shorty would have done it by himself.

Lost in these thoughts, Shorty seemed oblivious to his surroundings and in the dim light didn't even register the haze which floated on the concrete floor slab around the gas bottles, or the audible hiss as his gloved hand grew cold against the freezing metal valves. He turned to the computer and followed instruction no. 6 which told him to turn on the main gas delivery and the process was then vested in the control of the algorithms.

To his awakening horror, he grasped the significance of the gaseous haze on the concrete floor. He now had seven seconds left before the pumps started automatically. Those old pumps had always thrown off prodigious sparks and should this happen, Shorty knew instinctively the danger of the floating gas cloud.

He spun around and rushed towards the main power switch, the countdown screaming in his mind.

'All my fault … six …'

Stumbling over the jumbled mess on the floor and sucking in the noxious gas with his last breath, he picked himself up, screaming, 'Dear God, not like this, not me … five … fou …'

He reached desperately up towards the main power switch on the wall. 'Three … two … one …' and then oblivion. The explosion created by the old, sparking motors sucked all the oxygen from his lungs and thrust his 140-kilogram body back across the control panel.

A fire immediately took hold and flames were soon enveloping the gas bottles and heating the leaking valves. In no time at all, the bottles exploded in two spectacular blasts, hurling debris everywhere and stunning the last three of Shorty's gang before their reflexes kicked in and they rushed after the Mercedes on the safety of the access road. The police outside, transfixed by the holocaust before them, had no inclination to round them up. The clear moonlight over this frightening scene was slowly obscured by an acrid, red smoky haze.

Major Brand, at Kyalami Drive, was on the radio to the senior officer at Groenwater just as the plant exploded. Simultaneously, he was deafened by the noise from the speaker and saw a vast cloud of reddish smoke rising high in the south. Then he heard the dull, percussive thud of two faraway explosions. The dirty, red cloud continued to billow upwards and outwards, drifting across the moon and on the radio the roar of flames could be heard over the excited voice of the officer.

'My God, Major! There is metal flying about everywhere. We are pulling back; this is the biggest bloody fire I've ever seen!'

Hours later, after the blaze eventually died down and a forensic team was admitted onto the site, they found only enough to positively match Shorty with his voluminous criminal records. Shorty may have been obliterated, but he left behind an astonishing legacy of horror and corruption. How ironic someone with such a huge physical presence in life could exit in the way he had intended for the two scientists.

FORTY-THREE

Will was treating Margrit with great care, reassuring her Richard was only minutes away from being released when everyone in the room felt the distant blasts at the mine and heard the senior officer's shouted remarks on Major Brand's two-way squawk box. They rushed outside to see the rising plume of smoke above the horizon far to the south. Margrit was left lying on a couch feeling the full shock of her wound.

With stomach-churning horror, she listened to the excited conversation outside. She knew the blast's most obvious epicentre would be near where Richard would have been standing. He had no chance of survival.

The police had also reached the same conclusion and after some time Will came back into the living room with Brand. He spoke gently to Margrit, confirming her worst fears.

'I'm afraid things don't look good for your friend. It was a massive explosion and it seems impossible anyone in the building could have lived through it. We won't be able to get near the shed for a couple of hours, but we have to expect the worst.'

She sucked in her breath and despite her agony, waited as he paused, uncertain how to proceed. Brand helped him out.

'Dr ... er ... Margrit, you need to know a short time before the explosion, an unidentified driver left Groenwater in the big, silver Mercedes and my police were too pre-occupied to put a tail on him. It seems he picked up the rest of Mpane's gang and I can assure you we'll track him and see what he knows. And if we find he possibly was the one who set up the blast we'll make sure he won't pose any sort of threat to you or anyone else in the future.'

Margrit forcing away her anguish, asked what else had happened and Brand felt Margrit deserved to know more.

'I'm also sorry to tell you Winston Naidoo has recently committed suicide whilst in our custody. At least this is the official view, but I'm suspicious because he had been very forthcoming about what really happened on the night Denning died and also about your involvement. He confessed he had watched the whole thing unfold through CCTV and this means he wouldn't have been an ideal witness. While it seems so irrelevant now, I'm sure the story he told will match yours when you feel up to telling us more. Seriously though, he should have been as safe as houses. I put him under constant surveillance in witness protection. Something doesn't add up and I have suspicions about my sergeant, Ben Mgeni, but he certainly will never bother you.'

He stopped to gauge how Margrit was handling this information and Will looked on sympathetically.

'You may as well clear the decks and tell Margrit about Paesano too, man.'

Brand was abashed and seemed even more uncomfortable.

'As if we haven't made enough mistakes, you should also know we've lost track of Paesano and it seems he has Horsfeld with him. I'm putting you under twenty-four-hour guard in case he turns up, but I think he and his mate have done a runner and we won't see them again in this life.'

This reference to Paesano pulled Margrit up short. Through her foggy mind came the realisation of how lucky she was to have escaped Shorty's murderous intent. She turned to the Major and in a voice which could scarcely be heard, said, 'We are the only two left who witnessed Denning's execution and our chances of survival would have been zero if Shorty hadn't blown himself up.'

Margrit felt the full impact of all this on top of Richard's death and ignoring the pain in her arm, covered her face and sobbed uncontrollably. The other two turned away from her distress and Will lightly touched her free hand in sympathy. Soon an ambulance arrived at the flattened gates but couldn't get through and Margrit, protesting incoherently at the need for all the fuss, was carried to it on a stretcher.

Having ensured the mine site at Groenwater had been secured and having sealed off the crime scene at Kyalami Drive, Will and the Major headed for the Green Mines city building early next morning. There they were astonished to see, assembled on the pavement, a sizeable and noisy crowd of angry, black men. The Major made sure the mob was forcefully dispersed, and while some baton-wielding policemen chased the last of the malcontents from the scene, the others helped them gain access to the reception lobby.

Later that day, visiting Margrit, Will recounted the unfolding story.

'We found a desk bearing a notice saying the office was

closed indefinitely. On the twentieth level was a large office containing banks of filing cabinets along each wall. Drawers were open and there were papers everywhere. Clearly someone had been disturbed doing a methodical search. Have you any idea why that might be?'

Apart for some background papers on their scientific work which had been covertly copied, she couldn't help him. However, for Will this room was a treasure trove.

The disappearance of Paesano had eased the pressure on the Interpol investigations and he would have time to pore over these documents, hopefully to fill in the blanks. He had a cursory look at the papers on the desks and looked at the labelling on each drawer, flicking his way through until he came upon a file labelled 'IP' and found some damning material.

'Check this out, Koos. The scoundrels have set out to blatantly steal the intellectual property of Margrit and her friend. Here the jackal, Denning, has clearly explained how they were going to diddle the contract. The scientists would never be paid.'

Brand was not as experienced as Will, but he quickly got the gist of things as he scanned the document.

'Why wasn't Denning more security conscious, man? Why did he set it down in black and white like this?'

The answer was all too obvious to Will.

'While there is so much corruption in the public sector, the legal system and—I have to say it, Koos—,the police force, scum like him can do anything without fear of investigation, let alone prosecution.'

Brand was momentarily annoyed by his friend's sharp

comment, but knew it was well and truly warranted. Anxious to complete his inspection of Paesano's major properties, he decided to head for the Parktown mansion, while Will was far more interested in the office files and elected to stay put to begin a more detailed examination of the documents. Over the next few days, he and his hastily-gathered assistants were able to tap into the full spectrum of Paesano's corrupt and convoluted world.

They were helped by intercepting numerous telephone calls from anxious investors and minor bankers, keen to know if there was anything worthwhile left in the ruins of the Green Mines empire. There wasn't.

These connections were of great interest to Will and provided him more leads into the international racketeering. It was the breakthrough Will had desperately hoped for, and he was prepared to put everything else on hold until he had milked the files dry.

However, when Brand arrived at the mansion it had been completely abandoned and the police there told him the Argentinian guards had slipped away. This earned them a special rebuke from Brand who once again suspected some well-oiled connivance.

He found the place was in an incredible mess with papers strewn everywhere and remnants of a recent fire in the hearth. Whereas the search at the office had appeared to be calmly methodical, this one seemed to have been carried out in hasty desperation. It didn't take Koos long to determine there would be nothing incriminating on site. Then and there, he decided to leave the inquiry into Paesano's murky business life to Will.

FORTY-FOUR

Three days after the explosion, forensics experts were clear Richard hadn't died at the mine. However, the silver Mercedes had vanished. Brand brought Margrit the news.

'I am absolutely certain Richard has been extracted from Groenwater and the police believe the car may be easier to find now.'

It was the greatest comfort for Margrit to learn Richard had certainly escaped the blast although his fate was still a huge concern.

'But, Will, he might be only ransom money to those villains. Why are they stringing us out like this?'

From time to time, she shuddered with bewilderment at the way things had developed, feeling very much alone despite all the support she was receiving from Will. For his part, Brand was becoming less the formal investigator and was forgiving about her unwilling participation during the terrible night of Denning's execution.

She was thankful to be leaving Kyalami Drive and was at least finding solace in the fact that she held the only complete set of the IP material. While it seemed so unimportant now, she felt she could do something about it later after she settled down.

She couldn't even think about money at the moment and felt distressed each time she looked over the material which they had worked so hard to perfect.

At least in the short-term, money wouldn't be a problem. She had been living rent-free and saving the generous remuneration which had initially kept her tied to the project. Sensibly, she had rejected Denning's early offer to manage this nest egg for her and all her income was directed to her father's bank in Zurich. Nick had turned off her income stream when Richard arrived from England and the receivers weren't showing any compassion about her need for accommodation.

With help from Will, Margrit moved into a secure, quiet apartment and Brand ensured she was watched over by a really professional set of guards. She settled down to work on the reconstruction of an accurate and comprehensive presentation of the IP and was glad for the safeguards they had put in place. She focused on describing the outcomes she and Richard had achieved rather than the technological process itself. She recalled Richard's warning early on.

'Our portfolio should never reveal everything. The world is full of commercial sharks and it'll take time and money to get patent protection. This is what Paesano has on offer for us.'

Well, as it transpired, the offer was a travesty, but the warning still held good. Margrit hoped throwing herself into this work would keep her mind clear of morbid thoughts, but every page was a painful reminder of the challenging time they had spent together. 'If only he were here,' she said aloud in her loneliness.

After ten days of concentrated effort, she had developed a

tightly-honed presentation and thought wistfully how proud Richard would have been. As she was finalising the last few pages of her presentation, Will called with stunning news.

'The silver Mercedes has just been found, burnt out on a disused mine-site not far from Paesano's Groenwater mine.'

Her heart raced as Will added more.

'Koos thinks Richard may well have been held somewhere on the property as there are recently used things … a dirty bucket, quite a few food wrappers and used, plastic water bottles inside an old shed. It's all pretty disgusting and would have been awfully unpleasant for Richard.'

But this was a hopeful indication he was alive.

Will expanded on their findings.

'Curiously, they also found scraps of paper, stuff torn out of a notebook and strewn all over the floor. They are covered with mathematical jottings. The boys are wondering whether any of it may mean something. You can at least confirm whether the material is Richard's.'

Later that morning Major Koos Brand received a report from the inexperienced two-man team watching the SMGT offices and trying to keep tabs on Schneider.

'Sir, for the second time today, I have spotted a tough-looking, very large character coming out of the SMGT office building. This time he's loading a cardboard box into an old van. It could be a small TV or computer, something like that, but we're wondering why such a fellow would be taking such a thing from a place like SMGT. I'm certain I've seen him before in a police line-up, maybe one of the guards Mpane put on at the mine site after the intruders broke in. What should I do now?'

'Follow him at a distance! I'll get a team out to assist and one to replace you at SMGT. Just keep this squawk box open.'

Once again though, incompetence was to interfere and it wasn't long before Brand was told the van had been lost in the heavy traffic. At least its last direction towards Soweto was known. He immediately put out a general call but to no avail. There were so many similar vehicles on the road.

This incident was enough to confirm his suspicions about the possible involvement of Mpane's four Groenwater guards. Earlier, two of them had been beaten up by intruders while trying to secure the mine site for Mpane. Will had told him how aggravated Schneider had been about the rights to this IP. Had SMGT, perhaps even through someone as high up as Martine Monard, commissioned those intruders to steal the scientists' work?

It was becoming obvious Shorty's gang had abducted Curie right after the explosion and it was highly likely the SMGT thugs might also be making their own efforts to find him. If this was the case, he must have something of real value and it might also mean Curie was alive, possibly even cooperating under duress. Then came the confirmation from Margrit. The scraps of paper found in the shed were definitely his work and it was highly likely he was still alive.

Now Shorty was dead, it seemed his small off-shoot gang might well be looking to make mileage out of their former leader's Gold Bug obsession and prepared, perhaps, to use Richard as an income-producing, bargaining chip. With this in mind, Brand told Will that the police would ramp up their own search for Curie and keep clear of SMGT until they were on more solid ground.

'Look, Will, SMGT desperately needs great PR to get their shares out of junk bond territory and if the Green Mines IP project really works, all of their local problems can be put to one side. I don't think poor old Margrit is in any position to protect her interests, but if Curie was here, I think they could put up a formidable resistance to these commercial predators and also the receivers.'

Will reverted to his own obsession with the international financial manipulation.

'Man, you know how frustrated I am. All the global money-laundering investigations have been put on hold because of a lack of resolve in a couple of countries. Basically, this means SMGT is out of the woods for the moment, still short of cash. Capturing the complex IP ideas from Dr Curie to add to those developed by Margrit when she was with SMGT would be most valuable to them. We must find Richard before they do.'

Brand's response hit the nail on the head.

'At least no one wants him dead!'

Richard was indeed alive, in poor shape and not in a good place mentally. Later, his recollections of events which had occurred over many days would sometimes be hazy, but the first night often came back to haunt him in vivid detail. They had barely left the gate at Groenwater when two thunderous explosions hammered at his heart and he saw dazzling flashes of red light reflected on the car's ceiling above him. The driver shouted out.

'Jesus, with that blast, Shorty must be dead.'

The car screeched to a halt as its driver watched the growing inferno behind them. This gave the other three guards a chance to catch up and clamber breathlessly into the car. Richard, jammed between two of them in the back seat, tried to stifle a grunt of discomfort.

'What are we doing with this little English bastard? Shall I kick him out and shoot him?'

But the others seemed too intent on escape to make such a decision and Richard drew another sharp breath of relief.

The driver first thought they should put distance between themselves and the mine, but changed his mind to look for a closer hideaway. It would be days before the police refocused to look at sites nearer Groenwater. He manouvered through a rough, weed-infested patch on the rundown road, looking for an exit and constantly glancing back.

'How about that? There are no God-damned police chasing us'

He switched off the headlights, turned sharply to the right and drove between two old gates hanging awkwardly open. Then he threaded his way past several old buildings, clad in the typical rusting corrugated iron of the industrial district, and explained to the others

'I know this place well; they are too stupid to think of looking for us here on one of these old mines. They're tearing it all down soon, so it's safe to hide here for a while. The pigs will think we're already on the freeway and anyway, this big Merc is far too obvious. We can easily pinch a different car after things calm down.'

Driving past piles of rubbish, he hid the car under an old, lean-to shed and they got out, leaving Richard hunched up on the back seat listening to them briefly arguing his fate. Christian, the driver, had probably acquired his nickname through his constant use of religious expletives. He certainly wasn't filled with the milk of human kindness … in the changing circumstances; he assumed a loose authority over them.

To the others he had always appeared to be as close to Shorty as anyone could be. He was the one who had seen his partner killed in the first raid on the Kyalami house, who knew what had happened to Denning, and who had been beaten up by the intruding gang at Groenwater. He had watched as Shorty was being 'trained' by Richard. So it was logical Christian would have to make the decisions, albeit in a slightly more democratic fashion.

Having noted how much care Shorty had taken to understand the project and how close he was coming to success, Christian told them, 'This experimenting thing must be valuable to somebody. Now Shorty is very dead and the machinery in the mine must be repaired, it's only this foreigner and his girlfriend who know how the whole thing works. So why don't we get as much as we can out of this? We can trade this Englishman and his stuff for a huge bloody ransom. After all, we've got no money, and now all this shit has happened we won't have any other way of getting any. We'll not work in this crap town now people think we've started up the gang wars all over again. What do you reckon?'

With a very tense Richard well within earshot, the guards then began to dispassionately debate whether to kill him or to try to sell his knowledge. To his gut-wrenching relief, the outcome was three to one in favour of trying to exploit his experience in the short-term, particularly if they could somehow kidnap the woman scientist as well. Richard knew this addendum was far-fetched, but thinking of Margrit certainly weakened any resolve he may have had to hold out for too long. Christian now reminded them.

'The Englishman's computer is ash in the fire which is lighting up the sky over there.'

'So maybe he needs another one to write his stuff on,' ventured one of the thugs.

'We haven't got the money for that sort of thing, you dumb bastard. We have to steal one.'

Richard was pulled out of the car and without being asked for his opinion, muttered, 'It'll be a waste of time anyway, as there is no operating machinery left to demonstrate our process.'

However, not at all fazed by this negativity and after slapping Richard's face hard, Christian said, 'What other options do we have, smart-arse … put it all down on paper. We've got all the time in the world.'

Richard remained carefully obdurate for as long as he could, repeating he didn't know how he could capture all of the complex details on paper. He knew these rascals would have no idea of its value.

Of course, he held out some hope of being rescued and it was this which made him so determined to delay progress, just as he had done with Shorty, who after all, had been a country mile smarter than this tawdry lot. The lone dissenter in the debate must have had some clout, for as a sop to him they decided to put Richard into isolation for a few days to soften him up. They told him he'd have lots of time on his own to think out ways to document his stuff, and identify the people who would pay the most for it. As the hardliner so deftly put it, 'You'd better get it right, whitey. If you're the bloody smart-arse you think you are, you'll be able to do it all in your head. Now we must *hamba* out of here before it gets too dark.'

Richard was pushed into a small room, which must have been used in the past as a store for illicit goods and, by the smell of it, as a standby toilet. His wrists were re-tied in front of him before Christian confiscated his Rolex watch, mobile phone and wallet and in seeming recompense thrust a dirty, half-filled plastic bottle at him.

'Try to make it last, Englishman. You can piss and shit in the bucket. Here is a newspaper to wipe your bum.'

He slammed the door and the room was instantly pitch-black.

For the first hour or so it seemed to him, Richard gingerly explored his prison by working his way blindly along the walls. He knew it was early in the night, but there was not even a chink of moonlight slipping through anywhere. At one point he lost the plastic water bottle after putting it down to feel his way past the locked door and he had to search for some minutes in a rising panic attack.

The room wasn't entirely empty. He felt rough shelving along one wall and by kicking them over a wooden crate and a metal bucket. He sat down on the crate and spent time breathing deeply, trying to calm the knot in his stomach. After a while he had a better spatial perspective and also found a boarded-up window. Not even the hint of a draft under the door could make the air anything but foul. Even many hours later, thinking it might be dawn, not a vestige of light crept into his cell.

Eventually Richard made a space for himself by scraping out a smooth spot in the rubble under the would-be window and as he dozed fitfully on the cold floor his mind flew from one subject and image to another. He idly wondered if this was what it would have been like to be an underground geologist, an experience he had narrowly avoided earlier in his career.

More often though, he thought about Margrit and their work together, and how their feelings and regard for each other had grown so fast under such strained circumstances. He hoped desperately any rescue mounted by Brand would leave her unharmed. He deeply resented it had not been implemented much earlier to ensure their safety.

Try as he may, Richard was unable to plan a way to satisfy the loose demands of Christian and his pals and he began to dread their return. Then there was another fear. Perhaps they might never come back?

Time dawdled by. Finding some gravel near the crate, Richard used the pieces as counters and tried to 'guesstimate' the passage of time in piles of sixty. While he stuck at this diversion for nearly two hours, it provided him with a basis for assessing how long his captivity was lasting. His miserable source of water was finished far too soon and despite his fear, he was also desperately hungry and growing painfully aware of the hard floor. By his estimate, virtually a full day must have passed before the lock suddenly turned and he almost felt pain as a torch shone blindingly into his eyes. He staggered to his feet and tried to look past the torch-lit apparition but all was darkness.

'Before we start,' said Christian, 'go empty your bucket in the drain outside, this bloody place stinks.'

After the unpleasant task was completed, his captor said, 'I've brought you a pizza and more water, so what have you decided you're going to do for us?'

It was the question Richard knew he'd be asked but he didn't have a ready reply. After a while, and with as much firmness as he could muster, he stated, 'I can't do anything for anyone without a computer and it wouldn't work in here anyway as there isn't any power.'

Christian, who was proving to be a tad more amenable than his former boss, responded to this quite calmly.

'I'll only be able to fix the power problem later tomorrow, but I'll let you have paper and pencils before then. If you're a good Englishman I'll even give you a light to get your ideas down so someone can understand what they will be buying. If we get a bite, you can do your real stuff on a computer … as soon as we can steal one. In the meantime, don't forget to say your prayers.'

As the door was slammed shut, Richard faced up to another twelve hours or more of worry and darkness, eking out his pizza and replenished water. He had been in South Africa for only a matter of weeks and to find himself in this unholy mess.

The next visit was from the worst of the side-kicks. The same routine was followed after the door was unlocked.

'Phew, this place smells even worse than before. Do you have a secret supply of rotten fish?'

The thug gave a strange giggle at his own clever humour. The guard handed over more cold pizza, a couple of spiral-bound note-books, pencils, and a kerosene lamp. The thug looked Richard over rather theatrically as he prepared to leave.

'You must get on with your work in a hurry, Engelsman, these lights don't last forever. And remember I'm the one who wants you dead, so it had better be good.'

Again, the door slammed and Richard did get on with it. By the time the light eventually flickered out, he had a structure for the selling proposition down in draft form, carefully describing outcomes rather than processes as he had warned Margrit to do. The crate was covered in numerous drafts before he methodically sorted them and placed them in a pile on the shelves against the wall. Into this pile he slipped a coded note to Margrit, describing his current conditions and awkwardly declaring his deep affection for her. He could only hope desperately someone would be diligent enough to eventually find this note and work out its meaning.

Once again it was a matter of being alone in the darkness and the pizza, water, paper and light were replenished at quite regular intervals. Richard ground away, reliving the work he had done with Margrit while getting a final copy polished up. Without any connection to the outside world, he could only pace himself by the unvaried deliveries, which he assumed occurred each night. By now he realised he was no doubt financing those supplies through the money they had stolen from him, but regrettably it didn't mean a menu change.

Several more interminable 'nights' had passed and Richard began to feel disgustingly slovenly and unkempt in unchanged clothes and with heavy stubble. By now he had finished the first part of his task, but was still waiting on the computer he had asked for. He eventually plucked up the courage to ask about this. He sensed the guard bristling.

'It's not easy to steal stuff like that.'

At last, after what could have been a week or more, there was a short, frantic, final visit. He was told to pick up only his document and leave everything else behind and was rushed out of the shed into a nondescript, old, white van parked next to the Mercedes. The van pulled away in the dark and Christian barely looked back as flames suddenly shot up from the large silver car.

'My contacts have just told me the police are beginning to search all the old mine properties around here, especially the Green Mines' ones.'

Then he gave a sort of chuckle.

'The fire will distract them for a while, don't you think?' He paused and in a somewhat softer voice added, 'Shorty would be proud of me.'

Whereas working in the appalling conditions in the shed had been a horrible nightmare, the forced departure in the Kombi van from the mine shed started a period of relentless pressure for Richard. His captors seemed to feel time was running out. In the darkness at the back of the van, Richard was wedged between the worst two of his tormenters and could feel the rising tension as all four men tried to talk at once in Zulu. He was just able to sense the nature of their argument, but it seemed again the hardliner had to be put down by Christian for his worrying suggestion.

'The Englishman is too much risk for us. The cops haven't stopped looking for him and we don't know what to do with this nonsense he has been writing. We haven't even got the computer he says he needs, so let's kick him out now. But shoot him, he has seen too much of us.'

Christian was a lot more democratic than Shorty had ever been. He now had some authority flowing to him as the wearer of the Rolex watch. He became aggressive and for Richard's benefit said, in English, to the dissident, 'Just stop your nonsense, for God's sake, or we will kick you out of this van. I am still thinking of how to get a computer.'

They all quietened down and Christian drove on to their new hiding place in a ramshackle cottage which he told Richard was on the outskirts of the Soweto township. Richard only had a glimpse of the place behind its protective garden walls as he was frog-marched through a dark room to his third small prison in a fortnight. However, he did overhear his captors arguing about augmenting the size of the gang.

'When those other fuckers attacked us at the mine, we were too few to resist. We need more men.'

This, for Richard only added another element of risk to his predicament.

Evidently, the occupants of the cottage had been forced out in a hurry and a padlock had been installed on the door of his new, small prison. At least the room had an electric light even if it was unshaded and, in contrast with his last cell, it was left on day and night. After two interminable days of wakefulness, Christian came in to talk to him. He thought he had found a way to present his 'selling' document to SMGT, as his only customer, without giving his negotiating position away. He told Richard to write a short description of the work he had been doing in the mine shed and after Richard suggested the executive summary would suffice, Christian said it was too much.

'I'd fall asleep if I read it all, just put down the benefits ... I saw how excited Shorty and you were towards the end, so there must be a lot of good stuff to tell.'

After Richard had finished and tidied up his grammar, he said to Christian, 'I can't make it look real without using a computer to describe the reactions. It has to fit in with what Dr Dupain has been doing and SMGT would know a lot about that side. There's no way you can bluff them about this bio-metallurgical stuff.'

He may as well have been talking Chinese for all Christian understood.

'The bio what?'

He wasn't remotely interested in an answer, but he had a brainwave.

'I'll find a way of getting the first few pages to SMGT with a note asking for a deposit and a computer to finish the job. How much should I ask for the whole thing to show how it works?'

Richard really had no idea. Thinking about his own (mythological) fee in the millions of Rand, he judged the robbers would be operating in an unsophisticated world with low expectations. Still, the offer would have to seem realistic in SMGT's eyes and he suggested they ask for R750,000 with a deposit of ten per cent. Christian was staggered and looked at him with new respect.

'Come in here and listen to this, you guys.'

Richard repeated his proposal, but felt he had to cool their excitement.

'Of course SMGT will try to bargain you down so you might have to settle for, say, US$60,000, which is US$15,000 each.'

They gasped and clearly they would now treat him with kid gloves until the money was in their hands. The hardliner started to apologise for the thumping he had given Richard and for the others even the ten per cent deposit sounded like a fortune. On the other hand, the deposit would be nothing to SMGT and perhaps he would have gained more time in the hope of rescue.

The note was simply put with considerable help from Richard who knew he was working on a knife edge of duplicity. He had to balance realism against their overt greed.

To the Director of SMGT

We have access to the science which is partially described by Dr Curie in the three pages attached. It was proved to work successfully at Groenwater mine just before your gang broke in to steal the computer used by Dr Dupain.

We are looking for R750,000 in cash for the complete information with a deposit of ten per cent. Dr Curie needs a computer to finish the algorithms and to prove the process in stages. Further payments will also be staged. The details of the computer are attached.

If this proposal is agreed when we call your personal phone line in two days, we will send someone around to pick up the cash and computer from your reception. If this person is followed or the police are called in we will kill Dr Curie.

If this proposal is <u>not</u> agreed to we will have no further use for the scientist or his work.

However, as a sign of our good faith, one of our people will become a hostage for you until completion.

Richard knew his personal involvement in this approach would be blindingly obvious to SMGT and he also knew any politeness shown in the note could be withdrawn in an instant by the robbers. The offer of a hostage was pure theatre and, of course, there would be room for negotiation on the quantum of payment. The way the whole thing was written would be clear evidence the missing Dr Curie was alive, but Richard did not for a moment think this information would be immediately available to the police, nor could he see any mention of his personal position and whether his contribution would at least be rewarded with freedom.

FORTY-EIGHT

S chneider's secretary brought the note and attachments into his office the next morning and apologised for opening it.

'It looks like a scruffy, begging letter of some kind dropped off at reception, but I think there is more to it.'

It took him only a few minutes to go through the package and he immediately called his senior team together.

This team consisted of Martine running Finance, the Legal Manager, the Regional Manager of Africa, the Public Relations Officer and the Chief Scientist, whose recent appointment had raised derision amongst his professional colleagues.

He looked around the table and was met with quizzical stares. Starting with the Chief Scientist, he asked each in turn for their opinion.

'From what I can see on the computer which Martine's people recovered for us, the science part does work. The samples are clear proof. What we have only needs to be meshed with the actual operating algorithms outlined in these draft notes. And, clearly, they have had considerable success. This is unique stuff and will be very valuable.'

Schneider glared at him.

'This is a damned outrage. These crooks, whoever they are,

want to sell us something which was our idea in the first place, even if you haven't been able to progress things at all.'

He directed his venom at the Chief Scientist.

Martine rudely broke in, 'Not exactly, Herr Schneider. You dismissed Dr Dupain some years ago after she pointed out the need for a practical operating procedure.'

The Legal Manager also emboldened, added, 'And in her dismissal letter you said her part of the science would never work'

Schneider turned to the PRO who put a different spin on things.

'Herr Schneider, it's clear we have to think about a good news story right now to keep our share price up and if all this is true, we will have a short cut. Who knows or cares where those two scientists are? They can try to sue us for IP theft, but it will take forever and might just help to keep us noticed in the financial press. Where would they get money for a legal challenge anyway? This is a heaven-sent chance to raise our profile.'

Schneider said nothing for a while and the others had nothing to add, except the legal manager who suggested there was a real risk associated in messing with the scientists and they would need to involve the police at some stage, to which Schneider replied, 'We owe those dammed scientists, wherever they are, absolutely nothing. They can sue Green Mines or that bastard, Paesano, wherever he is. I am told the one called Curie has vanished into thin air and yet I can smell his presence in the stuff we have been given this morning. Maybe he has gone over to these robbers. Willingly or unwillingly? We could arrange to rescue him ourselves.'

He stood up.

'So let's give those extortionists a taste of money to see if they really have got something. Martine, I'll let you coordinate all this; just put your useless damned gang on standby and they can use all the force they need to get him as long as it doesn't come back to bite us. Last time the only useful thing your people got was the computer. If what you tell me is true, there is a hateful standoff between your lot and these other thugs who seem to have our man.'

He continued, his voice rising with his command.

'Don't even bother to negotiate down the fee to these clowns because we'll only be paying a token amount anyway. This will keep them hot and is only peanuts. It won't even be noticed in your budget, Martine. You seem to have shifted funds around quite easily, haven't you? Get it right and stay more in control this time. We need the doctor alive. And I'll work out what to do about him after I get back home to Switzerland.'

He ended the meeting and went out to settle his delayed travel arrangements now the threat from the syndicate was virtually dormant.

Like an incipient cancer, the main tumour of criminality had been excised, but the secondaries would re-appear in due course, something which did not engage his attention at the time. All he could think about was getting to Zurich to re-arrange his international money-dealing affairs before they were exposed. Little did he know the tenacious Will Wolhuter and his international cohort of investigators had not given up.

As far as his South African interests were concerned, it had all been a lucky escape for Schneider with some solid lessons learned from this local diversion. He felt disinclined to get directly involved in this piece of IP theft and the kidnapping of the scientist. Even though the rewards looked exceptional, there was dark work which might have to be done and he was keen to stay right out of the way.

Without any fanfare from his cowed managers, Schneider flew back to Zurich and Martine Monard took control, waiting for the call to come from Christian.

FORTY-NINE

The call was made from a pay-phone. It was brief indeed and Christian told the others there was no negotiation on her part. The arrangement to pick up the computer box, which would also contain US$8,000 in cash, was quickly fixed given SMGT's loose foreign exchange manipulations. Christian agreed he would email sections of Richard's procedures as each was completed, with partial payments being settled for each section. Martine had put a new spin on things.

'There is no need for a hostage. After all, we are doing this on a business basis, are we not?'

Two hours later, a tame courier arrived at the SMGT reception desk and sure enough the package was waiting. Christian allowed himself a large measure of satisfaction for handling the whole affair so well and told the others over and over again about his successful phone call. Richard on the other hand smelt a rat because it all seemed too easy, even inexperienced as he was in these matters. In his mind these negotiations could never be completed in such a simple fashion and he was the pig in the middle. He warned them they had no fallback position, but the gang members were too busy counting out the money to pay any attention to him.

He knew he had lost part of his safety net. Given the vengeful environment and the amount of money in prospect, his personal position was desperate. While he recognised SMGT could benefit by capturing him alive, he foresaw a dire outcome once Christian's gang had bled him dry. They now wanted him to get on with his scientific work and complete the next section of the IP.

He turned to the newly acquired computer to see whether by using it he could concoct some means of communication. The first things that popped up were the time and date. It was the 30th of April. He was astonished how short his imprisonment had been. He turned to Christian who was trying to give the impression he was supervising things.

'Is it only two weeks since the explosion? It seems so much longer for me.'

The gang leader looked down at 'their' Rolex on his wrist and then with disdain pointed at the computer screen.

'So what? They are both correct, just get on with it.'

And Christian, who had been standing behind him, moved away a bit as Richard really was ripe. He left him to set up the computer and after a while it dawned on Richard that among a number of standard applications, someone had included a subtle GPS feature which would identify the location of the computer whenever it was turned on. The someone at SMGT who had installed the application had foolishly overlooked it could be used by any outsider once there was a connection.

Now, his only issue was how to open communication with Margrit and through her to any rescuers. He decided to take the initiative and asked permission to send a request to his colleague at her email address, asking for the extra data he needed to complete the next section. To allay concern, he suggested Christian sit next to him to supervise the data request once he had it ready for transmission.

'Good, I can see you understand we mean business. Don't think you can fool me, man, I have seen how this email thing works, you know, and we'll be using it to send your stuff to SMGT as soon as you finish each piece. The computer won't stay in your room.'

Richard heard the padlock close on the door and settled down to write out by hand his information request to Margrit, ready for transmission the next day. It was complete nonsense of course and would have put her on alert as soon as she read it. There was only a string of numbers and letters, asterisks, exclamation marks and the like, as well as meaningless blocks of text statements. As had happened with Will early on, there was an embedded and coded message saying this computer could be located even in standby mode.

The next morning, with Christian beside him, he sat down and booted up the machine. He opened a number of applications, including the GPS locator before he pronounced the machine ready. He turned to Christian and asked him to read from the handwritten material while Richard typed. Christian now considered this put him in charge of the whole procedure.

'I was just about to tell you to do it. You can start now.'

And he began to slowly and painfully read out the request to Richard, battling with symbols in the text passages as Richard typed away. This was no secret service procedure. By any construct it was amateurish, but after thirty laborious minutes, it was complete and Richard thought he should reinforce Christian's belief in his grasp of computers.

'That's it. Well done. I won't even check it. It was all clear, thank you. May I now send it, please?'

The magnanimity of Christian's response was most pleasing and he even asked Richard how to turn off the machine. Richard responded without raising a vestige of suspicion.

'It will probably be better to leave it in stand-by mode in case SMGT wants to contact us.'

Which Martine Monard did later in the day, providing concrete evidence of her deep involvement in this wholly illegal venture.

FIFTY

From the moment Margrit had confirmed to Koos the scrappy message discovered in the mine shed really was authored by Richard, time had dragged on even more slowly for her. The brief personal message which had been hidden in the working papers had simply called for some action to free him.

Can't hold out much longer. Conditions awful here. Have to cooperate with them.

His longing for her was also evident and this brought colour to her face as she handed this roughly-coded message to Koos Brand. He politely looked away and then comforted her by saying they were now closing in on Richard and his abductors.

'All our usual sources are keeping quiet at the moment. It seems these guys are a residue of Mpane's old gang and no one wants to have anything to do with the matter. There is a feeling gang warfare could break out again.'

Three interminable days later, she was still polishing up her work, trying to keep busy and almost willing the phone to ring. The only calls were from Will or Koos, giving her progress reviews and discretely checking on her mood. There was a hidden agenda in this dual concern for her safety. Will did not share Brand's confidence in the re-vamped police team and also thought Margrit required strong support as matters escalated, besides which his international investigations were of much greater 'big picture' concern to him than this ugly township skirmish. For his part, Brand was keen to clean up the villainous gang which had been a long-lived problem in the township and he was less concerned about Margrit's mental wellbeing. Both men were working in concert but with different objectives.

Margrit was fearful about stepping outside the apartment despite the obvious police presence and she felt threatened by the legacy of violence left behind by men who now didn't matter at all, like Denning. Mr Paesano had vanished and Will told her Schneider had left the country.

'I think it's a bit rich that SMGT's in-house lawyer has continued to raise the issue of IP ownership. They have the cheek to demand from Green Mines' liquidator all documentation on the operational side of the pending patent. It seems the stuff on your stolen computer isn't detailed enough, because they are also putting out feelers all over the place trying to track Richard Curie down, with no more success than us, I might add. There are simply millions of people in those townships.'

He continued in a more understanding tone.

'You must know it is not out of SMGT's kindness of heart. I can sense some desperation and he will be spirited away if they get to him first. We will simply not let it happen.'

Margrit felt this was another pressure. Given her strong police bodyguard, her fear was irrational, but everyone could see she had been through a lot and couldn't distance herself from her recent horrors. Her strict daily routine started by her scanning a few emails, occasionally searching the internet for information on patent attorneys and becoming familiar with the patent lodgement process. And hoping desperately for any news about Richard.

On the fourth morning, she had just taken a coffee break and returned to the computer, when to her excited surprise, she opened a message containing the most extraordinary jumble of text and rubbish, asking for background data on the bio-metallurgical side of the IP. This was the message which had been prepared overnight by Richard and sent under Christian's supervision. Her heart nearly exploded as she noted the unique style of expression which clearly confirmed Richard's involvement in preparing those nonsensical requests. He was certainly alive.

After holding her breath for a minute to calm down, she called Brand and then Will, asking them to come to the apartment as quickly as possible. While waiting, she began to unstitch a simple coded message embedded in the nonsense on the screen. This took a considerable time as Richard appeared to be working under pressure and making many mistakes. Under this cover of a request for data was an instruction to keep her computer on standby, and to install a locator application which would pinpoint where he was being held.

There was also a warning in Richard's message. The gang holding him had probably now doubled in size. This information was of real concern to Brand as he would be struggling to put together an adequate number of trustworthy police and he knew he would have to scale down Margrit's protection at the apartment. He looked at the blinking blue icon on the screen as he summed up the situation.

'So there they are in Soweto! I guess this is the moment of truth, but it will be a very difficult place to surround and these guys always seem ready to shoot, so it will be dangerous in the extreme. However, they'll give up if they are losing. They aren't terrorists who will fight to the last. We'll have to plan things carefully and this will take time.' Margrit hardly took this in and her plea was desperate.

'I'll stay as far away as you want, but I must be near enough to help. Please do this for us. Please!'

Accepting she would have reduced protection at her apartment, he reluctantly agreed. After he eventually finalised his attack plan, he had to be very firm with Margrit. He warned her.

'Do not get out of the truck at any time, there could be a lot of metal flying about and you've been hit once before.'

Again, this was well beyond official rules of engagement, but Brand was never one for following these too closely. He set about briefing his team.

FIFTY-ONE

The computer-savvy operator at SMGT who had also been monitoring the locator signal from the Soweto cottage would not have known the police were committed to a rescue. However, this location information was enough to spur Martine Monard into action. Had he known, Brand would have been astonished how quickly Martine Monard had been able to put an extraction plan together. For his part, he completely overlooked the possibility that she might also have had access to the same location information.

She tried with great difficulty to assemble an extraction gang of toughs who would be working at arm's length from SMGT. This gang, guided by her instructions and with the incentive of even more money than their last commission, had only one task; to get Richard out of Christian's clutches as fast as they could with no concern for other lives. After they heard this mission statement and realised they would now be up against a vengeful crew, the SMGT gang reduced markedly in size and it took until late afternoon to find enough replacements to support the die-hard residual members. They were collected from all over the townships in a couple of SUVs for transport to Soweto.

So, two powerfully armed groups unaware of each other were converging on a third group in the small Soweto house. Given the need to protect community safety as well as to rescue Richard, the police operation also required tight planning, including the deployment of the police helicopter. This all took time, diverting it from another task and briefing the pilot, who was trying to sort out a crew shortage. Will suggested he make up the shortfall as an observer, reminding Brand of his army experience.

The police running late as ever, arrived after darkness descended on Soweto. While they were approaching the scene, the probability of surprise was markedly reducing. Christian's mob had already made themselves unwelcome in the district stealing food and money. Their neighbours had heard a rumour 'gang trouble' was brewing, so the nearest residents had prudently decamped at dusk. This news set minor alarm bells ringing for Christian.

'I want half you guys to stay on watch. There is something wrong. Everyone around here seems to have buggered off.'

The distant, distinctive thudding of a helicopter engine further aroused Christian as he dozed in the cottage. The tiny place was now a tight fit with all the extra people he had recruited and he couldn't afford a separate lock-up area for Richard. So, he trussed him up further and rolled him under one of the beds saying, 'We'll do the next section of your IP stuff tomorrow, no point in being too keen. And your friend still hasn't come back to us with answers to my ... our ... request this morning.'

Richard could see three pairs of legs in front of him with the old mattress sagging alarmingly. He only caught one comment from above.

'At least he smells better down there.'

There was a combination of quiet conversation above Richard and heavy snoring throughout the cottage as the men settled down. But then things changed very fast.

Brand was over a kilometre away from the cottage and approaching quickly through the narrow streets when the helicopter pilot signalled that he had sighted the headlights of two big vehicles pulling up about two hundred metres from the target. This was a real complication and knowing nothing about SMGT's mission, Brand wrongly guessed the gang holding Richard had called in further reinforcements.

Next, the pilot reported again.

'No one has yet left the vehicles. Where do you want us?'

Brand decided the time had come to act.

'Move lower and further away. Hold your position, but be ready to turn on the night vision equipment.'

The SMGT gang inside their SUVs had only just registered the presence of the helicopter. The engine note of the machine changed and thinking it was leaving, they leapt out.

Christian in the cottage made the same mistake about the helicopter. He looked out and urgently shouted for his men to get up. Down the narrow road, in the dark, he could see men jumping from an SUV and taking cover behind nearby buildings. There was a stentorian bellow.

'Give up right now, hand us the Englishman and there will be no shooting.'

Christian's first thought was the police had discovered

their hiding place and he blamed himself for not placating the neighbours more. Someone must have squealed about their bullying. But his mind took a different path and he muttered to a side-kick as they lay against a wall, 'The police don't bargain like this, it'll be the same gang which stuffed us at Groenwater. We are much stronger now, so let's give it to them!'

His men poured out of the cottage, breaking left and right and moving up towards their enemy under the cover of low garden walls. Christian adopted the classic role of driver rather than leader and hung back a bit, now worrying about the returning helicopter which he could hear approaching. Richard, a very unwilling participant in the impending violence rolled even further under the bed. He had no idea who was doing what to whom.

All the attention of the SMGT gang was focused on the men around the cottage ahead and they had not even considered leaving people behind to watch over the cars. The pilot directed the policemen to the SUVs which they secured behind the invaders. As a consequence, the SMGT thugs were now strung out between the police and the cottage. This was developing into a classic three-way battle without any party being too sure who really was their opponent. Will directed the pilot to move in closer and called Brand.

'My God, it's like a mini-Angola war starting down there. Tell your people to pull back a bit! I'm turning on the lights.'

In the aftermath, no one took the blame or the credit for firing the first shot of the night. But all hell broke loose between the three parties, and flashes could be seen from the handguns on every side with the police having the advantage of night vision equipment. Luckily for all, revolvers and pistols in the dark don't guarantee success and only two of Christian's people were knocked down near the house. And, until the SMGT men lost their nerve and decided to make a run for it hoping to escape in their SUVs, they were untouched.

However, they were now caught between Christian's mob and the police. The helicopter's floodlights caught them like deer-hunter's prey. The police megaphoned for their surrender and most lay down as soon as ordered. However, two of the boldest decided they had a chance in the township, but were easily brought down by Brand's marksmen as they tried to run off. A third thought about it, saw his comrades collapse ahead of him and he also dropped flat on the narrow roadway.

Christian's men, further away had quickly realised their predicament, and tried to escape through the labyrinth of passages behind them. The residents were disinclined to offer them any refuge and the night vision on the helicopter, manned by Will, proved its worth.

And Richard? Richard, bound up under the bed in the cottage, had called out desperately in the deathly silence after the shooting eventually stopped. From far up the road came a groan of pain and then he heard a lot of shouting as most of the fugitives were picked up despite the shortage of police.

The startled young policeman who dragged him out, expecting yet another criminal to be brought before the Major, was shocked by the appearance of the Englishman.

Unshaven, gaunt and stiff from the restraining tapes, his clothing was filthy and smelt foul. Richard could barely focus on the inquisitive throng crowding into the gloom, but his first words were to ask for Margrit. Brand who had just arrived didn't answer immediately, but his relief was obvious as he looked Richard over.

'So, this is Dr Richard Curie! My God, am I glad to have met you after all this time, even in this state. Your friend has been a good girl, stayed in the truck and will be with you in a minute.'

The young policeman was even more startled as a tall woman with her arm in a white sling rushed into the dingy room. Margrit clung to Richard desperately. They parted to look at each other; her sling was marked by dirt which Richard tried to brush away. There was nothing they could say for the moment and Will now appeared. He too was delighted by the outcome although a little shocked by the condition of the man he was seeing in person for the first time.

'From now on I am concentrating on those money-laundering matters which you'll know little about. So I have no urgent business with you two except to help close the net around SMGT. That can wait until tomorrow.'

Koos Brand added, 'I'm going to tidy up the events behind those murders and want to know the full story around Denning's death. You still have a bit of explaining to do. I'll be very busy tonight with this lot but we can save any debriefing until later. Richard, if you won't go to hospital, then you surely need a long shower and a good feed.'

He quickly commandeered a car with a driver and they hardly spoke a word during the trip to Margrit's apartment, just holding each other's hands tightly. Richard felt weak and smelled foul.

After a hot bath, an omelet, a stiff drink, another hot

bath, and a scrub-down from Margrit using her good arm, he painfully attacked his beard with her razor. His exhaustion seemed to wash away and at last the tension subsided as they began to recall and share the detail of their terrifying experiences.

And what of all the trauma surrounding their IP project and for which they had held such high hopes? Right now, for Margrit and Richard, it held no priority at all. Their conversation faded as they gazed at each other and looked away for an instant before folding together for their first kiss.